TURNBACK RIDGE

TURNBACK RIDGE

A NOVEL

Gerri Brightwell

TORREY HOUSE PRESS

Salt Lake City • Torrey

First Torrey House Press Edition, October 2022
Copyright © 2022 by Gerri Brightwell

Published by Torrey House Press
Salt Lake City, Utah
www.torreyhouse.org

International Standard Book Number: 978-1-948814-65-2
E-book ISBN: 978-1-948814-66-9
Library of Congress Control Number: 2021941410

Cover design by Kathleen Metcalf
Interior design by Rachel Buck-Cockayne
Distributed to the trade by Consortium Book Sales and Distribution

Torrey House Press offices in Salt Lake City sit on the homelands of Ute, Goshute, Shoshone, and Paiute nations. Offices in Torrey are on the homelands of Southern Paiute, Ute, and Navajo nations.

To my wonderful menfolk:
Cam, Conor, Ross, and Callum

1

That first evening after they fled Anchorage, the sun slipped beneath the spent clouds and hung huge and pale over the hills. Its light dazzled off puddles, off drops clinging to Nash's windshield, quivering in the rush of air as he sped along the highway. Here was the world washed clean: the road dark and gleaming, the forested hills razor-cut against the sky, the camping trailer like a new-made thing in Nash's mirror. He drove with his window cracked open and the cab filled with the earthy smells of life rousing itself, as though this was simply another weekend camping trip, just him and his boys. But those mile markers flashing past made his heart squeeze uncomfortably—it was still so far to the border.

Barely six in the evening, and the sun was high and would be for hours. If he kept driving, they'd cross into Canada during the night when the light had turned dingy. At this time of year there was no darkness, and now he wondered if the border would be open. He didn't know. In the panic of leaving, he hadn't thought to check.

He rubbed his chin. At least the numbness was almost gone, that awful feeling of his own flesh turned alien, though the tooth the dentist had filled was pulsing now. Yet another strand of misery on this miserable day, and the pain wasn't even bad enough to chase away the tiredness dragging at him. He pushed himself back against his seat and took a few deep breaths, as if that would help. He'd been up early to get the boys ready for day camp, packing their lunches, planning his work day because he had to be at the dentist's by one, and he had a report to finish, and Tony to fill in about what to present at the sales meeting. Now all that felt like days ago, before the moment this afternoon when his life had snapped apart.

He hadn't calmed down until the storm hit. He'd been blasting down the highway—taking bends too fast, hanging on the tail of the car up ahead because who drove at goddamn fifty out here?—when suddenly the sky had dimmed. Dense clouds had been piling up to the south and he hadn't given them a thought. Without warning, rain had come thrashing down so hard that the world beyond the windshield had simply melted away and he'd had to pull over. How long had he stopped? Half an hour, maybe longer. At first, he cursed and kept the engine running, but as he and the boys stared at the downpour slapping against the windows, their breath misting the glass, their heads filled with the din of rain and thunder, that fear in his gut let go. Eventually he shivered and looked around. Both of the boys had fallen asleep, Chris beside him with his teenage legs awkwardly folded so his feet could rest against the dash, and, in the back, Robbie slumped with his head against the window. Better that than them asking over and over why they were leaving home, and why they couldn't go back, and him trying to explain without letting on how badly he'd fucked things up.

And he had, hadn't he? Six months ago, when he'd tried to renew his permanent residency, he was denied, no reason given, so he'd paid for a lawyer to appeal and it hadn't made one bit of difference. His lawyer said, "It's happening a lot, you know. People who've lived in this country most of their lives are being turned down." Nash asked her what to do and she told him, "Pack up. Move back to Canada. And you'd better hurry—they took so long to deny your appeal, you only have twelve days." How can you let go of your life in twelve days? It was the middle of the semester for the boys, the middle of a big sales campaign at work. It was easier just to keep sending the kids to school and going into the office. The way he figured it, Immigration wasn't interested in law-abiding Canadians living up in Alaska.

Then this afternoon they'd come looking for him. He'd decided to go home after the dentist—one side of his face was numb, and if he was going to have food dripping down his chin, he'd rather do it in the privacy of his own kitchen. As he turned into his road, though, he noticed a black SUV outside his house. He pulled up in a neighbor's driveway and lowered himself in his seat. In the side-mirror he watched two men in gray track-suits knocking at his door. Across their backs, red letters in an arc, and a logo. This wasn't Immigration. This was worse: bounty hunters who rounded up *illegals* for profit. There'd been scandals—people snatched from hospital beds, from class-rooms, from gravesides during burials; people injured, killed even—and yet nothing had been done to rein them in, or the private companies they worked for. They were efficient, and that was all that mattered.

The two men knocked for so long that the old guy across the street had time to hobble over, smiling and chatting away. That bag of shit was probably telling them what time Nash got home from work. He stood by while they busted Nash's door open, even followed them in as they searched the place. After-ward, back on the doorstep, they slapped him on the shoulder, all smiles. The old guy walked home with something small and white cupped in his hand. A card. So he could call when Nash got home.

Nash parked in the back alley and let himself in through the kitchen. He used garbage bags, stuffing in clothes that had been strewn over the floor, and documents, photos, anything precious or necessary, and then heaved the bags into the bed of his truck. As for the camping trailer in the back yard—an old thing he'd bought years ago from a buddy who'd had enough of the US—he and his boys had been using it at the weekends to head out of town when the heat of the city was too much. The water tank was half full, the propane too. He hitched it up and took off with his heart thrashing in his chest. He made it to day camp just in time to pick up the boys. At first, Robbie had been excited—he kept asking where they were going and thought Nash was joking when he said Canada. Chris caught on at the sight of the truck bed covered with a tarp. He slouched in his seat and wouldn't look Nash in the eye.

The storm had stopped as suddenly as a cut in a bad movie, and steam wisped off the hood. Starting the engine hadn't woken the boys, nor had the bouncing as Nash steered back onto the road. They'd simply resettled themselves, and maybe it was the sight of them so tenderly asleep that made him feel emptied out by how badly he'd let them down. No wonder he drove cautiously, as though he were cradling them against the world.

The landscape beyond the windshield was nothing but hillsides bristling with charred trunks where once there'd been forest. In the last few years the whole continent, the whole world, had been raging with wildfires and droughts, massive storms and rising seas. Some winters, Anchorage was buried under ten feet of wet snow; other years, there was little snow at all. Farther north, buildings were sinking into the permafrost, and villages tipping into the ocean. Polar bears had been spotted roaming south, stark white against the tundra, and they were the lucky ones. So many had died. So many species were vanishing. This was a world gone crazy, and Nash pressed harder on the gas.

Before long the road curved into a slow descent. The fire hadn't reached this far so the hills were the fresh green of early summer. He let out his breath in a long slow sigh and resettled himself in his seat. Even here the landscape looked damaged: hillsides raw where slopes had slumped away, fans of debris heaped around their feet. Maybe it was because of all the rain, the earth so waterlogged that it gave way. It felt true, even if it wasn't. What did he know? He worked for a company that sold cleaning products, and that was the problem because nobody knew for sure how the climate was changing when government agencies were barred from collecting data.

He flexed his hands. Let it go, he told himself, just let it all go. Soon they'd have left this country behind, and he wondered why they'd stayed so long. But that had been the idea: to make a life here. His problem was that he'd refused to give up long after it was clear that giving up would have been the sensible thing to do.

The boys slept. Nash drove on with the pulsing in his tooth tugging at his attention. He pushed his tongue against it as though it needed warmth and kept the truck going at a steady seventy except where the highway turned sharply or rose in a long slog. In places the road crested, and there the land was laid out in all its glory with hills upon hills swelling away into the haze, and mountains magnificent and inscrutable in the distance. Then the road would descend again and there'd be nothing but the low sky, and trees pressing in.

He crossed bridges over rivers that thrashed past a few yards below. He passed dirt roads leading off into the forest, the occasional mailbox on a tilting post, and faded FOR SALE signs for plots of land that were nothing but wilderness. Where the road broadened into four lanes of perfect blacktop an RV overtook him, so sleek and enormous it blocked out the landscape as it slid past. Most of the highway hadn't been repaved in years, though, and was cracked and warped, or sagged into dips where frozen ground had thawed. In one place a wide puddle had gathered, and he had to slow way down to drive through it. On the side of the road, a moose. It swung its head to glance at him, then reached out with its lips and tugged at tender twigs, tugged harder, and down glittered a shower of rain.

So much rain. Everything drenched. Grasses beaten down, birches bedraggled by the weight of the water clinging to their leaves, bare rock turned dark and shining. The road was drying off to a pasty gray except where water had pooled. Small wonder so few people were out: no sightseers pulled up to take pictures, no tourists with binoculars. The only people he passed were a handful of men in yellow coveralls rooting through the debris of a rockslide. Their bus was parked close by—a short one painted gray.

Prisoners, then, perhaps even immigration detainees. The sight of them made a fizz of panic run down his back, and Nash looked away. He pushed his tongue against the tenderness of his tooth and focused on the endless band of road rolling toward the hood of his truck. His head was gritty with exhaustion, his thoughts clogged. He'd been in such a panic he'd just run, and now he wondered if he and the boys would be stopped at the border. It would make no sense to arrest them when they were trying to leave, but worse had happened: immigrants with legal status mistakenly detained, their kids lost in government bureaucracy for months, for years even.

Nash bent forward and rolled his shoulders to loosen them. The route was simple—up to Tok, then back down heading east to the border at Beaver Creek. All he had to do was keep driving. Up ahead, another bridge, longer this time. As he crossed, he stared out at the river. All that water twisting frantically, milky with ground-up rock and bristling with dead trees caught among the boulders. If you fell in, that was it—you'd be swept away and lost forever. He held the wheel tight and kept his eyes on the road.

Where the highway straightened up, the road was so buckled that the trailer lurched and bounced in the rearview mirror, and he had to slow again. He glanced at his watch. At this rate it'd be well into evening by the time they got to Glennallen, and he'd need gas and something for the boys for dinner—they would whine at having to eat in the truck, but he wasn't going to stop for any longer than necessary, not when he was already so goddamn tired. He switched the radio on low, something to keep him awake, and though he searched and searched, there was only a preacher talking about damnation, and a station playing Metallica. He sighed and turned it off.

A few beats later, like a strange echo of the music, a whomp-whomp-whomp started up under the truck. There was no mistaking it: a flat, out here where there was nothing but hills and the road, as if the storm and the desperate rush of leaving hadn't been enough. He pulled over onto the shoulder where it widened close to the debris from a rockslide.

Robbie groaned. "Is this where we're stopping, Dad? Are we getting dinner?"

Chris levered himself up and ran his fingers through his hair. "Robbie, look out the window, for crap's sake—there's nothing here." He'd had his dark hair cut short enough on the sides that his scalp showed through. On the top, though, it was so long and thick with hair product that it flared out. What would Maria have thought of it? That he looked like a feather duster, maybe, and she'd have said so, but she'd have stretched up to kiss him on the cheek, and he wouldn't have minded, would have laughed and said, "Yeah, Mom, that was the look I was going for."

Maria's son. Three years old when Nash met her, and Nash loved Chris because he loved Maria. Sometimes, though, like when Chris got that crazy haircut, or turned angry and sullen, to Nash he looked like a stranger, like the man who must have fathered him and who Maria had said little about except that he'd deceived her. A proud woman humiliated—no wonder she'd left behind her life in Mexico and brought Chris with her. At those moments when Chris was difficult, part of Nash hardened against him, never mind that he hated himself for it. Afterward he'd busy himself with dinner, or taking out the trash, anything but meet Chris's eyes, or Maria's. He'd always wondered if she suspected those flashes of resentment, those times when he hugged Chris a little too hard because he'd felt his love for him stumble.

In the passenger seat, Chris was frowning as he stared out the windshield to the road cutting through the hills, and the sky clotted with clouds. Nash took a long breath, kept his voice even as he said, "We've got a flat, that's all."

"But how long's it going to take to fix? Are we near the border?"

Chris rubbed his face. "Come on, Robs, it's not like Dad wants to get stuck out here."

"We're stuck out here?"

"Not stuck." Nash shut off the engine and felt Robbie's breath hot on his cheek. He turned and there was Robbie's face, so close he was all mussed hair and dark eyes. "I have to put on the spare. You know what, though? I bet this area's great for fossils. That rockslide, all that debris—that's the place to look. The storm will have washed away some of the dirt. Who knows what it'll have turned up. Why don't you two go take a look while I change the tire?" His voice sounded brittle and too cheery. Just a few hours ago he'd uprooted the boys and made them leave behind most of what they owned in the world, and now he was telling them to go hunt for fossils.

Robbie tugged on Chris's T-shirt. "You want to? Come on."

Chris batted his hand away. "We're supposed to go look for fossils? Jesus—" He made a sound that was half choke, half sob.

"Of course, if you want, you can give me a hand with the spare."

In the last year Chris had perfected looks of sourness, crooking his mouth, bunching the skin between his eyebrows—the face of the man who'd deceived Maria. Nash pushed that thought away. The face of a teenager, that's what it was, and those eyes staring at him from between thick lashes, those were Maria's. Then Chris looked away, swinging the door open and climbing out. A breath of cool air lingered in the cab as he slouched off with his hands in his shorts pockets.

How strange to be father to a sixteen-year-old almost as tall as him, who'd started shaving but could still sulk and snap. This last year he'd turned moody as hell. Maybe that was just hormones, or maybe the fact that his mother had disappeared and, despite all Nash had done, there was no trace of her. Chris needed her—they all needed her.

Nash unbuckled his seatbelt, said to Robbie, "You going to be pissy too?" When he glanced in the mirror, Robbie was staring back at him. A narrow face like his own, the same long nose, but the hair was a glossy black instead of his mousy brown, the eyes not gray but dark like Maria's. Robbie leaned forward. "No. He's just mad because you left his new hoodie back at the house."

"It was a crazy rush. I'm sorry." He sighed. "It's not like I wanted any of this to happen, you understand that, right?"

"Yeah, I guess," he said, but his eyes slipped away.

"I didn't want to pull you boys out of school during the semester. I didn't want your lives upset."

"I know, Dad. You don't have to explain it all again." Now he did sound pissy. Without another word, he got out and ran to catch up with Chris, his T-shirt flapping around him, so long it almost hid his shorts. It was a T-shirt Chris had grown out of, too big for Robbie really, and on the front was the surly face of some rapper Chris liked, or had once liked, and that was enough for Robbie to love it. Ten years old and he was full of yearning to be like his brother when he had the whole of the rest of his life to be grown up.

How quiet the truck felt now. The air hung still and accusatory. Nash pulled the keys from the ignition and held them hard enough that the metal dug into his fingers. So today was the day the boys had seen him frantic and scared for the second time in their lives, when no kid should ever see their dad like that. And the first time? Just over a year ago when Maria had vanished. She'd simply disappeared between the clinic where she worked and the parking lot across the street, and the cops hadn't done a thing about it because people took off all the time, they said, to escape marriages and debt and Immigration, and she was Mexican after all. Nash told them she had a green card, and one of the cops scowled, said, "Like you can't just buy yourself one of those online." Then he'd pushed his lips together and asked Nash where he was from, and when Nash told him Canada, the cop held out his hand and said, "Then we'd better take a look at your papers."

It was over a year since all that: the first few days of making calls to friends, to the hospital and the morgue, to government agencies that meant being left on hold for hours, and then the slow slog of posting her photo online, and putting up flyers across Anchorage. He'd found out nothing except that all over Alaska, all over the country, people were vanishing. These days it didn't matter if you were in the country legally or not: if you were foreign, or looked foreign, or sounded foreign, they took you anyway.

The boys were marching toward where the broken rock had slumped into an untidy pile. Here they were, growing up, and Maria was missing it all. When he thought about it too long, trying to weigh the odds of her being in a detention center against her being dead, or kidnapped, his life unbalanced like it might tip over. Sometimes he pictured her in a cell, dressed in coveralls and her hair grown long. Other times he imagined someone had warned her that the clinic was about to be raided, and she'd run. Maybe her bones were lying out in the forest where she'd tried to hide, or washed up on the edge of a river. Perhaps she was back down in Mérida with the man who'd deceived her because somehow he'd made amends, and she'd told her family not to say a word to Nash.

That wasn't Maria. A quiet woman but direct. She'd told him she loved him on their second date, and made it clear that any man in her life would have to be a father to Christofer. That wasn't the sort of woman who'd take off without a word, who'd leave behind the boys she loved with such passion.

He pushed open his door. The wind was gusting, brushing back the grass along the road, hissing through the trees. That wind was strangely warm and heavy, and he ran a hand through his hair, felt the stickiness of sweat. He shouted to the boys, "Stay where I can see you. And don't try climbing up the slope, you hear? We don't need anything else to go wrong."

Chris yelled, "Dad, for chrissakes—"

"Just be careful."

"It's kinda late for that, don't you think?" He stared back then let loose a kick that sent a rock bouncing and spinning across the dirt.

Last summer there'd been all those weekends to fill without Maria. When the weather was good, when the heat didn't summon up storms, Nash would drive the boys out of town to go fossil hunting. He'd never seen it so good—the extraordinary rains were washing away so much earth that new fossils were forever being exposed, and the three of them would walk and walk, concentrating on the ground in front of their feet, barely a word from Chris or Robbie once they quit complaining. There'd be only the hum of the wind, or the scuff of a shoe, and Nash would try to forget how he was doing his best to hold their lives together until he found Maria. Perhaps it was wrong of him to have made it seem as though everything was alright, that of course she'd come back. So much subterfuge—pretending to the boys that he wasn't broken apart at losing her, that they were still in the country legally when in truth any day they could be snatched by bounty hunters. Now he wondered if he'd pretended out of cowardice or mercy. And here he was, at it again, telling the boys to go look for fossils when the truck had a flat and a passing cop, especially a well-meaning cop, could ruin everything.

Chris was trailing after Robbie with his hands still stuffed in his pockets and his shoulders high as though this was oh-so-dumb. Nash hadn't expected enthusiasm, just cooperation, but maybe that was too much to ask of a sixteen-year-old, especially one who was pissed at him for wrenching him away from home. Any moment now, Chris might say something to sour Robbie on looking for fossils and they'd slouch back to watch him change the tire, and then—and then he might just lose his temper.

He was about to turn away when he saw it happen: Chris kicked at something, then crouched and touched it. When he moved on, he walked with his head down and his arms slightly crooked by his sides—the zombie walk of a fossil hunter. Robbie had noticed, and he called out to Chris. His voice carried to Nash on the wind, a pulsing of vowels, then Robbie trotted around his brother, darting this way and that like a dog trying to pick up a trail.

So there were fossils, or at least the boys thought there were, and that was good enough. Nash came around the truck with one hand skipping over the hot hood, then he stopped. "For shit's sake," he muttered and crouched beside the front tire. It wasn't just flat, it looked like it was melting onto the blacktop. They'd been lucky: if he'd been going any faster, he could have lost control of the truck. Old tires. He'd meant to replace them, had been waiting—for Maria, for his life to settle back to what it had been—because on top of the worry and grief of her vanishing he'd been fighting a riptide of cooking, and cleaning, and helping with homework, and driving the boys, and shopping, and trying to keep ahead at work, and to make matters worse, money had been tight with Maria's income gone. That was the worst—being at your lowest and having life kick you in the balls.

Still—he could have bought new tires. He cursed under his breath then straightened up and loosened the tarp he'd tied on over the bags in the bed of the truck. Water had pooled on it, and he folded it back carefully so that the water tipped off and splashed flatly to the ground. Beneath, looking like garbage, the full bellies of the trash bags that held all he and the boys had left in the world.

Rain had dripped into the truck box. The jack, when he dug down to it, was cold and wet, gritty with dirt, and the tire iron too. He wiped his hands off on his jeans and set up the jack. As he worked the wind huffed past, so muggy that soon his eyes were prickling with sweat and his T-shirt was stuck to his back.

He was down on his knees looking for a dropped lug nut when he heard the drone of an engine, then the crackle of tires on the blacktop just behind him. He lurched to his feet. In his hand, the tire iron, though what in hell he meant to do with it he had no idea. Stopped a few feet away was a black SUV. The driver's window hummed down, and Nash's fingers tightened around the rod.

From behind the wheel, an older guy stared out. He had a pouchy face with a mouth that turned down at the ends, and a cravat tied around his thick neck—who the hell wore a cravat? Not a bounty hunter, not a cop, and Nash let the tire iron dangle against his leg. "You okay?" the guy called.

"Yeah, I'm good."

The man glanced over to the boys climbing over the rocks and then back at Nash. "Anything I can do?"

"It's just a flat."

"That's really quite the flat. Jeez." He let out a snort of laughter. "You got a spare? Spotty cell service out here, you know."

"I'm good. Thanks for stopping."

"You sure? I can give you guys a ride into Glennallen."

"No, thanks. We're good." He gave a curt nod to signal that was the end of the matter.

The guy frowned and said, "All right, then," and took off with the window still open.

Nash had a spare, sure, but he hadn't looked at it in months, maybe years. He watched the car vanish down the road. A whiff of gas fumes hung on the air until the wind swept it away, and that wind was blowing harder now, licking up dead pine needles from along the roadside and sending them whirling into the grass. Above the boys, high over the hillside, more clouds were heaping up in great swollen mounds. Another storm was blowing in. He'd have to hurry.

He jumped up into the bed of the truck and heaved bags out of the way to get to the spare. It looked dry and cracked, and when he hefted it out and let it drop to the road, it landed with a dull thud. Even before he leaned his weight on it he knew: it was soft. Not unusable, not that bad, but the border was still hours away. So they'd stop in Glennallen, one of those dot-on-the-map places catering to tourists—there was sure to be a garage where he could get air. And if the spare had a puncture too, well then, a garage that could do a tire patch.

By the time he'd put on the spare it still felt early, the sun glaring above the dark clouds spilling over the hills, and yet his watch said it was well after seven. Chances were, no garage would be open this late, and a prickling unease stirred in his chest. He told himself that if they got to the border tomorrow instead it wouldn't matter, but he couldn't shake the feeling that things were falling apart. He hurried to put away the jack as the wind chased around him, whipping a candy wrapper across the dirt, tugging at his T-shirt as he tightened the tarp back over the bed of the truck, bringing the sound of the boys' voices to him. He looked up. At the bottom of the slope, Chris was holding onto Robbie's shirt as Robbie tried to run. Nash shouted, "Hey boys, cool it." Chris let go and Robbie staggered, half-fell, then came pelting toward him crying, "Dad! Daaaad!"

They'd found something. An ancient shell, most likely, or a

rock broken in half with part of a leaf imprinted on it. They had shelves of them back home—or had, he corrected himself. Come next month, the landlord would toss them in the trash when he noticed the rent hadn't been paid.

Robbie ran untidily with his thin arms flailing, leaning forward so far it looked like he was about to stumble again. A skinny boy who'd grow into a skinny man, just like him, Nash thought. A few yards behind, Chris trotted along half-heartedly with his elbows tight against his sides and his face set in a look of utter boredom.

When Robbie got to the truck he bent over, panting. "Dad—" He took a breath. "Dad, you have to see this." He held out one hand and unfurled his fingers. Lying across his palm was a gray lump of rock. Nash leaned closer. No, not a lump: something ovoid but long, one end a little tapered. He felt a smile start. Any moment now Robbie was going to ask if it was a T. rex metatarsal, or a stegosaurus egg, the sort of questions Nash had asked his own dad. His dad had loved all that stuff but he'd worked as a geologist because, he said, there was no point studying fossils for years and years when it might never lead to a job, and the oil companies would pay you an excellent salary. Besides, if you worked in Alberta, at the weekend you could drive out to some of the best fossil sites in the world.

Nash closed his fingers around the find. "Well, well," he said. When he lifted it away, it was surprisingly light. He brought it close to his face. Its surface was pocked with tiny holes like pores, except they couldn't be. So it was a volcanic rock and those tiny holes were made by gases, and yet it felt as though he was trying to explain it to himself.

Chris loomed over Robbie, his hair blown about and strands of it trailing over his forehead. "He's made an important find," he said deadpan, "and it's going to change the whole trajectory of science."

"What is it, Dad?" Robbie's face was shiny, and off him rose the sharp stink of little-boy sweat.

"It could be an odd-shaped piece of volcanic rock. See those tiny marks? They're probably from gases. And the thing's so light." He rolled it over. It had a strange, almost greasy feel, like nothing he'd ever come across. He glanced up. Robbie's lips were pushed together. He was disappointed, and no wonder when here he was trying to take the fun out of it. "It's weird that those holes are so even."

"It has to be a fossil, doesn't it, Dad?"

"He wants you to tell him it's a dinosaur egg." Chris swung open the truck door and heaved himself up into his seat. "Robbie, it's just a rock."

"Shut up, stupid head. You didn't find anything."

Nash weighed the thing in his hand. "Some eggs were long like this and had tiny pores. Eggs are incredibly rare, though, especially whole ones. It could be a coprolite—"

Chris tipped back his head and laughed. "You found really old shit. That's great."

"Then again, there are those tiny pores." He sighed. "It's a puzzle, and that's a good thing, Robs. It means it's something interesting. When we get to Calgary, we can show it to Gramps. Anyway…" He touched Robbie's shoulder and glanced away across the landscape as though it would give him some clue as to what this thing was, when all there was to see were just the same hills covered with spruce and birch that were everywhere around here, and those grim clouds rolling in. "Let's get back on the road. Maybe we can make it to Glennallen before it rains again."

Chris scowled. "Glennallen? I thought you were putting on the spare."

"We can't drive on it all the way to Calgary." He took hold of Chris's door then smiled, as though the spare wasn't soft, as though this wasn't a big deal. "Hey, we could find a place for dinner. What d'you think?"

Chris buckled his seatbelt. From his pocket he took an elastic band, then gathered his hair and tied it up into a sprig on top of his head. It made him look like a pineapple. "So now we're not in a hurry to get to the border?"

"Chris, you really—" Nash let the rest of his words fall away, and instead swung the door closed.

Robbie followed him around the front of the truck. "Can we get pizza, Dad? Can we get pepperoni?"

"Sure."

Robbie held out his hand for the find, and Nash hesitated. For a moment standing there cradling it he thought he felt a feathery vibration against his palm, but that was crazy. "Here," he said, and he plumped the thing down in Robbie's hand then wiped away the feel of it on his pants.

2

When at last they drove into Glennallen, crawling along because the truck was pulling hard to the right on the spare, Nash was worn out. The storm had blown off to the east and now the sun was slanting away over the mountains in a slow-motion descent that stretched the day on and on. Nearly two hours to get here, and the boys were hungry and bickering. Nash snapped at them to quiet down and slowed to get a look at the town, not that there was much to Glennallen. Most of the places he passed were already shut—a gift store, a small supermarket, a place that ran fishing and wildlife tours. Outside a Chinese restaurant hung baskets of yellow flowers, and the dusty red globe of a lantern that rocked in the breeze. A little farther down the road, the neon of a bar glowed trashily in the daylight. Nash told the boys to look out for a garage and the two of them stared sullenly through the windows. "There's nowhere to get pizza," announced Robbie.

"Right now we're looking for a garage. We're getting our bearings so we can make an early start tomorrow."

"Now we're camping here?" On top of Chris's head, the tuft of hair he'd banded together wobbled. "For crap's sake, Dad, you said we were in such a hurry you'd packed for us and we couldn't go home—"

"And now we're looking for a garage. All of us. Together." A sigh, close to Nash's ear, and he said, "You've got your seatbelt on, right, Robs?"

There was a soft click, and Robbie mumbled, "Yeah."

Just up ahead a garage, and he slowed. A sign behind the

office door said, *Yes, We're Open!* but the office was dark, and there were no lights in the windows upstairs. Chris said quietly, "D'you think it's closed for the night, or closed for good?"

Nash stared up at the gas prices listed on a tall sign. "Hard to tell. People here must get their gas somewhere, right? And they must need tires." A yawn climbed up his throat and he let it out, long and lazy, trying to push away the frustration in his chest. "At least we know where it is. We'll come back tomorrow. Let's find a place for the night and get something to eat." He sounded fake, as though he'd forgotten how to talk to his own boys. At least Chris didn't fling out a snarky reply. Instead, he just gazed out the window as they drove back through town to the RV park they'd passed on their way in.

It was a forlorn, windswept place run by an overweight guy with a bald head as brown as a loaf of bread. Fifty bucks for a patch of open ground marked by rocks—no hookup, no trees, nothing except a picnic table, but Nash paid and parked the trailer, then unhitched it and they drove back into town. The only one who talked was Robbie because there was a dog, a huge black dog with pointed ears who looked like a wolf, and could they get a dog when they got to Calgary? And there had to be a pizza place because everywhere had a pizza place, and he was hungry, it had been ages since lunch, and maybe he could have his own pizza because he could eat the whole thing. It calmed Nash, that little-boy chatter, as though they were off camping for the weekend, and tomorrow they'd head home to Anchorage.

In the trailer they had canned food and a stove, and no doubt that would have been quicker, but all Nash wanted was dinner set in front of him then to lie down and shut his eyes until the cramped feeling inside his head faded. He pulled up in front of the Chinese restaurant. Curtains shaded its windows, and the door was painted with a sinuous golden creature with a broad, frilled head and small crests running down its body. From its feet sprouted vicious claws, and yet it stared out into the street with a bored expression. A sign over the doorway said *Golden Dragon Restaurant.* It was going to be one of those places with dishes called Eternal Delights Pork, and One Thousand Blessings Chicken, and the prospect of reading his way through the menu made Nash feel tired.

Already Robbie was complaining. He said, "We should try the place up ahead because a Chinese restaurant definitely won't have pizza. And you said we were going to have pizza."

Nash glanced at him in the mirror. He had that wizened old-man look he got when he was tired, his eyes sunken and huge. "I'm trying my best here, but I can't make pizza happen."

"We could go in anyway. Just to see."

Chris heaved a sigh. "Robs, that's a bar."

"We could get carryout."

"Robbie—" Nash bit back his irritation. "We're eating Chinese because that's the only choice. Maybe you'll even like it."

Robbie's face tightened. "Chinese food sucks."

"You like chow mein. That's Chinese," and Chris nudged his door open.

"When Mom made it."

"Yeah, well—" Chris shrugged and got out, then stood fiddling with his hair.

Nash glanced up at Robbie in the mirror. "Come on, no point making a big deal over it, right? When you're on the road you need a sense of adventure." Robbie didn't look up, and he couldn't blame him. Christ, a sense of adventure—this trip might turn out to be one hell of an adventure. If the cops stopped him, if they ran his ID and realized he was in the country illegally, they'd detain him and the boys. Now that he'd lost his immigration status, they'd lost theirs, even Robbie who was born here. They'd be locked up too, along with the thousands of other kids who'd been detained in the last few years. His fingers curled toward his palms at the thought of it.

He shoved his door open and jumped down. How good it

felt not to be moving, though when he closed his eyes he could still feel the world rushing past him. "Come on, Robbie," he called. He was tired, he was hungry, and there was a dull ache in his tooth—he had the urge to leave Robbie to his sulk because for chrissakes, he couldn't magic up pizza. He glanced through the truck window. From the bend of his head and the way he was twirling his fingers in his hair, it was clear Robbie was trying not to cry. Nash told Chris, "Go get us a table. We won't be a minute."

"You totally baby him, you know that, right?"

"Younger sibling syndrome."

"Really? I'd have said it was single parent syndrome."

Nash's throat tightened, and he blinked. "Am I doing that bad?"

"Nah. But you are babying him."

"He's been through a lot. You both have." Nash straightened his back and took a long breath. "Just get us a table, will you?"

He waited until the heavy door had thudded closed behind Chris before he tapped on the window. Robbie peered up. "You alright?" When he turned away Nash gave him a few seconds before he opened the door. "Bet you're hungry." He squeezed his shoulder, then bent down to press a kiss into his hair. He smelled of dust and outdoors, the way kids were meant to smell. "I know all this is hard, especially on you. It must feel like your whole world has been turned upside down."

"We could've stayed in Anchorage."

He hugged him. "No, sweetie, we couldn't."

"You could have tried. You didn't really try."

"Of course I did. I got a lawyer and she helped me, but in the end there was no way. Things have changed in this country. Foreigners—well, the government doesn't think there should be so many of us."

"I know about that, Dad." He wriggled in Nash's arms. "Now Mom won't be able to find us if she comes back. Bet you didn't think about that."

He held him closer. "That was the first thing I thought about, but she knows how to get hold of Uncle Nolan."

"And Gramps."

"Well, Gramps has moved. Mom's clever, though. She'll know he's old and he couldn't stay in that house."

"I liked Anchorage. We had a good house. Mom liked it too."

"I know, sweet pea, but Canada will be great. At first it's hard to leave the place where you've been living, but then you get used to the new place and you like it just as much."

Robbie leaned against Nash, and his breath was hot on his chest. "How long will they let us stay there?"

"Forever. We'll never have to leave."

"Me and Chris aren't Canadian. Maybe they won't want us."

"You're Canadian because I am." He gave him another kiss then let go. Chris, though—he'd adopted Chris when he married Maria. Surely that counted. It used to, he was positive, but he hadn't thought to check, and fear pinched his gut. He made himself say, "It's just not something to worry about, Robs."

"You left loads of my stuff behind."

"You haven't seen what I packed. All the important stuff. And whatever I missed, we'll replace with better stuff, I promise."

"It's Stanley's party this weekend. I said I was going. It's laser tag."

"Sorry." He leaned down so his face was close to Robbie's. "And it doesn't help that you're hungry and tired. Come on, let's go eat."

Slowly Robbie uncurled himself then stood by the truck yawning. Already his clothes were filthy, as though he'd been wearing them a week—juice stains over the rapper's face on his T-shirt, a peanut butter smear where he'd wiped his hand, mud on his socks from traipsing around looking for fossils. "It's just not fair."

Nash laid a hand on his shoulder. "No, it's not. But let's eat anyway."

The Golden Dragon was empty except for Chris who'd taken a booth in front of an aquarium of paunchy goldfish moving so slowly it was like they were in a different dimension. He glanced up from his phone as they came in. In the electric light he looked weary.

Nash opened up a menu. "Okay, then, what sounds good?"

The waiter was an elderly man with graying hair slicked back and a narrow face who moved carefully, as though his joints hurt him. He took their order without saying much and carried it to the kitchen clutched in one hand. A few minutes later there were voices, and a din of clanging and rattling that echoed out into the dining room. The three of them sat in silence, Chris staring at his phone until Nash snapped at him to put it away. Through speakers up by the ceiling country music was playing, real old-time stuff that sounded lonely and sad. Nash took a breath to say something—anything—to get the boys talking, then stopped himself. Maybe they all needed a little quiet.

The menu had been straightforward to the point of abruptness—fried pork with vegetables, spicy chicken, sweet and sour shrimp—but when the food came it was good and plentiful. Big bowls of steaming rice, platters of meat and vegetables wheeled out on an old-fashioned trolley by the elderly waiter. No chopsticks, as though in this tiny town no one was expected to use them. Chris started right in, shoveling forkfuls into his mouth and chewing hard. Robbie sat with his hands in his lap until Nash said, "Come on—it looks great."

Robbie shook his head. "I'm not hungry."

"And I'm not finding something for you later when you tell me you're starving."

Robbie brought his hands up to the tabletop, and something clattered among the dishes. The find.

Nash laid down his fork. "Not on the table. Come on."

Chris snatched it up. "Oh right, your amazing discovery. You're keeping it safe by carrying it around. Or wait—" He cupped the thing in both hands. "You're keeping it warm because you think it's an egg and it's going to hatch."

"Give it back." Robbie's face flushed. "Fucking give it back."

Nash said, "Robbie! You're going to lose something for that."

Chris laughed. "Yeah, like your amazing dinosaur egg." He lifted it above his head, and Robbie leaped to his feet and swiped at Chris's hand. Nash hissed at them to stop just as Robbie lurched forward, bumping the table and slopping water from their glasses.

Chris leaned back. He held the find over the fish tank, fending off Robbie with his other hand. "Watch out, dude, or I might drop it in."

"Boys!" Nash pulled at Robbie's T-shirt but Robbie launched himself at Chris, climbing onto him, and with a yelp Chris let go.

The thing floated for a moment, its surface silvery with tiny bubbles, then it fell softly through the water as fish slipped out of its way and settled among the rocks with a hollow tap. Robbie let out a wail.

Chris frowned and eased Robbie back. "Jeez, you got me right in the balls."

Nash slammed his hand down on the table and the plates jumped. "For god's sake! What the hell are you two thinking?" Chris turned back to his dinner and Robbie dropped his hands to his sides. "Sit down." Robbie did, hunching over his plate. "Now eat, both of you, and if you step out of line again, dinner's over and we're out of here, and I won't give a damn if you're hungry."

Over by the cash register, the old man was watching. Nash gave him a nod, as though that would amount to an apology, and the old man got off his stool and vanished into the kitchen.

Sifting through the air came that mournful music, a man's voice bursting with melancholy over a slow guitar. The boys' forks clinked against their plates, and every few minutes Robbie glanced toward the tank. His face was wet, his dark lashes stuck together. "You know what?" he said at last. "I hate you. You're the worst brother ever."

Chris blinked a couple of times. "I didn't mean to drop it in, but you kneed me right in the nuts."

"You ruin everything."

"I was just messing with you, you know that." Chris gathered some rice on his fork and nodded. "I'm sorry. Okay?"

"You—"

Nash leaned forward on his elbows. "Robs, just eat your dinner. Come on."

He'd barely touched it. Now he slouched over his plate with his fork pointed to the ceiling and said, "Can we get it back? Can we ask the waiter to get it out?"

"Eat your dinner."

Scowling, Robbie stabbed up a piece of chicken and chewed with his eyes on the tank. One of the fish, a great fleshy thing with bulbous eyes and tiny fluttering fins, was poised over his find. The fish dipped forward for a nibble, and a small fizz of bubbles erupted from the thing. The fish wrenched itself away with a languorous twist of its body. It disappeared into a thicket of pondweed and left behind a thin string of shit that drooped in the water. Chris glanced around to watch. "Fish are gross," he said. "Imagine swimming in your own crap all the time."

Nash dabbed his mouth with a napkin. "In the wild there'd be other animals to eat it. It's not their fault if they end up stuck in a tank."

"Yeah, but eating crap is gross too." He laughed and looked at Robbie, but Robbie wouldn't lift his head. Chris nudged him. "We'll get your rock out. Dad'll stick his hand in there with all the fish crap, won't you, Dad?"

Robbie looked up, blinking hard. "Dad's not going to. You're going to. Isn't he, Dad?"

"Yup, that's the way it works. You mess it up, you fix it."

Chris said, "Yeah, yeah."

"You'll have to put your hand in there with all the crap. Won't he, Dad?"

Nash speared a piece of celery. "No gloating. Besides, we have to ask first."

In the end they didn't have to because the elderly waiter came back with a small green net held in both hands and silently fished out Robbie's find. He held it over the tank while it dripped, then pulled it free. With paper napkins he dabbed it dry before holding it in one hand and turning it toward the light from the aquarium. "Very curious," he said at last. He turned to Robbie. "Did you find it around here?"

"Our truck broke down and Dad made us look for fossils."

The old man's eyes brightened. "Lots of good places for fossils in this area. I go out looking all the time." He rubbed the thing with his thumb then balanced it on his fingers, as though he was weighing it. He bunched his lips. "I've hunted for fossils since I was a boy. I've got quite a collection. But this thing—do you have any idea what it might be?" He looked over at Nash.

"Obviously not a bone. It could be a coprolite, though there are those tiny holes all over its surface, and it's so light."

"Yes, so light." The old man held it out to Robbie with both hands, as though offering him a gift. "Some eggs are long like this."

"They're so rare, especially whole eggs. And just lying on the surface?" Nash shook his head. "I don't think so."

Robbie knelt on the seat with the thing gripped in his hand. "Have you ever seen anything like it?"

"I'm not sure. I've collected so many, especially in the last few years with all the rain washing them out. A lot of them are still in boxes and not even cleaned yet. If you're in town tomorrow, I can show you some of the more interesting ones I've found."

Robbie twisted around to Nash and his face was wide with excitement. "Oh yeah. Dad, that would be great."

Nash crumpled his napkin in his hand. "We're just passing through. Thanks for the offer, though."

"We got a flat tire," said Robbie. "Now we have to find a garage because we can't drive all the way to Canada on the spare, even though Canada's not that far."

The old man ran a hand over his thinning hair. "I hope you're not in a hurry. The owner of the garage is off dip-netting."

"When'll he be back?"

"The sockeye run's low, so it depends on when he gets his quota. Maybe tonight, maybe not until sometime tomorrow."

Nash felt his throat tighten. "There must be someplace else."

"You could head to Gakona Junction, but I'm not sure they're open either. Everyone's in Chitina trying to get their salmon while they can. How good a shape's your spare in?"

"Maybe not good enough. It needs air."

The old man tilted his head and gave a small nod, like that was too bad. "No air until Mike gets back. He keeps it locked up after some local kids got to bursting bike tires with it. Sounded like gun shots and scared the life out of him and his wife. The Tesoro on the edge of town doesn't do air, just gas and snacks." He sighed. "Can I get you anything else? You need boxes?"

"Just the check, we're done. And we're camping, so I guess we'll have to leave the leftovers."

"Which place?"

"The RV park on the west side of town."

"You're staying at old Standig's place? If you're here another night, you should try the state campground. It's a few miles out of town but much nicer. And cheaper." He stacked the plates and carried them away to the kitchen.

Robbie held his find to his chest. "Let's come and see him tomorrow, Dad. We can do that, can't we? We'll have time."

Chris leaned forward and hissed, "Weren't you listening? We're leaving tomorrow."

"He said the garage is closed, and he'll show me his fossils."

Nash dropped his head into his hands. "Shut up, boys. Please just shut up." Mercifully, they did.

It was too light to sleep, and too muggy. Even in nothing but boxers and with the trailer's windows open, Nash sweated into the sleeping bag he'd laid beneath him. He'd let the boys have the bed and now on this thing, a bed that was simply the dining table lowered with the bench cushions arranged across it, there wasn't quite room for his legs. He'd bent them this way and that, rolling over to where the sleeping bag was a little cooler, shaking his pillow to plump it, as though that were the problem. The blinds were swinging gently in the breeze, and he found himself staring at them as the minutes crept by.

A few feet away, the boys slept restlessly, shifting about and sighing. Chris moaned, "Mom! Mom!" How desperate he sounded. She'd been gone over a year and here he was, still calling for her.

Nash heaved himself off his bed and stood over the boys, then he leaned down and kissed Chris on the forehead. His skin was damp, and around him hung the cheesy whiff of damp clothes. His hair had come loose from the band and Nash smoothed it back, ran a finger along his cheek—how odd to feel bristle. He was almost a man, thick-chested with sturdy legs, like Maria's dad. Inside, though, wasn't he just a kid who'd lost his mom?

Chris murmured. Nash rubbed his shoulder to quiet him, but he fidgeted and his knee nudged Robbie who turned over with a groan. Nash straightened up just as Robbie flung his arm above his head, something dark clutched in his hand. That thing he'd found. Gently Nash tried to pull it away. His fingers slipped—the kid was so hot the find was slick with sweat, and when he tried again, Robbie tucked his hand against his chest.

Forget it, Nash told himself, just forget it. He stepped over to the sink and poured himself a cup of water. It was warm and tasted of plastic. He leaned against the counter and drank most of it down, then splashed his face with what was left. His shoulders felt strained from steering the truck forever straight, his hands achy from clenching the wheel, and he flexed them, shook them out, blew on them.

That was something Maria would have done. Whenever the boys had bumps and scrapes, she'd bend her head to their elbow, their fingers, and purse her lips to blow. It had worked: the tears would stop and she'd smile, tell them it was Mexican magic she'd learned from their Tata—Nash could understand that much of her Spanish. That was another thing that was gone—the sound of Spanish in their house, Maria chatting to the boys and them answering in English, and he'd joked that they'd think Spanish was the language of scolding, and she'd told him no, they'd grow up knowing it was the language of love. All those superhero movies they'd watched together, and she'd get so excited, shouting at the TV, insults, encouragements—Nash didn't understand it all, though the boys did, and they'd laugh.

The way Maria sat between the boys on the sofa, arms gathering them in, the boys melting against her, even Chris when he was taller than her, his cheek on her head, her fingers smoothing his hair. The way she slept with her arms up to her chest, or grimaced at bad coffee as though she was going to spit it out. He'd kept those moments nestled inside him, holding something of her close. Now, though—now he'd stopped believing she was out there, never mind that he knew better than that. All those rumors on the internet: tens of thousands of immigrants vanishing into privately run detention centers where they died from lack of food and medical care, or were forced to work for years to pay off the cost of their own detention—people who'd done nothing more than violate immigration law turned into indentured servants. Even if you were legal, there was no one to protect you. If you spoke Spanish, or had an accent, or were the wrong color, you could be taken into custody and disappear without a trace.

And for Maria, that was the best he could hope for. Online he'd seen pictures of women snatched by bounty hunters and sold to sex traffickers because the money was better than what the government paid. Those women—locked up in massage parlors for years on end. Even after they'd escaped, their eyes looked empty.

For months after she'd gone missing, the thought of what might have happened to her had invaded his dreams, and he'd startle awake with his T-shirt sodden and cold against his chest, and a poisonous fear running through him. In the mornings, worn out and gritty-eyed, he'd rouse the boys and feed them breakfast with barely a word, and if the boys talked about her he'd seize up. He couldn't live that way, just couldn't. Instead he pushed the thought of her away. This evening, telling Robbie not to worry because if she came back she'd be able to find them, that he'd thought of that. In truth, in the fury of packing up, the idea of Maria returning hadn't crossed his mind.

The air trapped in the trailer was so still it was suffocating. Nash lifted the blinds and ducked his face to the open window. There was not the slightest breeze. Beyond, under a sky drained of color, the campground lay motionless.

3

The sun rose hours before it would have been worth getting up and heading into town. Its heat gathered in the trailer and Nash sat up, boxers sticking to his skin. He raised his hand to unlatch the window over his bed only to find it was already open, and he lay back down in the sickly heat until he could bear it no more. Half-dressed, he went outside.

The campground was dotted with RVs, campers, and trailers. Close by, a VW bus had its top popped up and, over by the road, a massive brown RV sat with its generator whirring away. A breeze shifted air that was listless and heavy, and no wonder since the ground was soft underfoot and the grass sparkled damply. It must have rained during the night, and he'd slept through it. Yet more rain though what had already fallen had broken records. At this rate roads would flood, bridges wash out, hillsides collapse, and if the highway closed, it would mean a detour of hundreds of miles to get to the border. It wasn't even seven, but he had the urge to wake the boys right now, to get going. Instead he headed for the bathrooms, nodding hello to an old guy walking his tiny dog, catching smells of frying bacon and the tinny blare of the news: soaring temperatures across the Pacific Northwest, people dying of heatstroke in Seattle and Portland with no end in sight, while in the Midwest…Nash kept walking. He didn't want to hear the rest; he never did these days.

He waited until seven thirty to get the boys up and they complained groggily that he never let them sleep in. He shook them anyway, told them, "We've got a long day ahead of us. Come on now, get up and eat."

He packed his sleeping bag then hefted the small dining table back up and rearranged the bench cushions into seats. He set water to boil, though the heat of the burning gas bloomed out unbearably through the trailer. Chris was sitting up, slumped as though he was already worn out. Beside him Robbie was sprawled across the bed. His underpants looked dank with sweat. Nash called over, "You too, Robbie. And change your underwear." Robbie moaned and rubbed his face, and when he sat up Nash noticed the find still in his hand. "Come on, put that thing down and get moving."

Nash poured hot water over ground coffee in a paper filter and watched as Robbie scooted to the side of the bed and kicked at the clothes on the floor. "You boys need to pick up. This trailer's not big enough for dirty laundry everywhere." He rummaged in the cupboard, found the pack of muffins he'd bought for a breakfast treat a couple of days ago—a lifetime ago—and put one on a paper napkin. "I'll be outside. At least it's a little cooler out there."

He carried his coffee into the sunshine. Already it was growing hot, and he dragged the picnic table into the shade of the trailer then wiped away the tiny puddles of rainwater on its surface. The wood of the tabletop was rough and damp against his arms, and his coffee steamed lazily. Beyond the town, mountains loomed with snow dazzling on their peaks. He took a bite of the muffin. A store-bought thing that had the strange softness of food designed for a long shelf life. He ate it quickly, almost gobbling as though he were wretchedly hungry.

Somewhere close by a bird was calling, an insistent, slightly off-key song repeated over and over. Nash rubbed his chin, felt the pleasant smoothness where he'd shaved, and took a long sip of his coffee. Drinking it outside it tasted different, earthier, as though only now was it clear that it was made from the roasted seeds of a plant whose roots had sucked nutrients from the decayed matter they grew in. How very real the world felt, a place of soil and life and regeneration, not bounty hunters and detention centers.

He glanced at his watch. A quarter before eight. They should get going soon. If the garage was open, if he could get air for the spare tire, they could make it to the border by midafternoon, even driving slowly. Usually by now he'd be taking the boys to day camp. As far as work was concerned, he wasn't gone, he wasn't even late. The sun would be coming in through his office window, catching the models on his desk—Godzilla, Mothra, Kong. Gifts from Maria. In a little while, Tony and Wanda would head for the lunchroom and pour themselves coffee. They'd hang around for a few minutes, talking about their kids, and the news, and soon they'd wonder where he was. As the morning wore on more people would ask, "Hey, where's Nash? Did he call in sick?"

He took another sip of coffee. No, he thought, that wasn't right. Those bounty hunters had gone straight there yesterday to look for him, and Fran must have explained that he was at the dentist's and wouldn't be back until tomorrow. No wonder they'd shown up at his house, they'd known he wasn't at work, and the thought of it—that maybe while he was frantically packing, Fran had called a meeting to share out his clients, and Wanda had been in his office dumping his models into a box—it made him queasy, as though the world had lurched beneath him.

When the screen door slapped open, he set down his coffee and glanced behind him. Chris stepped out of the trailer in shorts and flip-flops, already eating a muffin. His hair was down, and he scooped it away from his face. On the roundness of his chin and upper lip, a shadow of beard was growing in. "You drink something already?" Nash called.

"Nope."

"Get yourself a juice box when you're finished with that, then go shave."

"Am I looking *sleazy*?"

Nash laughed. A word Maria had come out with years ago, caught off guard as she turned around with the phone in her hand, breaking off from Spanish when she saw the boys coming in from the yard covered in mud and Nash trying to shepherd them upstairs. She'd exclaimed, "They're so sleazy!" stretching it out, and it had sounded so deliciously scandalous that the boys had chanted it heading up to the bathroom. After that it had stuck—the family word for when their clothes were dirty, or their hair needed washing. "Yeah," Nash said now, "downright *sleazy*."

Chris grinned and sat down beside him, slid his phone onto the table. "I'll shave tonight. We want to get going, right?"

"We'll be crossing the border today. Looking sleazy doesn't help."

"Dad, honestly—you worry too much."

"I do worry." He stared off across the campground. "I don't want anything else to go wrong. I want us to get to Canada, then I'll stop worrying. About us at least."

Chris took another bite of muffin and crumbs sprayed down on the table. "You think Mom's still out there somewhere?"

Nash squeezed his fingers against his jaw. That soreness from having his tooth filled, only yesterday, a lifetime ago.

"Do you?" Chris's voice faltered.

"When we get to Canada, I'll call Tata and tell her where we are. In case Mom gets in touch."

"Tata always cries." With his fingers, Chris shoved the last of the muffin into his mouth and wadded up the wrapper. "She thinks Mom's dead too, doesn't she?"

"I don't think she's dead. I just don't know, I really don't." His voice sounded tight, forced, and he took a sip of coffee and held it on his tongue. He could understand it—deciding that Maria was dead. Maybe that was better than accepting there was a chance she'd been trafficked, that if she ever escaped she'd be so broken she might never recover. He ran his thumb over the rim of the mug. "Sorry, sweetie. I don't know what to tell you. I wish I did."

Chris stared out at the mountains with one hand shielding his face. "Yeah," he said and nodded hard, then nodded again. He flicked away the crumbs on the table, but they caught in the spots of water. "You did pack the chargers, right? My phone's dead."

Nash sighed. "Sure. In one of the boxes."

"Really, Dad?"

"It was a mad rush. It's a miracle I packed them at all."

Chris scowled. "Then let's stop in town and buy one."

"Oh, come on. You can live without texting for a day or two, can't you?"

He picked up his phone and rubbed its screen clean against his T-shirt. "I just wanted to let my friends know what's going on."

"Not until we're over the border. Just in case."

"Don't you think that's a bit paranoid?"

"It's not paranoia if they're really out to get you." Nash gave a quick smile. "Seriously, though—let's not tempt fate."

Chris shoved the phone into his shorts pocket. "Honestly, Dad—" but he swallowed back whatever else he was going to say. "I need another of those muffins. You?"

"No, I'm good. Tell Robbie to get a move on, okay?"

"Sure." The bench shifted as Chris stood. A few moments later, the screen door thudded shut.

Nash was drinking the last of his coffee when Robbie came out of the trailer, a muffin in one hand and his find in the other. He was wearing the same T-shirt as the day before, rap artist, juice stains, and all.

Nash said, "Hey, I told you to change, sweetie. And put that thing down."

He sat opposite Nash, in the sun, and blew the hair out of his eyes. They looked small and too bright, as though he was tired out. Maybe he hadn't slept well, but then, none of them had. He still had his fingers wrapped around the find, and Nash touched his wrist. "It's not going anywhere. Come on, put it down while you eat."

Robbie glanced at the trailer door, then he squinted at Nash. "Dad?" His voice was small.

"Yep."

"Dad, I can't let it go."

"Sure you can. Who d'you think's going to take it?"

Robbie shook his head. "No, Dad. I mean I can't." He stretched his hand across the table. Something inside the trailer rattled, and he startled and folded his arms against his chest.

Nash glanced over his shoulder and shouted, "Chris, put on more water for coffee, would you? Oh, and grab a juice box for Robbie."

He reached out for Robbie's hand, said quietly, "Show me." So Robbie did. He laid his hand on the table and tried to lift his fingers away from the thing, straining with the effort. "Really?" Nash said, and it wasn't until he saw the wetness in Robbie's eyes that he got to his feet and came around the table. He brought Robbie's hand up close to his face and angled it in the sunlight. He told him, "Try again."

This time, in the dazzling sunlight, he could see: between the thing and Robbie's skin were hundreds of tiny pale tendrils.

Funny how fast the panic overwhelmed him—one moment he was peering at those tendrils, and the next he had Robbie's arm pinned against his side, pressing Robbie's small hand onto the table as he pulled out his pocketknife and opened it with his teeth, bringing the blade down, and the whole time Robbie was wailing and beating on his back. It was only when Chris yelled, "What's happened? What's wrong?" that Nash looked up. An awful shrieking was running through his head, but the look on

Chris's face made him pause. A heartbeat, another, and his hold on Robbie's wrist slackened.

"Okay now—" and his voice was raw as he lifted the blade away "—this thing's stuck to Robbie's hand and I have to get it off. I need a little help here."

Robbie's face was flushed, his hair stuck to his forehead. He was trembling as he choked out over and over, "Dad! Dad!"

"It's alright. We'll take it slow. Chris—you help me, alright? Pull on that thing just a little so I can see what I'm doing when I get the blade in."

Chris let out a laugh. "What did you do, Robs? Glue it to your hand?"

Nash snapped, "Where the hell would he find glue?"

"I don't know, but if it's stuck, use soap or oil or something. That's what Mom used to do." He glanced at the knife. "You can't cut it off. For chrissakes, Dad!"

"It's not that kind of stuck," Nash said quietly.

Chris bent close and his hair flopped over his face. He tried to lift one end of the thing from Robbie's hand. "Holy shit. What is that?"

Against Nash's back, Robbie's head, heavy and hot.

Nash said, "Whatever it is, we're going to cut it off right now. Okay, Robbie?"

Robbie didn't say a word, and Chris ducked behind Nash. "Hey," Chris told him, "it'll be alright. This is some weird shit, but Dad's going to take care of it, okay?"

Robbie muttered something, then Chris said, "Why not? You can't go around with a rock stuck to your hand."

Nash felt Robbie lift his head. "I just don't want him to."

"You scared? I'd be too. Just be brave, okay? You can do this."

"You need a moment, Robbie?" Nash said. "I'm sorry I scared you, but we need to get this thing off. Ready, Chris?"

Behind him, Robbie grabbed a handful of his T-shirt. "Dad? Can't we just leave it?"

"No, I don't think we can. I mean, do you? Really?" Robbie's head came down against his back again, harder this time. "Right, let's do this. And Robbie? You let me know if I hurt you. Because if I do, then we'll try something else."

He had Chris gently tug up one end of the thing, then he crouched and was slipping the blade into the tiny gap between Robbie's palm and the find when Robbie cried out. Nash let go. "Sweetie, I hadn't even started. You're scared, that's all. Let's give it another go—I'll be careful, I promise."

Robbie held his hand to his chest. "You said if it hurt we'd try something else."

"I don't know what that something else is yet, Robs. I'd have to think."

Robbie's face bunched up. "Not the hospital, right? I don't want to go!"

Chris bent toward him. "Cool it, dude. Dad didn't say anything about a hospital, did he?"

Nash shot him a look and tightened his grip on the knife. Perhaps his medical insurance had already been canceled. If those bounty hunters had come to the office, by now Fran would know he was in the country illegally and she'd have yanked his coverage. No, he thought—she didn't have the authority. She'd have had to talk to Malcolm first, and he was out yesterday, meeting a client up in Utqiagvik, and today, well Malcolm didn't usually get in until at least eight-thirty. She couldn't have talked to him yet. He bent over Robbie's hand again. They needed to get the hell out of this country, that's what they needed.

He nodded to Chris to lift one end of the thing and delicately eased in the knife. So many tendrils, so fine and pale—he snagged one and sliced the blade through it. With a yell, Robbie wrenched his hand free, huddling over himself and sobbing, "That hurt, that really, really hurt."

Nash dropped the knife on the table and wrapped his arms

around him. He pressed his cheek against Robbie's head, said, "Oh god, I'm so sorry."

Chris was frowning. "You didn't cut him, I know you didn't."

Nash stretched his fingers through Robbie's damp hair. It was hot from the sun and had a slightly oily smell. "I wasn't listening, I just wasn't listening."

The bench creaked as Chris sat down. "He's scared, that's all. I'd be too, but it's not like the blade even—"

"Did you leave water heating on the stove?"

"Shit." Chris lurched up from the bench, then came the bang of the screen door swinging closed behind him.

Robbie was shaking, and Nash hugged him hard. "You okay?"

"I'm cold."

"Cold?" Nash let out a laugh. "When it's so warm out here?" Even before the words left his mouth he understood. He settled Robbie away from him and held the back of his hand against Robbie's forehead. Hot. Against the side of his neck. Hot. "Bet you don't feel so good."

"I just want to sleep."

Nash laid him back in his arms and Robbie closed his eyes. They looked a little sunken, as though he was exhausted. He ran a thumb along the top of Robbie's cheek. It gave softly, like rising dough, and that wasn't normal, it just wasn't.

"Sure, sweet pea, you lie there for a moment while I think." Nash rocked him, that small body burning against his.

"I don't want to go to a hospital."

"Well, you're in luck. The nearest hospital is hours away," he said and ducked his head to hide his fear.

4

Nash told Chris to make sure everything was stowed, and then he locked up the trailer. From the back of the truck Robbie was staring out at him, face ghostly behind the glass. It made no sense to think the dead thing attached to his hand was making him sick—that was what Maria used to call crazy American thinking, the sort of logic that came straight out of movies. Sometimes watching the news with her—a preacher proclaiming the Midwest's massive floods part of a Chinese plot to destroy the country; militia members holed up in a bunker, waiting for a civil war—she'd shout at the TV, "You people, movies are for fun, not for living your life," and she'd get to her feet and pace across the carpet, fists pressed against her head. He'd loved that about her, the way she took it all so personally.

Maria was a nurse. If the boys were sick, she was the one to decide if they stayed home from school, or went to the doctor, or needed to be driven straight to the ER. Surely she'd have said that they needed to get Robbie looked at, and soon. But heading back to Anchorage meant risking running into bounty hunters. There was a hospital up in Fairbanks, too. The problem was, these days a lot of hospitals ran IDs through government databases. One phone call and you could be snatched, right from the ER.

He slapped dust from his hands and stared off toward the mountains. Canada, that's where he'd get Robbie looked at. It would be safer. At the border, there was only the tiny town of Beaver Creek. No hospital, maybe not even a decent clinic until they got to Whitehorse, and that was well past the border. In his chest, fear dug in its claws. He couldn't risk it, he just couldn't. They'd have to find a clinic somewhere near here, because there had to be less chance of getting reported in a tiny out-of-the-way town. Maybe there was a place right here in Glennallen, and he pulled out his phone and searched, damp fingertips leaving smears on the screen until he pulled up what he needed: a walk-in clinic. They could be there in a few minutes. Most likely whatever was wrong had nothing to do with that thing stuck to Robbie's hand and he just needed antibiotics, or antihistamines, and they could be on their way again. Still, he'd feel betrayed— there was no avoiding that.

"What's the plan? Are we hitching up the trailer?" Chris was leaning against the truck. He'd pulled his hair together in an elastic band again, and it stood up from the top of his head in a tuft.

"Not now."

"We're not leaving?"

"There's a clinic in town. We'll take Robbie there first, then come back for the trailer."

His face stiffened. "Dad—"

"I know, really I do. But what are the chances they'll run our IDs in a tiny place hours away from Anchorage?" He pulled out his keys.

"I could stay here with the trailer. In case anyone comes snooping around."

"So they could take you? No!" He pushed back his hair. "We need to stay together."

"Even though we're hours away from Anchorage?"

"Chris—"

"Yeah, yeah, I know. We're playing it safe, we don't want anything else to go wrong." He gave a sad smile and climbed into the truck.

He must have said something to Robbie because when Nash started the engine, Robbie leaned forward and said, "Dad, I don't need to go to a clinic. I'm fine, really."

"Just in case, Robs."

"Dad—" He clutched the headrest. "I'm not sick."

Nash turned, and Robbie's face was just inches from his. His skin looked smooth, taut, the cheeks round in a way they hadn't been since he'd lost his baby fat. "Sweetie, it's probably just a bug, or an allergic reaction, but we need to make sure."

"I don't want to get caught."

"Is that what you think's going to happen? Where did you hear that?"

"On the news, Dad. Stuff like that's always on the news. You know—bounty hunters catching people."

"That's not going to happen way out here. The doctor'll just give you some antibiotics or something, and we'll be off." He gave a quick smile and looked away. He hoped it was true.

Chris caught his eye. He pressed his lips together in a way that Maria had when she wanted to say something but couldn't, and in reply Nash just shoved the truck into gear.

The clinic turned out to be a tiny white building with dusty windows. In the few minutes it took to get there, Robbie fell asleep, or at least pretended to fall asleep, slouched against the window. Nash shook him, then lifted him out onto the dirt of the parking lot where he stood swaying and blinking in the sunlight. "Do you really feel that bad? Or are you just pretending to be tired so we don't go in?"

Robbie leaned against him. "I'm really tired."

"We're still going in."

Robbie wrenched himself away and stood with his arms by his sides and his mouth contorted. "This sucks."

"So does being sick. Come on," he said and beckoned for Chris to get out too.

The receptionist was a large woman with hair scraped back from her forehead into a pony tail, and small unblinking eyes. Nash explained that his son had a fever, and his face had swollen a little, and oh yeah, he had a rock stuck to his hand. "Well, these things happen, right, hun?" she said easily, then smiled at Robbie who stared back stony-faced. Handing her his health insurance card, Nash felt like a fraud. For sure it would be canceled by the time the clinic submitted the claim, still he went ahead and confirmed all the information on it, gave her the address of the house they'd just fled in Anchorage and a made-up phone number. He had to nudge Chris when he started to correct him. In his throat his heart pulsed as he waited to be caught out, right up until the receptionist handed back his card and told them to take a seat.

The waiting room was as narrow as a bus. On its walls hung oversized paintings of bull moose standing in lakes, and bears snatching salmon from rivers. Overhead a speaker churned out vapid pop music, and the smell of floor polish plus something chemical and heady lingered on the air. A few other patients trailed in: a skinny woman in tattered Carhartt's, a man with a toddler who writhed in his lap then grizzled quietly, an elderly couple in ball caps that said *The Last Frontier*.

Robbie sat swinging his feet hard, rocking the row of plastic chairs and making them squeak. Every few minutes he muttered something like, "This really sucks," or, "This is dumb, Dad, I'm fine." Nash gave up explaining that they were getting him checked out just in case. Chris was slumped in his chair with his eyes shut, as though this was all more than he could bear.

When at last the nurse called them in, Chris made to get up only to have the nurse shake her head. "Three's a crowd in our tiny rooms." Chris sighed and flopped back onto the chair.

Trailing down the corridor beside the nurse, Robbie looked small and bedraggled, and Nash felt his heart contract. It didn't help that the nurse was all hearty efficiency, getting his height and weight at the end of the corridor and then shooing him into a small room where she took his blood pressure and temperature. "Well, you got a fever of a hundred and three. You're not feeling so good, huh?" She popped the cover off the thermometer, straight into the garbage. "Don't worry. There's stuff going around. Always is." Then she tipped her head. "That thing stuck to your hand?"

Robbie nodded.

"What did you do? Superglue it?" Robbie kept his head down and she let out her breath, caught Nash's eye. "Kids get up to some crazy stuff. Well, don't worry. The doctor will be right in, and she's seen it all."

Nash laid a hand on Robbie's shoulder. "Yeah, I bet she has," he said flatly.

When the door closed behind her, Nash took the seat beside Robbie and put an arm around his shoulders. How hot he felt, heat radiating off his small body. "You poor thing," Nash whispered. "You're pretty sick."

Robbie tried to pull away, said something so quietly that Nash didn't catch it.

"What's that?"

Robbie heaved in a breath and said more loudly, "We should go. Before the doctor gets here."

"You've got a fever. It could be an infection."

When he looked up, his face was fierce. Already the delicate bones of his cheeks looked a little blurred, his eyes narrowed by the swelling. Whatever this sickness was, it was affecting him fast. Robbie said, "She's just going to be like the nurse. She's going to think I'm some dumb kid who superglued this thing to my hand and that's why I'm sick."

"Then she'll take a look and see it's not superglued."

He broke free of Nash's arm and rocked himself. "I'm so stupid," he said, "so stupid, so freaking stupid."

"Sweet pea, you didn't do anything stupid—"

Then he craned his head up, burst out with, "I should have left it! Why didn't I just leave it where it was?"

"Because I sent you off to find fossils, and it looked like a fossil. So it's my fault, not yours." Robbie wasn't even looking at him, but Nash kept going. "Besides, who'd have thought this could happen? Inanimate objects don't usually attach themselves to people, right? Maybe it's a coincidence that you got sick today, or maybe you're having an allergic reaction to it—I don't know, but we'll find out. That's why we're here."

"Dad?"

"Yeah?"

"You're full of shit."

"And you don't get to talk like that just because you're sick. You are so grounded."

Robbie was shaking, and it took Nash a moment to realize he was laughing. "I'm grounded? To the trailer? Or are you going to take away my video game time?" He was blinking fast, his hands jammed against his thighs. "Or what else are you going to do?"

"Dunno," said Nash, "glue a rock to your other hand?" and Robbie shoved him with his shoulder.

A rat-tat at the door, then in came the doctor with a laptop under her arm. An older woman in pale green scrubs, her hair held back by a couple of steely barrettes. "Mr. Preston?" She shook Nash's hand and gave a businesslike smile that fell away as she settled herself on a stool. She opened the laptop on her knees and ran a finger down the screen, her lips working. "This must be Roberto. You're not feeling too good, hmm?" She glanced at him, then back at the screen. "Some swelling, a temp of a hundred and three—that's quite a fever. And something stuck to your hand?"

Nash explained—the fossil-hunting, the find, Robbie holding onto it and how he couldn't let go because of the tendrils, how now his face was a little swollen and he'd come down with a fever. The doctor's eyebrows lifted, and her pale gaze went to Robbie's hand. "Tendrils?" she said sharply.

"That's what they look like. I tried to cut through them, but Robbie yelled like I was cutting into his hand."

"I see, I see." She slid the laptop onto the counter then scooted her stool over to Robbie. She didn't touch the thing on Robbie's hand, just stared at it then tugged on a pair of purple surgical gloves from a box on the wall. "Well then—" she gestured to the bed "—let's take a proper look."

Robbie moved like an old man, hefting himself out of his chair, heavy-footing it to the bed and hauling himself up. He sat there until the doctor waved at him to lie down. Beneath him the paper sheet crackled drily, then came the metallic snap of the doctor turning on an adjustable lamp, the squeak as she moved it to examine his hand. She turned it this way and that, even hoisted it to eye level and took hold of the thing and tugged. She brought her face closer and pulled again, then sat back and blinked, as if to clear her eyes. "Well, well, well," she said at last, and the faintest of smiles tugged at her mouth.

Nash said, "I thought maybe he was having an allergic reaction."

The doctor peered at Nash, all trace of the smile gone but a liveliness playing in her eyes. "He hasn't taken a new medication? Nothing over the counter? He hasn't eaten seafood or nuts or anything else he's allergic to?"

"No, nothing like that. Couldn't it be an allergic reaction to that thing?"

"I doubt it." Her lips closed, and they looked thin and mean.

Nash leaned forward. With one hand he pushed back his hair. It felt gritty. "Do you know what it is?"

"It's certainly worth a closer look." She got to her feet peeling off the gloves and balling them together, tossing them into the trash where they landed with a light thunk. Then she snatched up the laptop and stepped toward the door. "If you'll excuse me for just a few minutes—"

"Wait." Nash stood too. "It's that thing making him sick, isn't it? And you can—"

"One step at a time, Mr. Preston."

"It's not just a bug, then?"

The doctor hesitated, one hand on the door handle. "A bug could very well be the culprit. There are always illnesses going around, especially among youngsters." She nodded a couple of times, as though she was seriously considering that possibility. "Now, I need to make a call. I won't be long but I must insist that you wait here."

"Call? Who do you need to call?" He heard his voice pinch tight.

"Mr. Preston—"

"I want to know what's going on."

"We all do, Mr. Preston, so please—you two sit tight, and I'll send the nurse in." With that, she slipped away into the corridor.

As soon as the door closed, Robbie sat up. Perhaps it was the washed-out light, but his skin looked dingy, like old sheets. "Dad?" he whispered. "What's wrong with me?"

"I don't know, sweetie. The doctor doesn't know either." He wrapped an arm around Robbie's shoulders. His T-shirt was damp, and from close by came a whiff of burned sugar, sweet and foul at the same time.

He was to keep Robbie here and wait because look at Robbie, there was something wrong with him, something serious, and yet anxiety squirmed in Nash's gut. Doctors didn't leave in the middle of consultations to make phone calls. The receptionist could have run their information and told her they were illegal, and right now that doctor was turning them in—no, that didn't make sense. So perhaps she was calling a specialist. She'd been excited about whatever was wrong with Robbie: that small smile she'd tried to hide, that eagerness to get out of the consulting room and on the phone. Nash lifted his head. The doctor had barely examined Robbie. She'd looked at that thing on his hand then said she had to make a call and hurried away. This wasn't about Robbie, it was about the find. Nash took hold of Robbie's arm. "Let's get out of here."

"Dad! She said we had to wait."

"So? Is she the boss of us? She's just a doctor."

Robbie glanced toward the door. "I didn't like her."

"Come on, then. Before the nurse comes back."

The corridor was empty. Nash gripped Robbie's wrist and fast-walked him along its scuffed flooring. They passed a door cracked open. The doctor was bent forward with a phone pressed to her ear. Her fingernails were tap-tapping the desk, and she let out a noisy sigh and said, "Well, alright then, alright." Nash nudged Robbie to keep going just as the doctor's head jerked toward them and she cried, "Hey! I told you to wait!"

Nash dragged Robbie into the waiting room where Chris jumped up at the sight of them. Then Chris was rushing for the door, holding it open, and they were outside running for the truck.

It took all of Nash's concentration to keep the truck in its lane, to stop at the stop sign, to drive like a sane man. He checked his rearview mirror, checked it again because his thoughts kept scattering. That doctor. So furious. Charging after them in her scrubs as they took off from the clinic. Nash told himself, this is batshit crazy, it really is, and he let out a bark of a laugh that made Chris say, "Dad?" The engine was roaring and he glanced down. Fast. Way too fast. He forced his foot off the gas, and when he glanced in the mirror he saw Robbie curled up in the back seat. He told him, "Everything's okay, Robs, everything's okay," even though it wasn't. He'd been a fool to go to the clinic, and an even bigger fool to leave the trailer at the campground because now they had to go back for it, and he called out to the boys, "Keep your heads down, okay? Just in case they come looking for us."

Chris shot him a look as he scooted down in his seat. That sprig of hair on top of his head had sagged to one side. His lips were a flat line, his eyes wide. He was frightened. Of him, his own dad, and what he'd unleashed. Nash wanted to make him understand—this wasn't his fault, he was doing his best, for crying out loud.

In front of the truck, a woman in a sun hat was leisurely crossing the road. Nash braked. He saw her lurch out of the way and her hat tumble off to the pavement. He took a breath and let it out as slowly as he could, despite the burning in his chest, and when she'd picked up her hat and set it back on her head, he drove past so sedately that it felt like he was mocking her. In the mirror, nothing but a red minivan coming closer. No flashing lights, no one watching except that woman staring out from under the wide brim of her hat, and already she was shrinking into the distance.

Nash shifted his grip on the steering wheel to where the plastic was cool. He couldn't panic. He needed to think clearly. No shady government bureaucrat was going to swoop down and take Robbie away, no bounty hunters were going to appear out here in this tiny town, at least, not this quickly. In sight just ahead was the entrance to the campground. Before turning on his blinker, Nash slowed to scan the place—for unmarked vehicles, for black SUVs that menacing men could spring from. Ridiculous, he told himself, and yet his heart throbbed uncomfortably.

He drove across the campground slowly, glancing around. The trailer looked small and shabby among the RVs. Everything was still except for dead leaves whirling over the ground, and the old guy walking his tiny dog.

"Really, Dad?" Chris let out a laugh. "You think they're on our tail already?"

Nash stepped a little harder on the gas and drove carelessly over the lumpy ground, sending the truck bouncing and swaying, and Chris braced himself against the window, his topknot dusting the ceiling.

"Just trying to be careful."

Chris twisted around in his seat. "Yeah, right. I mean, I don't know what went down at that clinic, but you and Robbie running out like that—"

"Not now, Chris."

"The doctor could barely have had time to look at Robbie, so what—"

Nash pulled up close to the trailer and jammed the gearshift into park. "Please! Enough! Do you understand? We have to get out of here."

Chris held up both hands. A familiar gesture—Nash's own, he realized. "Sure, whatever. It just seemed like we were in Crazy Town, you know?" Chris's mouth was a little slack, like this was all a joke and maybe Nash shouldn't take it so seriously.

He killed the engine. In the silence his ears hissed with an empty sound like static. Under his breath he said, "Chris, don't make things worse. Alright?"

Chris stared back, eyes hard, pushing at him. "You haven't even explained what happened back there. I mean come on, I'm not a kid anymore!"

"I need you to help me get the trailer hitched up so we can get back on the road."

"Another change of plan? The tire's still flat, Dad."

"It's only a few hours to the border. We'll find a place to get air on the way." How hollow his voice sounded. He'd forgotten about the spare, even though the truck had been pulling the whole way back from the clinic.

"Did the clinic say they were reporting us? What happened, Robs?" Chris twisted around in his seat and one knee, crooked up, jerked and jerked at a manic speed.

Nash took a breath. When he glanced in the mirror, Robbie's eyes were watching him. "The doctor wanted us to wait while she made a call. It didn't seem like a good idea to hang around."

"I didn't like her," said Robbie. "Neither did Dad."

"So we just ran?"

"Yeah." Nash pushed open his door and got out.

There was a breeze, and despite the sun he shivered—no wonder, his T-shirt was stuck to his back, wet through with sweat. He plucked it loose as he walked over to the trailer.

Inside, the air had the funky whiff of dirty laundry. He pulled off his shirt and wiped his chest with it then took a fresh one out of his bag. All he needed was to put it on and hitch up the trailer so they could get going, and any moment now he would: he'd shake out that clean T-shirt and duck his head into it, but not yet, not quite yet.

The panic that had propelled him back to the campground was gone, and in its place was a sick feeling and a fizzing in his head. He laid one hand on the rickety dining table and levered himself down onto the seat, gingerly, as though he was lowering himself into a hot bath, then he rested his head on his knees and pressed his hands against his temples. His nose filled with the meaty smell of his own skin. For a moment he thought he was ill, but it wasn't that, it was fear. The only other time he'd been this afraid had been when Maria hadn't come home. At first there'd been a slight worry tinged with irritation—she was late and hadn't called. Then as one hour tipped into another that worry had been swamped by the cold, unrelenting certainty that something awful had happened. He'd sent the boys to bed so he could shut himself away in the living room and make calls without them hearing the strain in his voice as he tried to stay calm.

Whatever had happened to her, Maria must have felt this same gut-gnawing dread. If she'd been locked away—in a detention center, or forced to work for her keep, or pimped out by some gang—before long that fear would have turned into despair. Once she'd given up, perhaps any way out looked worth it, even if it meant never seeing her boys and her husband again. A jump from a high window. A piece of glass slicing along her wrist.

How hard it had been when those cops were convinced she'd run off. They'd talked to the boys, dazed from being woken up, and afterward Robbie had cried and said over and over that Mom wouldn't have left him behind. What the hell had he been thinking, letting the cops talk to them?

Now he wondered what else he was fucking up. He'd behaved like a lunatic, fleeing the clinic when maybe the doctor had been calling a specialist. He closed his eyes and tried to replay what had happened, to hear again what she'd said, though when he reached back to those minutes in the consulting room, all he could see was the way the doctor's eyebrows had lifted when he'd mentioned the tendrils, the way her gaze had sharpened. She'd known who to call, had been furious at Nash and Robbie for escaping—and they had been escaping, though from what, he wasn't sure.

A scuff of noise outside the trailer. Nash opened his eyes as a shadow came stretching over the dirt beyond the doorway: Chris, ducking his head and peering into the semi-darkness. "You okay, Dad?" There was a quaver to his voice.

Nash pulled on the T-shirt. "Yeah, just coming." He snatched up his keys from the table. "How's Robbie doing?"

"He's a bit freaked out." He lifted a hand to shield his eyes. "You've got your T-shirt on backwards."

"Shit." He pulled his arms back through the sleeves and twisted it around. "Well, let's get this show on the road."

Chris didn't even roll his eyes. Instead he watched Nash lock up the trailer, as though he needed watching.

5

They drove back through Glennallen with the trailer, past two sleek buses that had pulled up nose to tail on the roadside across from the bar. Tourists were drifting around in shorts and pastel-colored shirts, in sneakers white as sunblock, as though they hadn't noticed the storm clouds banking up on the northern edge of the sky. On the doorstep of the bar, a woman with bleached hair and a creased face sat tapping ash off her cigarette, staring at the tourists and blowing out streamers of smoke that were snatched away by the breeze. She glanced at Nash as he drove past and then flicked what was left of her cigarette into the dirt.

In the morning light, the Golden Dragon looked dingy. Its curtains were faded, and dust clung to the red lantern swinging in the breeze. Beneath the hanging baskets, the ground was dark where water had dripped, and in the window a sign said *Closed.* Nash drove slowly, carefully, past an ice-cream shop, a burger joint, a hardware store, a men's clothing outfitters that had transparent yellow plastic in the windows to protect shirts and pants that looked thirty years out of date. A little farther on, an unmarked white van was turning into the side road to the clinic. Nash's neck went stiff. Nothing remarkable about an unmarked white van, he told himself, it didn't mean a thing, still he sped up and hung behind a rusty blue pickup. A couple of teenage boys with a large dog wanted to cross, and when the pickup stopped for them, Nash braked hard, muttered, "Goddammit." A shout from close by, but Nash stared straight ahead. Out of the corner of his eye he saw someone waving, striding closer.

Beside him, Chris was looking out the window. "Dad? That old guy's saying something."

One of the teenagers was tugging on the leash and laughing because the dog was lying in the road, legs in the air as it wriggled in delight, and these kids—these kids had their phones out to take photos. Nash muttered, "Oh for fuck's sake."

From close by that voice again, yelling.

Chris touched Nash's arm. "Dad!"

"Ignore him."

The old guy was determined. He'd caught up with the truck and now he stepped into the road and laid one hand on the hood. "Mister! You can't drive on that tire!"

There was no helping it—Nash turned toward him. Chris wound down the window and the old guy gripped the top of the glass with his thick fingers. "Sir? You've got a tire going flat. You need to get it taken care of." His face was large and round, and a fluff of white hair stood up on his scalp. "You drive on it, you're going to have an accident. I worked twenty-four years as a state trooper, and I've seen what happens when a tire blows out on the highway."

The teens had coaxed the dog to the side of the road and were laughing now as it jumped up, a young dog, its sides still fluffy with puppy fur. The blue pickup was easing away. Nash glanced back at the old guy. "I'm sure you have," he said, and he touched the gas to edge the truck forward.

The guy followed, still holding onto the window. "There's a garage a little ways up the road."

"That's where I'm headed, if it's open."

"It's open, alright. You think about your kids and go take care of that tire, you hear?" He gave the side of the truck a slap like it was a horse he was sending on its way, and Nash hit the gas. The truck lurched off, and the old guy had to jump back.

The old guy was right: coming up to the garage Nash slowed and there, on the forecourt, a white van was pulled up. In the office, hardly more than a shadow behind the glass, someone was moving about. So, the owner had caught his salmon and was back. Nash parked and told the boys, "Wait here. I won't be long."

Before he'd gone more than a few yards, a guy unfolded himself from the driver's seat of the van and sauntered toward him. He was well over six feet with a chest that filled out his dark zip-up jacket, and a thick neck like a bull's. On his forehead his sunglasses were propped up like a second set of eyes. From beneath them he looked down at Nash with a tight, steady gaze. "Can I help you, sir?"

"I need air."

Without a word, the guy crooked his head a little.

"For my spare." Nash gestured behind him to the truck and its tire.

"Looks like you need more than air."

No wonder the old guy had wanted to get Nash's attention: the spare looked like it was squatting on the concrete.

"Could you patch it? We need to get back on the road as soon as we can."

"I'm sorry, sir, the garage is closed for electrical work. Could take a couple days."

"Oh." Nash nodded as though that made sense when this guy looked nothing like an electrician, when in the office another man was dumping out drawers of papers onto the counter. Maybe they were undercover cops, or bounty hunters—but in that case, they weren't looking for him and the boys, and Nash made himself turn to the guy standing over him. The guy stared back, and how curious it was to be watched by someone whose face was a blank. A squirming stirred in Nash's belly. He wanted to climb into the truck and get the hell out of there, but he told himself that wasn't normal behavior and he should act normal—he was just a man pulled up at a garage, that's all. "Could I get air, at least?"

"Sorry, sir, that won't be possible."

Nash looked off toward the road and a motorbike buzzing past, then nodded again. He'd been standing here a couple of beats too long now, and he licked his lips, felt the soft suck of them parting as he opened his mouth to say, "Anywhere else in town with air?"

"Not that I know of." The guy shifted his feet, set his hands on his hips. He lifted his chin a little to say, "Anything else I can help you with?"

"No. Thanks." It took an effort to pivot around and walk back to the driver's side of the truck. His feet were far away, the air curiously dense so that he had to push himself through it. Behind him, footsteps. His shoulders stiffened and he dragged his keys from his pocket. When he took hold of the door handle his hand slipped with sweat, and he had to grab it a second time before he could swing the door open.

He was starting the engine when he heard a knock on the glass. The goon was staring in with his hand still raised. Nash wound down the window. His mouth was so dry he could barely speak. "Yes?"

"There's a Tesoro just where you hit the Richardson highway. You could try there."

"Thanks. I'll try there then. Great," he said, and he shoved the truck into gear.

It took a huge effort not to stamp on the gas, to drive off down the road at a sane speed. When he glanced in the mirror the goon was still watching, the sunglasses on his forehead catching the light.

Nash turned off his phone. Even out here where coverage was spotty, they could trace him, he was sure. He wondered who exactly *they* might be.

Paranoia, he thought. Chances were, the garage really was

closed for repairs, and yet he double-checked his phone was off. The doctor had been furious. By now she could have worked out that Nash had given a made-up cell number and reported him as suspicious. In his head he heard Maria's voice: he was being ridiculous—this was crazy movie thinking. Whoever those guys were at the garage, they weren't looking for him.

They were coming up on the Tesoro at the edge of town when Robbie wailed, "Dad!"

Nash glanced back. "You okay?"

Robbie was bent over. When he looked up, his eyes were squeezed half-shut by the swelling of his cheeks, his mouth open and wet. This thing—it was making him sick so fast, his face round as a baby's but the color all wrong, so very pale.

"My god, Robbie," he said.

Robbie groaned, long and hard: he was going to throw up. Nash pulled in at the gas station, parked any old how and flung open his door. He opened Robbie's door too and hauled him out just in time—Robbie crouched and vomit splashed onto the ground in front of his shoes. Nash held his shoulders, felt his whole body stiffen as he retched and retched.

At last Robbie settled back on his heels. He whispered, "Wow."

"Wow?"

"That was gross." He shuddered as though ridding himself of something and let Nash help him to his feet. His chin was slick, and dribbles ran down the front of his T-shirt. "I feel better now."

Nash stroked back Robbie's hair. A sickly sweet smell was rising off him. "Really? You don't look so good."

Robbie gave a half smile. "Do I look sleazy?"

"You're beyond sleazy."

Robbie dabbed at his chin with his hand. It looked swollen too, the fingers thick and ridged like old carrots, the knuckles dimpled.

"I'm hungry, Dad."

"Hungry? You just threw up."

Here they were, taking off for the border when Robbie was sick. They should have stayed at the clinic, no matter that he didn't trust the doctor. Nash stared off toward town and wondered how it would be to walk back into that place. He would do it if he had to, he would do it for Robbie.

Robbie was watching. He said, "I'm not going back to that doctor. I'm not."

"I didn't say you were."

He peered up at Nash. "But that's what you were thinking."

"Let's just get you cleaned up."

He helped Robbie to his feet then led him into the icy air of the gas station. At least the bathroom was clean. Under the vapid light, Robbie's skin looked grayish like a sick old man's. Nash turned on the faucets then beckoned him over. "Rinse out your mouth, sweet pea, and wash your face."

Robbie leaned over the sink and held both hands under the rush of water—that thing, the water racing over it, and Nash said quickly, "No, no—don't get it wet again."

"But there's puke on it."

"You need to keep it as dry as you can."

Robbie was staring up at him through his half-shut eyes, the thing shining darkly in his fingers. "Dad, it's just water."

The find falling into the fish tank—that's when all of this trouble had started. Maybe it hadn't been dead but dried out, and the water had brought it back to life. It felt like crazy movie logic, and yet when Robbie had put the thing in his hand there'd been the slick feel of it, the tickle against his palm before he'd passed it back.

He turned off the faucet and tugged paper towels out of the dispenser. "Here, dry it off."

"It's still got puke on it."

"So wipe it off the best you can." He leaned against the sink and watched Robbie dab it. "After it fell in the fish tank, did it feel different?"

"Yeah, I guess. Not straightaway but later."

"Different how?"

"Not hard anymore. More kinda squishy, and a bit slimy."

"Dry it off real good, sweetie."

"It's not like being wet is going to make any difference now. It's already gone soft."

"Soft?" Nash stepped closer. "Show me."

Where the thing was exposed between the swollen ends of his fingers and his palm, Robbie touched it with his index finger. For a moment there was a slight dimple, and then the indentation vanished. Nash steeled himself and touched it too. Against his fingertip it felt cool and a little sticky, the way he imagined a snail would. He wanted to wash the feel of it away but he didn't, because here was his son with the damn thing stuck to his hand.

Robbie gazed down at it. "It's alive."

"It can't be. Something you pick up off the ground that feels like a rock, that thing's dead. That's about as dead as a thing can be." He didn't sound convincing, even to himself.

"Maybe you just don't know." He bunched up the wet paper towel in his hand. "Maybe it's sick too."

"Sweetie, it isn't even alive." He took the paper towel from Robbie and tossed it in the trash. "Even if it was, no way should it be stuck to your hand."

"It's making me sick, isn't it?"

"Could be. We don't know for sure."

Robbie pushed his elbows against his sides and shivered. "I don't want to die. Do you think that's what happened to Mom? Something made her sick and she died?"

Slowly, Nash let out his breath. "Here's what we're going to do—even though we don't like that doctor, we're going to head back to the clinic."

Robbie's lips bunched together. "No, Dad—"

"We don't have a choice. Listen," he said and leaned down close enough to catch the sickly smell rising off Robbie, "we need to make sure this isn't anything serious."

"If it isn't serious, why do we need to go back?"

"Because we don't know." He sighed. "Come on, Robs, help me out here."

"I don't want to get caught. I don't want us to be locked up."

"Neither do I. If it looks like that could happen, we'll just walk out of that place again, I promise." He pulled open the bathroom door. "Now let's get out of here."

Robbie was still beside the sink. He looked rooted in place, his mouth set. "Dad, I can't. I've got puke on my T-shirt."

"All you have to do is walk through the store."

"Da-ad!"

"Fine." Nash yanked off his own T-shirt and held it out. In the mirror, he glimpsed himself—his bloodshot eyes, his hair sticking out to the side. Like a mug shot of a celebrity caught drunk driving, that wild look of going off the edge.

He glanced back at Robbie, blurted, "Shit—no," but it was too late. Robbie had simply pulled the T-shirt on over the dirty one. "Come on, Robs. Really?"

Robbie shrugged, then seemed to sag. "You didn't say."

"I didn't think I had to." It hung halfway down Robbie's thighs and there, huge across his small chest, lay the shadowy egg from *Alien* with its glowing crack. Of all the shirts to grab, and he hadn't even noticed.

Robbie trailed along behind Nash into the store hissing, "You need to buy me a Sprite, Dad. That's what Mom always gave me when I threw up." The moment the clerk looked over he went quiet and slunk out the door.

From the fridge Nash grabbed three cans of soda. He stood at the counter with them cold in his hands, shivering in the air conditioning. The clerk glanced at his bare chest. "Sir? I can't serve you like that."

He set the cans down on the counter. "My kid just threw up and I gave him my T-shirt. It'd be quicker to take my money than argue about it."

The clerk stared at him with weary eyes and snatched up one of the cans to run over the scanner.

From outside came the distant wail of a siren, and Nash glanced through the window. A few heartbeats later, the dazzling flash of red and blue lights came tearing along the highway into town. That damn doctor, she'd made her call, alright. Nash crossed his arms over his bare chest and stepped behind a tall wire stand. He peered out just as a second cop car came racing up. This one slowed by the gas station, crawling along as though the driver was taking a careful look around. Shit—the truck was out there, the boys.

Behind him Nash heard, "Hey buddy, you checking out or what?"

Nash muttered, "Just a moment." His hand trembled as he looked through the wire rack to follow the dancing lights. With predatory slowness, the cop car was gliding along the road toward town.

Cops gathering in tiny Glennallen: there was no going back to the clinic, not now, and his focus snapped to what was in front of him. The display. Maps. Honest-to-goodness real paper maps and he pulled one out, then another. Their paper had a dusty feel, and the corners were crumpled. Maps of Alaska. Maps of the Yukon. Old technology that no one could track him with. He picked out two and slapped them on the counter in front of the clerk.

The clerk raised his eyebrows. He lazily waved the maps in front of the scanner then took Nash's card and jabbed at the register as though he meant it harm. Finally, he slipped the maps into a thin plastic bag with the sodas and leaned his elbows onto the counter. As Nash made for the door, he called out, "Have a better one."

Nash took off out of the gas station as fast as he dared. What with the soggy spare and the weight of the trailer, he couldn't do more than thirty-five. This, he thought, was the slowest, saddest get-away ever, him bare-chested, glancing in the mirror to check for flashing lights, as though he had any chance of outrunning the cops if they came after him.

Chris shifted in his seat. "Dad—what the hell? Robbie's sick and we're still heading for the border?"

Nash didn't look at him. "Yeah, that's the plan."

"Don't tell me you think those cops are after us?"

"We just can't risk it." His words came out more harshly than he'd intended. He took a breath and added, "Listen, we can be in Canada in a few hours."

"And we're in such a hurry you couldn't even put on a shirt? What's that all about?"

"Yeah," he said, but he didn't say more.

It took miles before Nash's panic died down. In its place washed in fear about Robbie. He tilted the rearview mirror to keep an eye on him, and every few minutes he called out something like, "You doing okay back there?" or, "You tell me if you feel sick again." Robbie was leaning against the window, staring out groggily with the Sprite held under his chin. Nash made Chris dig through the glove box for Benadryl. He'd bought a bottle a few weeks ago when the pollen was bad and Chris's eyes were watering. He popped off the lid with his teeth and passed a couple of pills back to Robbie. Maybe it would help. At least, he thought, it wouldn't make things worse.

Chris had one of the maps open across his knees. Nash had

had to explain how to refold it so they could see where they were going without Chris holding the whole thing up like a screen then complaining it was impractical, and maybe even dangerous, because how the hell could you see out the windshield?

Over the hum of the engine Nash said, "How far's Gakona Junction?"

Chris dumped the map on the seat between them. He'd managed to unfold it so it slumped like a failed piece of origami, and now he picked up Nash's phone. Nash barked, "No, don't turn it on!"

"For real? Come on, Dad."

"Humor me, okay?"

"Fine, fucking fine." Chris tossed it back onto the console. "You scared the government's tracking us?"

"They can, you know that."

"But who's going to track *us*?" He let out a laugh. "Bounty hunters? Or d'you think some men-in-black dudes from the CDC are after that thing stuck to Robbie's hand? Bro," he said and looked over his shoulder, "sounds like you could be famous. You should sell your story to the *National Enquirer*—'Boy taken over by ancient alien creature.' Sheesh, you'll be so loaded, you'll be able to buy us a house with a pool and a home movie theater."

In the mirror, Nash watched as Robbie nodded. His head was low, and it bounced loosely with the motion of the truck. Nash said softly, "That's enough, Chris, okay? He isn't feeling too good."

Chris rested his head against the window. His tuft of hair splayed against the glass. "No one's after us, Dad. You don't have to act all paranoid, that's all I'm saying."

"If I get caught, we all get caught. They don't take sick detainees to the hospital, you know that. They get left in cells, and they—" He glanced in the mirror again. "Well, you know what I'm talking about."

"What if there's no hospital at the border?"

Nash didn't take his eyes off the road. "We just need to get there. Let's focus on that, for the time being."

He couldn't remember how far Whitehorse was from the border. He grabbed up the map and shook it out, holding the steering wheel with his knees so he could snap the map into a rectangle. With it propped across the wheel, he took quick glances. Whitehorse was farther than he thought, at least five hours from the border, and probably much longer at the speed he was driving. How sparse the map looked. Most of the places marked along the highway were probably only a gas station and a diner, maybe a motel or RV park too. So much green, so much wilderness—the sight of it made him uneasy. If Robbie got any worse, there was going to be no way to find help for him out here. Nash called out, "You feeling any better, Robs?" and peered in the mirror. All he could see was the top of Robbie's head, and if he answered it was too softly for him to hear.

Instead, before long, Robbie started coughing. Nash saw his hand go to his mouth and he pulled over to the shoulder as hard as he dared. He shouted, "Robbie—window!" and spun around to guide Robbie's head, but he wasn't fast enough.

The smell of vomit filled the cab. Chris moaned, "Oh my god, Robs!"

Nash got out of the truck and opened the door. Green vomit had pooled in Robbie's lap, right over where the T-shirt said ALIEN. Nash's favorite T-shirt. Vintage too.

From under the seat, he took a roll of paper towel and gave Robbie enough to wipe his hands, then mopped up as best he could. "It's okay, sweet pea," he told Robbie, and stroked his head. Robbie was shaking and, when he looked up, his face was ghastly and wan. "Soon as we get to Whitehorse, we're going to take you to the hospital, okay? For now, just sit tight. And if you have to throw up again"—he reached past him for the plastic bag from the Tesoro—"here."

Nash dug a couple of fresh shirts out of the trailer. As soon as he pulled his own on, the sudden warmth was cloying. The other he held bunched in his hands. No point in Robbie putting it on before he could get him properly cleaned up, so he tossed it next to Chris and got back behind the wheel.

Chris was scowling. He said, "Dad, we can't drive to Canada like this. Robbie's covered in puke, and the truck reeks."

"We'll stop up the road somewhere."

"Where? There's nothing here." With his chin, Chris gestured out the window at the forest, and the stark hills rising behind.

"There's a campground a couple miles farther on." Nash tapped the map with one finger. "We'll stop there and clean up."

"Don't you think we should take him to a hospital right now? I mean, maybe it's—"

Nash raised his hand to tell him to be quiet, and Chris looked away out the window. He rested his chin in his hand and clamped his fingers across his mouth, holding in whatever else he was going to say.

6

The turnoff to the campground was a narrow dirt road. Ruts and potholes glimmered with rainwater, and Nash steered around them, keeping an eye on the mirror because the trailer was pitching and swaying behind the truck.

A state campground: a pay station by the entrance, a hand pump for water, a bear-proof dumpster, plus a shelter with notices about bear safety and hiking routes. He and the boys had stayed in countless places like this. For an instant, it felt as though this was just one of those weekends when they'd headed out of town to hunt for fossils, or go fishing, anything to take their minds off the emptiness left by Maria.

Between the trees the pale bulk of RVs gleamed, and here and there the brilliant colors of tents like party balloons. A large white dog was loping around, and it came dancing toward the truck with its tongue dangling pink against its fur until, suddenly, one paw lifted and its ears pricked, it dashed away. Nash drove on to where the loop curled back on itself close to the entrance and pulled into a campsite canopied by birch and spruce trees. In the quiet after he turned off the engine, he stretched. His jeans were damp against his thighs, his belly sour with anxiety.

Chris propped his feet up on the dash. "Now we're camping? Robbie needs help."

Nash looked away out the windshield. "We're going to get him cleaned up, then be on our way. By tonight, we'll be in Whitehorse." When he glanced back at Chris, he'd folded his arms over his chest and his eyes had a faraway look, as though part of him had retreated. "You do understand, don't you? What would happen if we were detained?"

Chris muttered, "I understand that you're gambling with his life."

"There are no right choices here." Nash climbed out of the truck and slammed the door behind him.

Here in the campsite's small clearing, the light was dappled and green. A cool wind was pushing around the smells of rotting wood and pine sap, sending the grass rippling, making the leaves whisper like soft rain. Nash's throat was tight, his tongue pressed up against his teeth. He took a breath then let it out, slowly, and hung his head. He was doing the only thing he could, though Chris was right, it was a gamble, a huge goddamn gamble. Robbie was sick, and here they were, in the middle of nowhere. What would Maria have said? He cringed away from the thought of it.

A whoosh of wings overhead. A raven sweeping through the air, something in its beak. If they were going to make it to the border today, he had to focus: Robbie needed to be cleaned up, his clothes rinsed or thrown away, the inside of the truck wiped down. Nash came around the front of the truck. When he caught sight of the spare his hands tightened into fists—the tire looked as though it was sinking into the ground. He shouldn't be driving on it but hell, he had no idea what else he was supposed to do.

He unleashed a kick at a rock that spun away and clanged against the rim of the fire pit, then he booted another into the bushes. A squirrel took fright and skittered off up a tree, and he grabbed a rock and hurled it after the squirrel so hard it bounced off the trunk. His breath was coming fast, the inside of his head so tangled he let out a half-cry that echoed through the air. When he turned back to the truck, Chris was watching him through the glass. He strode away with shame prickling down his neck.

At least the business of finding what he needed calmed him: a bucket and soap, washcloths and a towel. He carried it all out to the picnic table where rain had gathered in small shining blisters. He swiped the water away with his hands and swatted at the mosquitoes twitching around his head. The boys were still in the truck. When he opened Robbie's door, the air inside smelled rancid with vomit. "Come on," he said, "let's get you cleaned up."

Robbie blinked at him. "Not now. I don't feel good."

"I'm sure you don't." Nash reached out to touch his cheek— so round, so full that his eyes and mouth looked shrunken. Robbie batted his hand away, and instead Nash scooped him into his arms, never mind the puke, and never mind that he was too big for that and protested and wriggled until Nash set him down on the picnic bench. "Come on," Nash said, "let me help you."

"It's not like I'm a baby."

"I don't want you dripping puke everywhere, especially inside the truck. We've still got a long way to go."

"You said the border was close."

"Calgary's a long drive from there." He bent down in front of him. "Are you feeling any worse?"

"I just want to sleep."

He tried to touch the back of his hand to Robbie's temple but Robbie ducked away. It didn't matter. It was clear he still had a fever—his hair sticking to his forehead, his eyes too bright. "You can sleep in a little while. First we need to get you cleaned up."

"Is there a bathroom here?"

"Robs, it's a state campground. Just outhouses and a pump."

"A pump? Dad!"

"You have a better idea?"

"In the trailer."

"You're covered. Come on, there's no point having to clean the trailer too."

Robbie scowled and waved mosquitoes away with one hand. "I can't wash at the pump. People will see me."

"C'mon, you can't stink of vomit until we get to somewhere with showers." He ruffled Robbie's hair and walked away to the truck. From under his seat he took a can of mosquito repellent and sent a shower of it over his head and hands. He brought it over to Robbie. "Want me to spray you?"

"What's the point if I have to wash?" Still, a moment later he snapped, "Well go on, I'm getting all bitten."

Nash told himself, the poor kid's feeling bad, and he's got that thing stuck to him. Even so, he sprayed Robbie a little longer and harder than he needed to. "Better?"

Robbie hadn't lifted his head. His shoulders were slumped, and they shook now. Shit, thought Nash, and he smoothed Robbie's hair, felt the heat of his head against his fingers. "Sorry. I guess we're all in a bad mood."

"Well, you are." Robbie got to his feet then marched away down the dirt road toward the pump, so small, so furious.

There was an edge to the air as Nash followed him—bloated clouds had glided in over the sun and now the wind was picking up, flapping the towel he'd slung over his shoulder and nudging the plastic bucket in his hand. Down at the pump, Robbie was peeling off his clothes and dropping them to the ground. Then he stood waiting in his red underwear, his back turned, hunched against the cold. His spine stood out like a string of beads under his skin, and that skin—it was mottled gray, as though it had been rubbed with ashes. No, realized Nash as he came closer, not mottled. His heart caught: spreading over Robbie's spine, over his shoulder blades where the skin was thinner, was a fibrous mesh like the outer layer of a cantaloupe. Nash raised his hand and touched it, tried to peel it away, but it seemed to be melded to his skin.

Robbie wheeled around. He must have seen the look on Nash's face because he said, "Dad, what's wrong? Am I swollen up worse?"

"No, no, it's not that." He set down the bucket and held out his hand for Robbie's, the one with the thing stuck to it. Running up the delicate skin of his inner arm, more of that gray webbing, and it stretched out over his shoulder, down his chest, around his neck, pale but distinct.

Robbie's mouth, when he looked up, was wide with fear. "Dad, what is it? What's wrong with me?"

"A rash, sweetie." Nash hugged him rather than look him in the eye. "I'm sorry. We should have stayed at the clinic."

Robbie struggled in his arms. "No, Dad. And I'm not going back there. I'm not going to any clinic."

"Sure." He gave him a squeeze.

"Dad, I mean it."

"Let's get you cleaned up before you catch cold." He tried to smile, and when that smile faltered, he set the bucket under the pump. He worked the handle in long, hard strokes, heaving water up from under the ground. "Ready?" he said.

Standing there in his underwear, Robbie gave a quick nod and Nash sloshed the water over him. He gasped. He curled in on himself with his eyes shut and his arms clutched to his chest. In one hand the thing glistened, and Nash made himself look away from it as he held out the soap. "Wash your chest or you'll still smell of puke."

Robbie rubbed it over his skin in quick, jerky movements, and when Nash raised the bucket to rinse him, he flinched away. The water hit his back, sliding off, leaving the fibrous mesh dull against the gleam of his wet skin. "You're doing real good," Nash told him, and how hollow he sounded. "Real good, sweetie. But we have to get your chest this time and then we're done."

The pump creaked as he worked it, and the smell of iron rose off the handle. When he hefted up the bucket he told Robbie, "Shut your eyes so you don't know it's coming. You ready?"

Robbie stood with his chin raised and his eyes closed tight like someone waiting to be shot. Nash tipped the water over him in one long silvery arc and slid the towel from around his neck. He wrapped Robbie in it, whispered, "Sorry, Robs, you must be freezing." Against his cheek, the awful coldness of Robbie's skin, and the clammy warmth beneath it. He held him close as he rubbed him and planted a kiss on the side of his face. "You go back to the trailer and get dressed while I rinse out your clothes, and don't dump the wet towel on the bed, okay? Chris knows how to turn on the propane—tell him to make you hot chocolate." He let go but Robbie just stood there, shivering. "Go on— go dry off before you catch cold."

Robbie clutched the towel to himself awkwardly, that thing stuck to his hand, before heading stiff-legged back up the dirt road to the trailer. Above him in the massing gray of the sky, the single black cinder of a raven floated on the wind.

Robbie was in the trailer asleep under a pile of blankets by the time Nash started cleaning the truck. Where vomit had splashed up it had dried, and Nash had to scrub it off with wads of paper towel. The reek of it was everywhere, even though he'd opened all the doors and the wind was buffeting through.

Whenever he sat back, to watch the storm clouds heaping up, or to tear off more paper towel, a part of him must have noticed someone close by on the dirt road. He didn't pay much attention—that's what people did at campgrounds, they strolled around, they walked their dogs. It wasn't until he'd finished scooping dirty clumps of paper towel into a garbage bag and was knotting it shut that it struck him: it wasn't people lurking but one man in a bucket hat and blue raincoat. Nash came around the truck. He zipped up his jacket and made a show of staring at him, and the guy ducked his head and took off, as though all of a sudden he had something urgent to take care of. In Nash's chest, an itchy fear, even if it was ridiculous: bounty hunters didn't wear bucket hats and loiter in campgrounds.

From the trees, a shushing as leaves lifted and showed their pale undersides. Then, as though the wind had taken a breath and was letting it out, raindrops slapped against his face. Nash went around the truck slamming the doors and locking up, then he locked the trailer too—just as a precaution. Most likely that guy was just some tourist who didn't know to mind his own business, or had seen him washing Robbie at the pump and wanted to complain—well, screw him, and Nash picked up the bag of garbage and strode to the road.

The guy was still there, only now he was crouched down and poking at something in the dirt. Nash shouted, "Hey! You!"

He looked up. An old man, his hat pulled down so low the brim hid half his face, and yet there was something familiar about him. He raised himself stiffly and came close holding up both hands and patting the air. "I'm sorry," he said. "I wasn't sure it was you. You remember me, don't you?" He snatched off his hat. "From the restaurant last night?"

The old waiter who'd fished Robbie's find out of the aquarium. Nash tightened his grip on the bag of trash. "Sure, I remember you."

"Good, good," he said and nodded. "I thought it was you, but I wasn't certain. I didn't see your boys."

"Well, it's me."

The man nodded some more, as though thinking things over. Down his face raindrops were leaving shining trails, and he pulled his hat back on. "You must think it a little strange—that I came here to find you. Because I did, you know." He shot a glance at Nash. Up close, his eyes were the uneven brown of old wood.

"Why would you—"

"That object your son found, do you still have it?"

"That's what you came to ask me?"

The old man took hold of his arm. "Where is it?"

Nash yanked his arm away. "Hey—none of your business."

"Does your son still have it?" The old man was breathing hard. He stood so close that Nash caught the garlicky smell of his breath. "You have to take it away from him. It's dangerous. Do you understand? Go back and take it away from him right now."

"What's going on? Do you know what that thing is?"

All around, the crackling of rain coming down hard, slicking over Nash's face, his hands, onto the bag of garbage he was holding. Beside him the old man stared into the downpour as though it wasn't falling on him, then he turned his gaze on Nash again. "You take that thing away from him, then I'll show you."

"I can't do that."

"Can't?" The old man's eyebrows lifted in surprise. Then he must have understood because his face sagged with weariness. "Then you'd better come with me."

His RV was parked past the dumpster and up around the bend, a big white thing tucked in a stand of birch trees. Inside, at the top of the stairs, the old man stepped out of his shoes and walked through the kitchen with his bare feet gently slapping the linoleum. Nash kicked off his shoes too. The interior was like a different dimension: the sudden warmth, the rage of smells— spices and some kind of flowery soap—the rattle of the rain on the roof. This wasn't like Nash's trailer with its tiny galley and cramped dining table: the RV had a booth with a roomy table, and a full-size fridge.

The old man beckoned Nash to follow him into a short corridor. At the end, he paused and listened at a door before opening it, slowly, glancing around as though expecting to be startled.

With the blinds pulled down, the bedroom was all shadows and the pelting of the rain. On the air hung the stinging reek of ammonia, and beneath it something nastier, earthier. Most of the room was taken up by a bed, and he gestured Nash toward it. In the middle lay the indistinct lump of someone beneath the blankets. The old man waited until Nash stood beside him. "My wife," he said softly, and the head on the pillow pivoted toward his voice. "It'll agitate her too much if I open the blinds, but you need to see."

He took something from the bedside table, and the beam of a flashlight slicked over the bedcovers. A white nightgown.

A wrinkled neck. Long dark hair threaded with gray. The light touched her face and her head jerked, her whole body wrenching itself toward the beam, scrawny arms wheeling and a thin, ugly scream trailing from her mouth.

Nash staggered back with his hands raised, and his shoulder hit the wall. He said, "My god—what happened to her?" though he didn't want an answer, he just wanted to flee. He watched as the old man carefully laid a small towel over his wife's face, and she quieted to twitches and shudders. Her arms, though, stood out rigidly, one hand with its fingers crooked like tree roots, the other wrapped in gauze.

The old man said, "This is how I found her this morning." Tenderly, he eased the bandaged hand down to the bed. Beneath her skin, the muscles and tendons stood out as though she was resisting with all her might, and he set himself to unwinding the dressing. It spiraled to the floor, and when the last of it had fallen away, he shone the flashlight onto her palm. He gestured for Nash to come close and look. Across her palm and the belly of her fingers gleamed wet wounds, as if the skin had been torn away. All around the flesh was scorched and cracked, and oozing a yellow fluid that gave off a strangely sweet smell. Without thinking, Nash pressed his fingers against his nose.

"You see?" As the old man glanced at Nash, the beam of the flashlight flared up over the towel. The woman convulsed and her fingers scraped at the air, frantic, until he turned it off.

That raw flesh, that awful sweet smell, that woman who'd been reduced to something barely human—Nash steadied himself against the wall. "Did she touch one of those things?" His words came out groggy and slow, and he shivered. How cold he felt, cold through to his bones. Darkness was swamping him, dizzying, hissing as loudly as the downpour above his head, and he couldn't see, couldn't think—

A hand on his arm, the old guy saying, "No no no," and steering him away. Something against the back of his legs, and he was being pushed down into a chair, and his head bent toward his knees. When he tried to sit up, the hands wouldn't let him. With his head low, the reek was worse and a gagging rose up his throat. His mouth was filling with saliva. He couldn't swallow, and he tried to get to his feet but the old man told him, "You must sit still. Keep your head down and take some deep breaths."

Each breath dragged that foul smell into his lungs. In his head, the sight of that poor woman wrenching herself toward the light, and he wanted to scratch it out of his mind, to get the hell out of there, and he heaved himself up again. The inside of his head slipped as though it had broken loose from its moorings and he stumbled against the wall.

The old man took hold of his arm. "I'm sorry. I didn't prepare you, I didn't think." A sigh. "Come on, sit down before you fall."

"No, I'm good," and Nash wrenched himself free. He steadied himself against a closet while his eyes found the outline of the door, then he went reeling toward it as fast as he could.

From across the dining table, the old man—Jimmy Cho—was watching him, a cup of tea in both hands and steam wisping off it. Delicate creases ran down from his nose to bracket his mouth, and between them his mouth was tucked in on itself. He said for the third time, "I didn't mean to upset you."

Outside, thunder crashed across the sky. Even from here Nash thought he could smell the sickening odor of the bedroom. He leaned forward with his elbows propped on the table. "Did she have a fever? Is that how it started?"

The old man gestured at the cup of tea he'd set in front of Nash. The cup was small and brown and had no handle so Nash used his fingertips to pick it up at the rim where it wasn't as hot. The tea tasted of tree bark but he sipped it to rid himself of the awful chill inside him. "My son—" he started. "That thing he found. It's stuck to his hand, and now he's sick. Not like your wife, nothing that bad . . . " His voice trailed away, and it took an effort to raise his eyes to the old man's. "What happened to the thing stuck to her hand? There was one, wasn't there?"

Jimmy slid his cup back onto the table with a grimace. "Yes, there was." He got up and set more water to heat on the stove, never mind that his cup was still nearly full. As the burning gas hissed, he moved around the tiny kitchen touching a clay tea-pot, a canister of tea, a spoon, and then he stopped and looked back at Nash. "Last night after we closed up, I got out the fossils I've collected. I was sure I'd seen one like your son's. I emptied my boxes on the kitchen table, and my wife wasn't happy about that—dirt all over the place, messing up the kitchen."

"Did she hold it? And it stuck to her hand?"

He sighed. In the garish light above the stove, his face looked as soft and creased as old paper. "She tipped everything in the sink and filled it with water. It took quite some time to scrub them all—I've got a bunch of finds I haven't had time to look at properly." He gave a little shrug. "I wiped down the table and laid it with newspaper. She'd washed most of them, then she reached into the water and flinched. I didn't understand. When she brought her hand up, she was holding one of my fossils and she looked startled. I thought maybe she'd scraped her hand, or bro-ken a nail. What else could it have been? They were just rocks."

Nash wrapped his hand around his cup. It was too hot, but he gripped it until the clay was scorching his skin. "And it was like the one Robbie found?"

"It was one of the last ones she washed. It must have been in the water some time. Twenty minutes, maybe longer."

Steam was lifting off the water heating in the pan. A flash from beyond the window—lightning—then the massive rumble of thunder. "It all happened so quickly. She shouted at me to help her, and I didn't know why. It sounded like she was hurt. There was no blood, though, just that thing dripping in her hand. I tried to take it from her, and I felt it—a strange stickiness. Why would a fossil be sticky? I put on rubber gloves and tried again, and it wouldn't come off. We tried soap, and oil, but nothing helped, and when I got my glasses on I saw—well, it looked like tiny roots growing out of that thing and into her hand." He turned off the gas. The water pouring into the teapot sounded thin and hard. "My wife told me to use a knife. She wanted me to cut it off. I could tell she was scared, even though she tried to hide it."

"Did it hurt?"

"Susan's a tough woman, but it was too painful. She couldn't bear it. We put salt on that thing, we tried bleach. Nothing worked. In the end she got out the iron and burned it until it let go. The smell was terrible, like burning trash." He shook his head. "I couldn't believe what it had done to her. It looked like she'd been bitten by a thousand small teeth. I was worried she'd get an infection but she said she was fine. No more bringing home those dirty rocks, though—that's what she called them, dirty rocks. I bandaged up her hand and she went to bed, like it was all just a strange accident."

He swirled the teapot, puffs of steam pulsing from the spout, and set it on the table. "I couldn't sleep. Part of me was worried. I mean—what sort of thing could do that? So I called Mike's wife—he's the one who owns the garage in town. His wife's a paramedic. She's from Korea, like us, and she misses home, and of course—well, she's become like a daughter to us. I knew it was late but I called her anyway. She was working the night shift. Maybe she'd know what it was, or if it was dangerous."

Jimmy topped up his cup. When he blew on his tea the surface wrinkled. "Ju-Yeong said she'd make a few calls. That was at one in the morning, and I haven't heard back from her. Then this morning—you can see what has become of my wife." He tilted his head away, eyes shut.

Nash said, "I'm so sorry." Rain was washing down the window in jellied wakes. An electric snap of white cracked through the trees, and then thunder rang out as loud as dropped rocks. "This morning there were men at the garage. They told me the place was closed for electrical repairs."

"I saw them too. I keep an eye on the place when Mike's away and Ju-Yeong's working. In town there's not much for kids to do and sometimes they get themselves in trouble." Jimmy sighed. "We have blackout curtains for the summer. Usually my wife's up first—not this morning, though. I knew she hadn't slept well because I hadn't either. She'd been restless—that thing sticking to her hand had upset us both, that's what I thought. And there was an odd smell in the bedroom, like bad honey. I did notice that."

Jimmy ran a hand over his face. "I went downstairs without waking her and had breakfast. It was when I was watering the hanging baskets outside the restaurant that I saw those men over at the garage—I tried calling Ju-Yeong to ask her what was going on, but her phone was off. I knew right then that something was terribly wrong." He sighed. "I went upstairs to tell my wife. I pulled back the curtains, and that's when I saw what had happened to her." His voice wobbled and strained, and he fought it back. "We're not legal anymore, so we have to be careful. Can you understand that? Susan needed medical help, but instead I carried her out to the RV and left town." He twisted his head away and stared out at the storm.

Nash drew his cup closer. The clay was gritty against his fingertips. He did understand. He understood perfectly. He licked his lips, ready to say so, then instead he lifted his cup and took a sip of tea. He said gently, "So you just left? Did you hear back from your friend?"

"Her phone's still off. She should've been back from work by eight thirty this morning, but her car wasn't there when I left town. She's a good young woman, and now I've made trouble for her."

"Maybe she had to work late."

Jimmy shook his head. "Not that late."

"If those men wanted to find your wife, why would they go to the garage? Why didn't they come to the restaurant?"

"Ju-Yeong wouldn't have told them it was me who called her. She knows better than that." He swung his head back to Nash and sat a little straighter. "Until last year we were citizens of this country. Now we could lose everything because, just like that, the government changed its mind and we're not supposed to be here. Where else can we go? We haven't lived in South Korea for decades—to the South Korean government, we don't exist anymore." His voice had risen. He swallowed it back down and said quietly, "We've done nothing wrong, nothing."

He carried his cup over to the sink and rinsed it out. Against the window he looked small and bony, his fleece hanging loosely from his shoulders. He set the cup to drain and turned back to Nash. "Sometimes I forget myself—I'm sorry." He dried his hands on a cloth. "You haven't told me what happened to your boy."

"He held onto that damn thing all night, and this morning he couldn't let go. I took him to the clinic because I didn't know what else to do, and next thing I know, the doctor's telling us we mustn't leave and she's going to call someone." He ran a hand through his hair. It was still wet from the rain and clung to his fingers. "We got the hell out of there. I swear, there was something not right. The doctor was more interested in the thing stuck to Robbie's hand than in Robbie."

"And now?"

"He's been throwing up, he's got a fever, his face and hands are swollen. On top of that he's got some sort of—well, it's like a rash. I don't know if it's that thing making him ill. Kids come down with bugs all the time, right? Or could be it's an allergic reaction. The doctor didn't explain anything. She took one look at that thing on Robbie's hand then told us not to leave and rushed off to make her phone call." How bitter he sounded, and he picked up his cup and finished the tea. There was a little sediment in the bottom and it caught under his tongue.

Jimmy looked away. He rested one hand against his cheek as he stared out into the rain. "Your son's young. Maybe it'll take longer."

"But your wife doesn't have a rash. Chances are, Robbie's come down with some allergy, that's all. You just—" and he took a breath against the tightness in his chest "—you just can't assume it's the same thing."

"No, no, of course you're right. We don't know anything, not really."

Somehow the reasonableness of Jimmy's voice only made it worse, and Nash got to his feet. "I need to get back. My boys'll be wondering where I got to."

Jimmy bent forward to stare out the kitchen window. "It's not letting up. You're going to get soaked."

"Doesn't matter." When he pushed his feet into his shoes, they felt clammy, and when he opened the door the world outside was trembling in the downpour.

The old man came down the steps after him with an umbrella. "Please—take this."

"I'm fine." Nash zipped up his jacket. The trees, the road, everything was blurred by the rain.

Behind him Jimmy asked, "What will you do?"

"I need to get help for my son." He glanced back. "I hope your wife gets better, I honestly do."

Jimmy pushed the umbrella into his hands, and there was the fleeting warmth of their fingers touching. He said, "Maybe your son will be fine. Kids get sick all the time, right?"

"Right," said Nash, and he opened the umbrella and stepped beneath it. The rain battered down against it, all the way back to the trailer.

7

There was no driving in the storm. Instead, he and the boys sat in the trailer watching the rain thrash down, and Nash was careful not to mention Jimmy Cho. He tried to not even think about him, or what had become of his wife, and it left a strange hole to tread around. Perhaps the boys noticed it—that something was there but not there—and they sullenly shrugged at him when he asked if they were hungry, and lay on the bed dozing as the day wore on and the storm didn't let up. Nash couldn't help himself. He'd shake another Benadryl into Robbie's hand then lean close and ask how he was doing, or he'd shine a flashlight into Robbie's face, just for an instant, to see if he jerked toward it.

That poor woman. He wondered if that thing had hurt her because she'd burnt it off her hand. Sometimes he told himself there was no way to know; other times, there seemed no better explanation, and he held his head in his hands as though he could will himself back in time, and instead of sending the boys off to find fossils, he'd kept them safe in the truck.

Every now and again when the rain eased up a little, he'd peer outside, heart tight. Then lightning would crack across the sky, and thunder boom overhead, and the rain come pounding down again. As soon as the rain stopped, they'd leave. For now, he sat at the table with a map spread in front of him, knee bouncing, fingers tapping the paper, because he couldn't decide whether he should drive north to the hospital in Fairbanks and risk getting caught or turn east to Canada. He stared at the rain beating against the window, as though it would help him make up his mind.

As the hours wore on, Robbie's swelling went down. His eyes opened wider, and when Nash touched his cheek, the softness had lessened. As for that strange rash, it crept up his neck to the delicate skin under his chin, but no farther. Nash told himself to stop fussing and made coffee. An allergic reaction, then, maybe to something Robbie had eaten, and he stood at the window with his mug in his hands, his heart calming as he watched the storm seethe on the other side of the glass.

Sometime during the late afternoon, a gray bus pulled into the campsite beside Nash's. He didn't notice it arrive. The day had turned so dark he couldn't see the map, couldn't do much of anything, so he'd lowered the table and made up his bed. He lay there listening to the rain rage down against the roof, and the thunder hauling itself across the sky, and it wasn't until he pulled on his jacket and let himself out for a piss in the bushes that, with a shock, he noticed: a few yards away behind the trees stood the broad gray side of the bus. A short one, its windows painted over. Like the buses they used to transport prisoners. A stillness hung about it that seemed unnatural, and he trod through the mud to piss on the far side of the clearing, then hurried back inside.

That bus unsettled him: the way its blank windows stared out as he heated beans for dinner; the way lighting a lantern made it vanish into the dreariness of the worn-out day; the way he could sense it out there even as he slept, tangled up with nightmares that kept startling him awake. He checked on Robbie so often that he dreamed he was checking on him, and when he got up for good in the morning, he wasn't sure if he'd really tried to wrench that thing off Robbie's hand, or only dreamed it—he could recall it dry and flaccid against his fingers, even as he shivered in the damp air.

The morning had brought a clinging fog that erased everything. Nash fumbled his way through the whiteness, past the picnic table to the bushes. He was pissing when a cry came trailing through the air like the ragged echo of his nightmares. He glanced over his shoulder to where the bus was hidden in the murk. The thought of it—prisoners locked onto that bus all night, only a few yards from him and the boys. When the storm hit, they must have been on their way to a different facility, or heading back from work duty. There'd been those inmates he'd seen combing over a rockslide on the way to Glennallen—Christ, perhaps they were using them for search and rescue. He zipped up his pants and felt his way back across the clearing. There he listened, gazing into the whiteness before he pushed through the undergrowth, thorns snagging his jeans and wet leaves swiping his face, only to find the campsite empty except for the churned-up mud the bus had left behind.

Back in the trailer, he set water to boil and woke the boys. By the time he'd balled up his sleeping bag and set up the dining table, they still hadn't moved. "Come on," he told them, "let's get going." He snapped up one blind, then the next, and Robbie rolled over. In the shabby light it looked like he had something laid over his face, pale netting that didn't drop away when he sat up.

Nash's heart strained and he lurched toward him. When he touched Robbie's cheek with his fingertips, the rash felt rough as string, and he rubbed it because some part of him believed it would come loose, it had to. Robbie blinked up at him. Over his eyelids, over the delicate skin around his eyes, that white mesh, and Nash gathered him to his chest, said, "Oh Robbie, oh my god."

The bed bounced as Chris sat up. "Dad? What the hell?" He got to his knees, breathing hard, and threw back the blankets. Robbie's legs were covered too, but it wasn't just that—they were thicker, sturdier, corded with muscle. "Holy shit, bro!"

Robbie stared down at them. When he looked up, his eyes focused somewhere beyond Nash, and though his mouth opened, no words came out.

Chris was on his feet. "Dude, you look like one of those melons, only you're not green. Or not yet, at least. You want to see?" He pulled open a drawer beside the bed and took out a mirror.

Nash batted it away and it fell to the floor with a thud. "It's just a rash, Robs, you're okay."

Robbie craned his head toward him. For a moment, his eyes couldn't quite find him. "Okay," he said.

"Okay?" Chris gave a flat laugh. "That's all you have to say? You've got some weird-ass rash all over you." He held both hands to his head and stared down at Robbie. "Listen, Dad's going to take you to the hospital to get it looked at. They'll give you some medicine, and you'll be fine." Chris glanced up at Nash. "Right, Dad?"

"Chris—"

"You have to! Look at him!"

"It's not that simple. If they catch us . . . It's not like detention facilities have even basic medical care."

"That's not true."

Nash let out a bitter laugh. "Come on, Chris. You think they'd medevac him down to Seattle? It can take days just to process detainees, and in the meantime people—" He turned away. "Just trust me."

"People have died?"

Nash raised his hands to quiet him. "Come on, Chris." He glanced at Robbie, but Robbie was staring down at his legs. Nash picked up a fleece throw from the end of the bed and wrapped it around Robbie's shoulders. "At least the swelling's gone down. We'll be in Canada by this afternoon. We'll go to the hospital there."

Chris's forehead creased. "Dad! For crap's sake, look at him!"

"Think about it. Consider our situation." Nash glared at him until he looked away.

Chris snatched his jeans off the bed. As he yanked them on, he said, "In case neither of you has noticed, that thing stuck to Robbie's hand has fallen off. Or maybe that's not important either." He plunged his head into a hoodie and pushed past Nash. With a slap the trailer door shut behind him.

Nash took hold of Robbie's wrist. "Well, that's good news."

Robbie's head tipped, as if he wasn't sure. Over his palm the webbing was little more than a few long strands fanning out from where the thing had been attached. There his skin was stippled, as though it had been resting on a bed of nails. The bottom of each indentation gleamed slightly, and Nash ran his fingers over them expecting wetness, but Robbie's palm was perfectly dry. "Does it hurt?"

Robbie tilted his head again.

Nash said, "You've barely said a word. That's not like you. You really okay?"

Robbie stared back at him. "Okay."

"Okay? You must be sick. I've never heard you so quiet." Robbie's eyes followed him as he stepped back, and Nash said, "Let's see if we can find that thing. You going to help?"

As Nash flung back the bed covers and swept his hand over the sheets, Robbie only watched. Nash reached right down to the bottom where his fingers found grit and a tissue and a candy wrapper, and then something long and crisp. When he pulled it out it looked shrunken, a dried-out husk that had flattened and buckled like an empty seed pod. He fetched a plastic bag from the kitchenette. On the stove, water was boiling away. He turned it off—coffee seemed beside the point—then scooped the thing up like a dog turd and knotted the bag tight. It was so insubstantial that the bag felt empty.

Nash told him, "I guess it's dead now. Well, that's a relief, right?" In the thin light of the fogged-in day Robbie looked exhausted, his face all bones, that rash growing over his skin like the web a spider uses to trap prey. Nash shied away from that thought. He laid a hand on Robbie's forehead—at least he didn't feel hot anymore—and pushed back his hair. Even over his scalp, those pale threads were everywhere, and the sight of them made him wince. "How do you feel? Worse?"

Robbie was staring at the whiteness beyond the window, and he got to his feet strangely, jerkily, and pressed his face up to the glass.

"You need to pee? We won't bother with the outhouse, okay?"

"Okay."

"Come on then," Nash said and took his arm. It felt hard as wood, and when Robbie walked through the tiny kitchenette, he rocked quickly, stiffly, like someone rethinking the mechanics of locomotion. "You really okay?"

"Okay."

"Wish you'd say something more than okay, Robs. You're weirding me out, you know that?" He gave a small laugh.

Outside, Nash led him to the edge of the clearing where he let loose a stream of urine that steamed in the damp air. He looked so small standing there beneath the dark shapes of the trees, so vulnerable. When he'd finished Nash said, "Do you blame me for all this? I can understand if you do, but I want to know."

Robbie turned and stared at him. "No."

"That's it? Just no?"

"No." Robbie trod past him and headed for the truck. "No, no, no, no, no."

That strange repetition, as though Robbie was learning to speak all over again, as though he was so sick he wasn't himself any more. Nash opened his mouth to call out to him, then swallowed away the words and clutched the plastic bag more tightly. Maybe it was just a sulk: self-consciousness about the rash, or disappointment because that thing had fallen off his hand when he'd had little-boy hopes it would grow into something he could nurture.

Out by the road, Chris was waiting. He hissed, "Dad, you can't be serious. We should go back to Anchorage."

"What if we get caught? You want to end up in a concrete cell with a dozen other kids? You think they're going to take care of Robbie?"

"You can't know that."

"No, I do know that, and it's not worth the risk." He strode past him out to the road, mud sucking at his shoes and the bag rustling in his hand.

Chris followed. "He's gone all quiet and weird. Doesn't that worry you? I can't believe you think he's okay."

"You think that's what I said?"

"Yeah." Chris wheeled around. "Pretty much."

"Then you weren't listening, were you?"

Beyond Chris, the road was all broad puddles turned bright with reflected fog. So much for taking the bag to the dumpster. Nash knotted it tighter and pitched it into the undergrowth. It was so light it caught on the air before dropping gently into the bushes a few feet off.

From behind him he heard, "Nice one, Dad." Chris turned away and strode toward the truck.

How it stung: the curl of sarcasm in Chris's voice, the look of disappointment before he walked off. He was doing his best, for crying out loud, and here was Chris, punishing him for it.

Neither of the boys looked at him as he climbed into the truck and revved the engine. The fog was dulling everything, and he pulled out of the campsite too fast, the trailer scraping against branches and jolting through puddles. Nash didn't say a word and, mercifully, neither did Chris.

8

That fog. It reduced the world to black and white. Out of the blankness shapes materialized on the road: a dead dog that was nothing but wet leaves heaped up, twisted hands that resolved into clumps of twigs. Everything except for a few yards of blacktop was blotted out—the road signs, the forest, the mountains, all gone.

Chris sat hunched away from Nash with his hands shoved between his knees. "We should turn back to Anchorage. Instead, we're heading to the border in this? We can't even see where we're going."

Nash spat back, "There are no good choices, okay? This one's just less bad." He'd been driving hunkered over the wheel, but now he made himself sit back as though he could see just fine when in truth his eyes had to feel out the line of the road. He told himself perhaps the fog would keep them safe because no one was going to be out chasing illegals in this weather. Still, as he wove around debris left by the storm—tongues of mud washed onto the road, the broken-off top of a spruce—and a pair of headlights materialized behind the trailer, he startled. He couldn't stop himself snatching glances in the side mirror, trying to size up whether the vehicle was a white van, or something larger and innocuous like an RV. It hung there, too close, edging out into the road then, in a blast of horn, it pulled past. A courier van. In a matter of seconds it had vanished, all except for its tail-lights that floated, disembodied, before winking out.

Nash's shoulders were burning from fighting the pull of the soft tire. If he couldn't get help up the road, he had no idea what to do. Just drive on, he told himself, even if he was driving on the rim, even if it wrecked the goddamn truck.

In places where the fog thinned, the forest massed over the slopes stood out starkly. Then the road would pitch down again and the whiteness flooded back in, and all he could do was watch the few yards of highway rolling toward him, delivering up its debris and potholes. Without him noticing, his anger fell away. All that was left was a gritty irritation whenever Chris turned around and made a point of checking on Robbie, saying, "You okay back there, dude?" or "You tell me if you feel worse, or if you're gonna puke, right?" Robbie must have been leaning against the door because all Nash could see of him was the blanket he'd pulled up over himself.

Trees and fog and that endless road, and soon Nash worried that somehow he'd missed Gakona Junction and its garage, and the turnoff to the border crossing at Beaver Creek. There had to be mile markers but he hadn't seen one in miles, since the top of a hill where the road was laid out ahead of him, black and shining, before they'd plunged back into the fog. His phone, he thought—if he could get bars out here, he'd be able to check. With one hand he grabbed it, was about to turn it on when he stopped himself and tucked it away in his pocket.

Paranoia. Or maybe not, whatever Chris might think. He slowed instead so he could scan the roadside. Beside him Chris sighed. He said, "Wow, really? All of a sudden, the fog's that bad? That sucks because there's nothing here, no hospital, nothing."

Nash felt the root of his tongue tighten, said sharply, "I don't want to miss Gakona Junction." He glanced up to the mirror. "Robbie, you doing okay?" Robbie lifted his head and stared back. He held Nash's gaze, and it was Nash who looked away.

Up ahead now, unmistakable, the straight lines of buildings, and he crept along until lights grew out of the fog: the garage. He pulled in, said, "Robbie, you need the bathroom?" He twisted around, meaning to lay a hand on Robbie's knee, but the way

Robbie was watching him, eyes unblinking, baleful, his fingers folded back toward his palm—that look, like a dog about to bite. He pushed that thought away. "If you feel worse, you say so. Chris is going to stay with you. I won't be a minute."

The garage office smelled of oil and cheap coffee. Behind the counter, a hulking man in stained overalls was talking on a landline. When he saw Nash he hung up and leaned against the counter. "Let me guess. You want air."

Nash shoved his hands into his pockets. "Yeah."

He lifted a stained, oversized travel mug, took a sip, and rested it against the slope of his chest. His beard was long enough to touch the rim, and he smoothed it with one beefy hand and nodded out the window. "You plan on going far on that?"

"Far enough."

"Hope you got life insurance then." His lips twisted into a sort-of smile.

"I'm in a hurry."

"Everyone's always in a hurry." He took another sip of coffee. "If your flat's not in too bad shape, I can do a patch in a half hour. It'll cost you, but you'll get there in one piece."

Nash let out a ridiculous laugh. "It's been a crazy couple of days."

"You don't fix it, things'll get a whole lot crazier." He ran his hand down his beard again and propped his elbows on the counter.

Having this immense man stare right into his face felt like a rebuke. Nash took a breath to tell him to forget it—he could feel the way he'd march out of that office and drive away—but when he looked out the window Chris was leaning against the truck, watching.

"Okay then," he said. "I'll go get it."

The edge of the truck bed was cold and wet as he hauled himself up. Already this tire felt like a relic from long ago, before the thing on Robbie's hand, before Jimmy's wife. By the door the guy was waiting, tipping up his mug to drink the last of his coffee. Nash rolled the tire to him, and he scooped it up under one arm as if it weighed nothing at all.

Chris was coming across the forecourt. He'd pulled up his hood, and when he stared out tiny droplets of moisture were clinging to his lashes. "I thought we were just getting air."

"He can fix the flat. We'll make much better time if we're not driving on the spare."

"For chrissakes, how long's that going to take?"

"Thirty minutes."

Chris jammed his hands into the pockets of his hoodie. "Well—" He looked around, then at the ground. "I need to take a leak."

"You alright?"

"Course I am," he said and pushed open the office door.

Nash moved the truck to the far side of the forecourt, then dug peanut butter and pilot bread out of the trailer for Robbie. He hadn't said he was hungry. Then again, he hadn't said anything. By the time Chris came walking back past the gas pumps, Nash had passed one cracker after another to Robbie who'd taken them without a word and eaten them quickly and messily before holding out his hand for more. Nash had tried kidding with him, saying, "My god, Robs, you having a growth spurt?" and "You trying to make up for puking yesterday?" but Robbie didn't look at him. All he did was push another piece of cracker into his mouth, crunching it so fast that crumbs fell from between his lips, and as he swallowed, Nash caught the soft creaking of his throat trying to squeeze it all down.

When Chris opened his door, a bloom of cold air swept into the cab. Nash said, "Wow, you took long enough."

He didn't look at Nash, just heaved himself up into his seat. "What—now you want to know what I was doing in the bathroom?"

"Come on, Chris, I was just making conversation." He was

spreading another piece of pilot bread with peanut butter, and now he held it out to Chris. Chris gave a quick shake of the head and turned away, and they sat in silence as Nash passed it back to Robbie. The cloying smell of peanut butter filled the cab and, beneath it, the sour-honey smell that clung to Robbie.

Before long a vehicle pulled in, the glare of its headlights softened by the fog. Chris perched forward to watch as it turned toward the gas pumps. An RV, and Chris let out his breath, turned around in his seat. He said, "Robs, slow down, why don't you? You're going to throw up again."

Nash held out another piece of pilot bread for Robbie, but Chris smacked it away. "Dad, he's going to make himself sick."

"He's hungry. He hasn't eaten much the last couple of days."

"You still hungry, Robs?" Chris dipped his head to look at Robbie. "What's wrong? You lost your voice too? I mean, come on, say something, you're freaking me out."

Nash pulled on Chris's arm. "Really?" he said under his breath. "How's this helping?"

"It's the truth."

"Leave him alone."

"Dad, he's being all weird—"

"Chris—" Nash squeezed his arm to shut him up and glowered at him. "Let's not make matters worse, okay?" He got out and took a few breaths of the clammy air, then climbed into the back with Robbie and wrapped the blanket more tightly around him. Robbie didn't resist. He didn't do much of anything except stare out the window, and it was weird, Chris was right, and he was worried, but maybe Robbie was just feeling sick again. He whispered, "If you think you're going to throw up, you tell me."

Up front, Chris drummed his fingers against his knee. Beyond, the RV lingered. It looked familiar, a long white RV like Jimmy Cho's. That woman, or what she'd become—Nash hugged Robbie closer, and this time Robbie let himself be pulled in tight to his chest, and the warm, sweet smell of him filled Nash's nose.

Nash whispered in his ear, "We'll make a new life for ourselves in Canada. Things'll be easier there, you'll see. Calgary's a great town—there's so much to do. Movie theatres, ball parks, a terrific music museum, and if you drive out to the lakes in the summer, there are beaches. You can go windsurfing, or kayaking. You're going to love it."

Chris craned forward. Headlights, their glow haloed by the fog, and a second vehicle close behind.

Nash settled back a little. "Gramps is there, and he'll be so pleased to have you boys around."

Chris glanced behind him, then bit his lip and stared out through the fog.

The first vehicle was coming in close to the truck, so close its headlights glared into Nash's face. He mumbled, "Oh come on, really? There's all this space here."

Someone was getting out. A big man with a second set of eyes high up on his forehead. Not eyes. Sunglasses. The goon from the garage in Glennallen. Nash gripped Robbie to him, said under his breath, "What the hell?" His hand went to the door handle, but it was too late—the goon was already standing just beyond the window. Another man lurked a few feet from the hood of the truck, watching as the second van turned in a tight arc and pulled up beside the trailer.

The goon stepped closer. With one knuckle he knocked on the glass and peered inside. When he recognized Nash, the skin between his eyes puckered and he said, "Come on out, Mr. Preston."

Nash was breathing too fast and too hard, staring at that guy whose face was just a few inches away. "You can't do this!" he blurted.

Chris called out, "Dad, don't, just don't!"

"Mr. Preston, I won't tell you again—step out of your vehicle."

"I don't know who the hell you are." Nash's voice lurched. His tongue felt large and clumsy, his mouth dry as dirt. He couldn't look away. Those dark lenses clouded with condensation, those flat eyes beneath. At one corner of the man's mouth, a patch of stubble he'd missed when he'd shaved.

Nash fumbled his phone from his pocket and held it up. "Get away from me and my boys or I'm calling 911."

The guy turned away with a shrug as though to say, *Can you believe this?* Then he swung back and his elbow whipped out so fast that all Nash saw was the window breaking apart, and an instant later a hand reaching in and grabbing him by the throat. The guy's face was too close, his breath loamy with coffee. "You still want to mess around? I enjoy this kinda stuff but you," and he dug his thick fingers into Nash's throat, "I figure you're not having such a good time. Is he, boys? He needs to do as he's told." He tilted his head to look at Robbie and Chris.

Nash couldn't breathe. He tried to pull those fingers off. Someone was shouting, "Dad! I'm sorry! I'm so sorry." Chris, desperate, but how far away he was, beyond the awful grip of those fingers on Nash's throat. In Nash's ears, the sound of his own death was coming to him in raw gasps while there, clinging to the ceiling, crisp and perfect, hung the small plastic cover of the dome light. That ridiculous thing was going to survive him, and he yanked at the goon's thumb, got a grip and still couldn't pull it away, tried pounding on the guy's arm, but the guy just squeezed harder.

Then the pressure was gone. Nash fell onto the seat gasping in air, and more air, his hands at his throat to shield it, though it was too late for that. It took him a few seconds to make sense of the quiet settling around him. The truck was empty. Its doors had been left open like a winged beetle about to take flight. As for his boys, they were gone.

A door slammed, and Nash sat up. The goon was behind the wheel of the van parked just ahead, and another guy in a dark uniform was walking around to its passenger side. As soon as he'd shut his door the van backed away, dragging with it the blaze of its headlights, and then taking off onto the highway.

Nash scrambled out. From his clothes broken glass tinkled prettily onto the ground. Nearby, a third guy was waiting with a gun held lazily in one hand. With it he gestured for Nash to step toward the hood of his truck, and Nash cried, "Whatever the hell this is, keep me with my boys. I'll do what you want, just don't take them from me." Already the buzz of the van's engine had been swallowed up by the fog. He glanced toward the highway. The van hadn't headed south. It hadn't taken his boys to Anchorage.

The guy lifted the gun. "Hey, hands on the hood, feet apart." He sniffed richly and swiped his sleeve beneath his nose. "Come on, come on," he said and waved the gun. He looked weary and sick: shadows beneath his eyes, his eyes watery.

Under Nash's hands the metal of the hood was wet and still a little warm. His boys, gone, and how vast the world felt. The highway was nothing more than a strip of tarmac vanishing into the mist, carrying his boys away, terrified, snatched from him and bundled into the back of a van. He could taste the panic they must have felt, and beneath it the suffocating sense that he'd failed them.

The scrape of feet on concrete, a long, bubbling sniff, and then the guy's hands were patting down his sides, his back, his waistband, doing a half-assed job, and Nash was gauging how it would be to swivel around and punch the guy in the face, or sweep his legs from beneath him, despite the fact that he was leaning on the hood and off balance, and the guy had just seized his wrist—to cuff him, surely, and then there'd be no chance of escape—when he heard a wet crack and the guy's weight collapsed on his back. Nash's arms folded up and his cheek hit the hood. Everywhere, suddenly, a strong, fruity smell. He twisted himself to throw the guy off, and the man fell solidly to the ground. Behind him, the broken neck of a bottle in his hand, stood Jimmy Cho.

9

Jimmy grabbed Nash by the arm and yanked him across the forecourt toward his RV. "This way," he hissed, "quick."

"My truck!"

He dragged at Nash's jacket. "No, just get in."

As soon as Nash had climbed up into the passenger seat, Jimmy jammed the RV into gear.

"All my stuff! That's everything I own!"

But Jimmy stamped hard on the gas and sent the RV wheeling around the pumps and out toward the highway. He gestured over his shoulder with one bony thumb. Nash turned to look: the second white van, the guy Jimmy had hit sprawled like the chalk outline of a murder victim, the door of the trailer wide open—and there in the doorway, a pale face staring out.

Nash pushed himself back against the seat. "What the hell?" He reached up to smooth back his hair. His fingers were trembling. "What's going on?"

A pinging was coming from close by. He heard Jimmy say, "Put your seatbelt on or it won't stop."

"My seatbelt?"

"Or it won't stop."

In the wan light, Jimmy's face looked hollowed out. He had a wool hat pulled down to his eyebrows, and he drove perched close to the wheel with both hands at the top. There was a flutteriness to how he dabbed the back of his hand against his mouth, or reached up to touch his hat, or turned to look in the side mirror, which he did over and over. He said, "Please—your seatbelt.

That noise is driving me nuts." He let out a strangled laugh as he glanced at Nash.

There was fear in that look. Nash pulled on the seatbelt, awkwardly—not the accustomed gesture of reaching over his left shoulder—then he leaned forward against it to urge the RV on, staring through the fog for the taillights of the van that had carried away his boys. There was nothing except the road vanishing into the blankness, and beside him Jimmy sitting rigid at the wheel.

Jimmy said, "The van headed east on the Tok cut-off."

"They took my boys, right in front of me."

"I saw everything." How old Jimmy looked, how fierce too. "Some of those men were at Mike's garage yesterday. They trashed the place."

"I stopped in. I thought the garage was open, but it was them." Nash crossed his arms over his chest and tucked his hands beneath them. The shaking was still there, his fingers twitching, and now his knee bouncing crazily. His body, still terrified, the feel of that thumb pushing against his windpipe lingering.

"I tried calling Mike but there's no cell service down in Chitina. I called Ju-Yeong too and some other woman answered. She said she was her friend and could take a message. I hung up." He dabbed at his mouth again and glanced in the mirror. "They'll come after us, you know. It's just a matter of how long we have."

Nash peered into the side mirror, trying to see the road behind them. The angles were all wrong and the mirror showed nothing except the side of the RV. "Who the hell are they?"

"Everyone in town has seen those white vans around." He licked his lips. "Please don't think I'm nuts—for a couple of years there's been talk about a secret facility up around Slana. Alaska's huge, but even here you can't hide what you're doing. All your equipment has to come along the highway from Anchorage, right through Glennallen. People are going to notice construction vehicles, and unmarked white vans." He gave a tight smile. "A secret facility, though—I thought it was crazy talk. In this country, people love conspiracies and that sort of nonsense. No offense." He gave Nash a quick, apologetic look.

"A secret facility? What on earth does that even mean?"

"Listen, I don't know—for research or something, I guess. Maybe it's to do with national security. You know, because the climate's changing so fast."

"Wouldn't that be more the university's thing? Up in Fairbanks?"

"What's left of the university, you mean, after all those cuts?" He blinked fast.

"Building a place like that in the middle of nowhere doesn't make any sense."

Jimmy shrugged. "I'm just telling you what I've heard."

Nash stared out into the gloom. The wet road, the debris, the shapes of trees faint in the fog. A world in which nothing made sense. A secret research facility? A secret detention center, more like, if the place even existed. The sort of place Maria could have ended up in. He pinned his hands between his knees to still their shaking. "Well shit, is that where they're taking my boys?" He let out a thin laugh. "And somehow we can get in? Is that the plan?" The words sounded dumb the moment they left his mouth.

Jimmy lifted one hand from the wheel and patted the air. "My plan? My plan was to stop them taking you. I couldn't help your boys."

"So what are we going to do?"

"It's not like I've thought this through. We're following the van. That's as far as I've got."

Nash's chest felt tight, the air thin. He was breathing fast and he tugged at the seatbelt, only that wasn't the problem and loosening it didn't help. Through his head came a crazy whirl of ideas—overtaking that white van so they could force it off the road and snatch the boys away, storming into whatever facility the boys were being taken to and rescuing them and, by some miracle, Maria. Dumb ideas, he realized. Movie ideas. He glanced over at Jimmy. "What you did for me back there—that was brave."

Jimmy's hands tensed on the wheel. "And stupid. They'll have more reason to come after us both now. Anyway, it wasn't just for you. I'm an old man. I can't do much single-handed to find Ju-Yeong." He took a deep breath and let it out almost in a whistle. "Apparently she was picked up before the end of her shift. Some sort of emergency."

"Picked up? Who picked her up?"

He shot Nash a quick sideways look. "Good question."

"Her husband?"

"No, they said it wasn't Mike."

"Maybe something happened to him. Chitina can be dangerous. A friend of mine says the only reason to tie yourself off when you dip net is so they can haul your dead body out of the river if you fall in."

"So why was someone else answering her phone? If something had happened to Mike, she'd have told me. She'd have kept her phone with her." He tipped his head, as if against a stab of pain. "I called her because I was worried about my wife, and now this young woman's vanished. It's my fault, and my wife—" His mouth hung open for a moment, then he shut it without saying more.

"You couldn't have known," said Nash.

"Ju-Yeong's a foreigner too. Can you understand what that means? For her, any trouble and they'll detain her or send her back. It doesn't matter that she's married to an American, all that matters is that she's foreign. Unless you've got money, they come after you. Anyone can betray you—they just call the hotline and say you're here illegally, and those contractors come and take you away."

"Contractors? You mean bounty hunters?"

"Whatever they call them. You end up in a detention center for months, for years, no matter if you did nothing wrong. There's no fairness anymore, and no one cares."

"You think that's what happened? Immigration came for her?"

"This has to do with those fossils. It has to, right?" He glanced at Nash. "But whoever took her, that's where she'll end up in the long run. That's where all us foreigners end up, even over the smallest thing."

Nash nodded and rubbed at a mud stain on his jeans. He still hadn't told Jimmy he and the boys were illegal, and he gazed out the window rather than look at him. It was a betrayal of sorts, when this man had taken a huge risk to help him. Now he wondered if he'd betrayed the boys, too. For all those months, he hadn't told them the danger they were in. Chris had been pissy with him in the truck, and he couldn't blame him. After all, he hadn't turned back to Anchorage, he'd taken the risk of driving on when Robbie had been acting downright weird—he didn't seem the least bit bothered by the rash, and there was that eerie silence, that ominous stare, as though it wasn't him looking out from behind those eyes. No, Nash told himself, that's movie logic. Robbie was worn out and sick, a little boy frightened by what was happening to him, that was all.

Another few hours and they'd have made it to the border, and to safety. Those stories in the news the last few years: kids being kept in cages at detention facilities, kids getting sick and dying for lack of medical help. All Chris had understood was that his dad wasn't paying attention to what was happening right in front of his eyes. Of course he'd been sullen, taking off to the bathroom at the garage to sulk.

Nash cupped his head in his hands and stared down at the grit on the floor mat. Chris coming back from the bathroom and not looking him in the eye. Chris sitting silent in the passenger seat, disgust and disappointment radiating off him. Then those headlights had appeared and he'd strained forward. Eager. Expectant. Nash shivered. A ghastly chill was sinking through him. That phone on the counter in the garage office—Chris might have been worried enough to make a call. And if he'd said his brother was ill because a fossil he'd found had stuck to his hand, would a bunch of goons have been sent to pick them all up? No wonder Chris had shouted *I'm sorry*—he couldn't have been expecting that.

Nash heard Jimmy call, "You alright?" and he nodded.

"It's shock." Jimmy's voice was thin and scratchy. "That can happen. Your boys grabbed like that, and you attacked. It's a shock to the system. You need to calm yourself. Close your eyes, if you can."

They drove on, and Nash didn't close his eyes. Maybe those goons were bounty hunters taking his boys to a detention center. Maybe they were contractors for some other government agency because it was Robbie's find that they wanted. What did it matter? His boys were gone, and whether they were being taken to a secret research facility, or just detained like so many thousands of others, it made no difference. After all, it was just him and the old man trying to find them.

Occasionally a clatter came from the kitchen cabinets when the RV hit a dip in the road. A wind must have picked up and soon it tore the fog apart, giving glimpses of hills and rocky slopes. Nash said, "I haven't said thanks for what you did back there."

"You think I killed that man? Because I didn't look back to see." He threw a glance at Nash, and his eyes looked scared.

"I don't know."

Jimmy sat shaking his head, and shaking it, then he braked hard. Nash grabbed the edge of the seat and yelled, "We can't go back! No!"

The RV bumped and lurched as it left the highway onto a turnout. Jimmy's face was bunched up. He steered the RV across the gravel to the far end where spruce trees arrowed up toward the sky, then he plucked his hands from the steering wheel. His fingers seemed molded to its shape, and he stared at them, his breath coming roughly. All in a rush he said, "Excuse me," and fumbled for the door handle. Cool air swept in as he crouched on the gravel and vomited.

As the morning wore on, the last of the fog dissolved and the mountains revealed themselves. There was little traffic, just a few camper vans and RVs, a pickup truck or two, and three motorbikes that swarmed past close together, their riders dark and shiny as beetles in their leather. A couple of times Jimmy pulled over so he could check on his wife. Nash didn't ask how she was: Jimmy's face was grim as he buckled himself back in his seat and eased the RV onto the road again.

On his knee, Nash had a map—Jimmy had a whole drawer of them, and this one showed in detail the dirt roads and trails leading off the highway. He said, "How sure are you about this?"

Jimmy shifted his grip on the wheel. "They didn't drive your boys off toward Anchorage, so do you have any better ideas?" He pitched his head toward Nash. "Anyway, it's not too far, somewhere up around Slana."

"And all we have to go on is perhaps it's a secret facility?"

"I've driven past that place. I've seen trucks turning in. If it's not a mine, what is it?"

"How can you know it's not a mine?"

"One of my regulars, this old fellow, he used to be a mining engineer. He thought it was odd—there are plenty of mines in that area except they're abandoned because their seams are worked out. Besides, there's no ore being trucked out of that place."

"Seems like a long shot." Beneath Nash's hand the map had grown warm and a little damp.

Jimmy scratched his neck, slowly, as though giving himself time to think. "If you wanted to hide a facility, where better to put it than in an old mine? Those places aren't ancient history. Some of them were being used twenty years ago, even ten years ago, so the buildings would still be in good shape, and the tunnels wouldn't have caved in." He sniffed. "I know it all sounds crazy, but everything's crazy—fossils making people sick, children being snatched from their parents, the weather turned upside down. What kind of world are we living in?"

"You think this is the government?"

"So much has been privatized—prisons, detention centers, you name it. I'm not sure there's much difference between the government and the big corporations it hires to do its work."

Without the fog the landscape looked bleak, rocky crags scraping the bellies of clouds, the marshy land below full of trees tipping toward each other where the ground had melted, or tilting into ponds where, ten years ago, there had been no ponds. A world gone crazy, alright—a world falling apart because it had been warmed beyond the point of repair. That thing Robbie'd found—it should have stayed safely buried, but now he was sick, and Jimmy's wife as well, and who knew if they were the only ones.

"Those fossils, or whatever they are," said Nash, "if they're a health risk, they're the CDC's responsibility." His fingers were tapping the map, making a soft patter until he folded it and tucked it under his arm. Maybe the doctor had been worried about a public health problem, and that was understandable— no, he told himself, that wasn't it. There'd been that look in her eyes, excitement, not concern.

"You think the CDC detains people?" Jimmy sucked at his lips. "Or hires some corporation to do it for them?"

"I don't know—no, that's nuts." Nash turned away to the window and sighed. "But whoever they are, it's not like we'll be able to just walk in. Maybe this is a terrible idea—who knows what we'd be getting ourselves into. That installation could be military."

"No military around there, I know that much. Besides, isn't it worth finding out?" A little sun was filtering down. Jimmy pulled off his wool hat and replaced it with a ball cap he took from the dash, scooping it onto his head then angling it low against the glare. "Ju-Yeong's missing, and my wife's not going to make it unless I find someone who knows what those things are. I've got nothing to lose. How about you?"

Nash opened up the map again. "I guess not."

10

The place was easy to spot: a hefty metal gate blocking a dirt road leading off the highway. Beneath it ran tire marks so crisp they had to have been made that morning. With the fog gone, the air had a crystalline quality that meant the dirt road stood out as it cut its way across the scrub and onto the lower slopes of a ridge. There it climbed and twisted back on itself a couple of times, ending at a cluster of buildings. Behind them towered a rocky scarp that rose almost vertically.

Jimmy pulled up by the gate. A few yards away a large sign displayed a logo of a circle cut in two by a thin, black line, the top of the circle green, the bottom white. A short statement declared that the Turnback Ridge Facility belonged to GES Holdings and access was prohibited for any purpose, including but not limited to prospecting, hunting, fishing, hiking, and other forms of recreation, and that the property was under twenty-four-hour surveillance.

Nash muttered, "Well, shit. This doesn't tell us anything." He couldn't help glancing around, as though that goon was going to appear out of nowhere to smash the window and throttle him again.

"Except that they don't want anyone going in there."

"A warning and a padlocked gate? They're not trying too hard." He let out a loud breath. So this is what they'd come here for—those distant buildings at the bottom of the ridge. This place was probably just some small-scale mining operation, and while he and Jimmy sat puzzling over it, his boys were being carried farther away.

"Maybe they just want us to think they have good security." Jimmy reached down and pulled a pair of binoculars out of their case. He gestured for Nash to sit back out of the way before lifting them to his face. As he scanned the hillside, his fingers fiddled with the focus, then he held still. "Behind the building on the left—I think that's the back of a white van." He passed the binoculars to Nash.

They were heavier than Nash had expected, and he lifted them with both hands. How odd to have the world lurch close—the blurred green of grass and bushes, the brown band of the road. He followed it up to the buildings. "Which side? The right?"

Instead of an answer the engine surged and the RV jolted forward, throwing Nash so that the lenses blurred with the rocky face of the scarp. He cried, "Hey! What the hell?"

Jimmy lifted one finger and pointed out the windshield. Nash ducked to look. At first there was just the sharp mass of the ridge with scree scattered down its lower slopes, and then he caught it: a disturbance on the air. A speck of something pale with a slight fuzziness around it. As he watched, it dipped and wobbled. He muttered, "What on earth?" It wasn't until it slid horizontally, an unmistakably mechanical movement, that he understood: a drone.

Nash braced his arms against the window. Trying to find the drone with the binoculars was like peering at the world through a pinhole, all that mountain and brush that looked so much the same until there it was for an instant, a massive robotic mosquito with crooked legs and a white cylinder for a body, dropping away so fast he couldn't track it. One thing was evident, though—which way it was moving. "Shit. It's headed for the road. We're driving right toward it."

"We can't stop. That would look suspicious." Jimmy sat as stiffly as a mannequin with his arms held straight out to the wheel and his shoulders high. Every few seconds his head twitched as he glanced through the side window. "We're just tourists taking in the sights, that's all, just driving along this road minding our own business."

Nash steadied himself against the motion of the RV and looked through the binoculars again. The drone was easier to find this time because it was flying in a straight line toward the highway. Magnified, it looked menacing: a shiny black eye that must have been a camera, a spikiness to its legs and antennae that suggested a vicious nature.

As he watched, it swooped downward in an elegant arc then settled above the road, hanging like a spider from a thread, and there was no choice but to keep driving toward it. Maybe it was standard protocol for a surveillance drone to fly in on any vehicle that stopped by the gate, but he dropped the binoculars into his lap and set his elbow on the windowsill, his cheek against his sweaty palm and half his face hidden, as if this was just a comfortable way to sit. The drone waited. They were so close that in a few moments they'd pass right beneath it.

"Just act natural, just act natural," Nash said under his breath, though he couldn't remember what natural was. Then the drone danced up as though it had been yanked by a string, and when he looked back, it had tipped to the side and was bouncing in the RV's wake. Soon it steadied itself and swept along behind them until, where eventually the road curved around the bulge of the ridge, it plucked itself away and vanished into the distance.

"Well shit," Nash said, and let himself slump back against the seat. He glanced at Jimmy, but Jimmy just stepped hard on the gas.

When they finally stopped, at a pullout that was little more than a stretch of cracked blacktop, Jimmy sat with his hands on the wheel and gazed down the road. His face was shining with sweat but he didn't wipe it away. Instead, with a moan, he let his head tilt back and closed his eyes.

Nash said, "We need a plan."

Jimmy didn't say a word. He sat with his ball cap askew and his mouth open as he took shaking breaths. He gathered himself up, straightening his cap and hoisting himself out of his seat. Nash caught the bitter smell of fresh sweat as he squeezed between the seats and made his way through the RV. There was a squeak of hinges as he closed the bedroom door.

Nash sat alone with the map on his knees, everything quiet except for the blustering of the wind and the ticking of the engine as it cooled. He ran his hand over the map. By the look of it, this road looped around the ridge so that the gentler slopes outside the window were somewhere on the far side of the scarp behind the facility. Perhaps the drone was going to appear over the crest of the ridge and find them—surely they hadn't driven far enough to have doubled back on themselves, but he wasn't positive.

He gazed out of the windshield, just in case, then moved through the RV checking through the windows. He told himself he was being paranoid because there was nothing out there except the hillside and the highway, though even after he sat down at the dining table he couldn't help peering through the blinds and scanning the sky.

From the wall came the ticking of a clock. It wasn't even eleven, and he watched as the second hand measured out each moment, as if time still ran straight and constant when that wasn't true at all. No, it was full of pockets and branchings that meant, since he'd stopped at the garage, there'd been time for his boys to be taken, for him to have fled with an old man he barely knew, for him to realize that Chris had brought this disaster down on them. He laid his head on the table and let its top cool his cheek. Chris coming out of the garage office, that determined sourness to him. He should have guessed right away what he'd done.

Chris, he thought, why couldn't you just trust me? But he knew why—he'd lost Chris's trust when he hadn't turned back. But whether he'd taken Robbie to the hospital in Anchorage or kept going, he was risking his life. That was what the system did: it caught you out, and then it ripped your soul apart by giving you choices that were impossible to live with.

A knot of fury lodged in his throat. He wanted to roar out his rage, to rip down the blinds and snatch that damn clock from the wall, to get behind the wheel and pelt madly back along the road because by now his boys could be miles up the highway, and perhaps there was a detention facility in Tok, perhaps that was where Maria had been taken, he didn't know, he just didn't know. His head was filled with the wash of his own frantic breathing, the thud of blood in his ears. Then he heard it: a distant beating on the air. He half rose out of the seat and rested one hand on its back: yes, there, the buzz of an engine coming closer. In moments the air was vibrating, the inside of the RV too, its windows, its walls, the thin plastic slats of the blinds, and he parted them with his fingers and stared up at the sky, horrified. A drop in pitch and there it was, a small yellow plane slogging upward and veering off to the south. Not coming after him and Jimmy. No, just a plane. He pushed his fingertips hard against his temples—he had to get a grip, he really had to.

Jimmy came hurrying out of the bedroom. "You see that?" he hissed. "We have to get out of here." He lowered himself into the driver's seat.

Nash called out, "It's headed south to the mountains."

Jimmy drove the RV back onto the road, and as it bounced and rocked Nash held onto the table while beside him the blinds rattled. "Jimmy, it's gone. There must be an airstrip around here. It's probably just tourists being flown off on a tour."

Jimmy scowled. "There's no way to be sure." He accelerated so hard that Nash had to lean forward and haul himself along to get back to the passenger seat. "The government uses planes.

Did you think about that? That could be Ju-Yeong or your boys being taken away."

"South of here there's nothing but mountains and wilderness for hundreds of miles." Nash let himself down into his seat. It was still a little warm. "We don't know what we're doing. We need to think. I mean, how sure are you that you saw a white van back there?"

Jimmy didn't answer. The RV was going fast, way too fast, the ridge outside the window wheeling past.

"Jimmy? How sure are you?" He glanced at him now. "You okay?"

Jimmy gulped in a breath, spat it out, tried again. "My wife," and his voice cracked. He turned to Nash. His eyes were small and uncertain, and then they flinched away.

"What's happened?"

"She's not moving, not breathing. I don't know." He shook his head. "I just don't know."

"If she's not breathing—" The engine was straining hard and the road pouring toward them so dizzyingly that Nash yelled, "Hey, slow down, you've got to slow down."

"We need to get out of here."

The speedometer needle was leaning far to the right. Nash blurted, "For chrissakes, you're doing eighty-five!"

Jimmy must have lifted his foot off the gas because the shriek of the engine dropped away, and soon the roll of the landscape past the windows slowed. "I don't know what to do, I just don't know."

"We need to pull over. We need time to think things through."

"Somewhere out of sight." He looked over at Nash. "You've got the map. Find us a place."

"You think we can hide a big white RV out here?" He almost laughed. Beyond the window there was scrubland, and the rocky slope of the ridge easing up to the sky, but he lifted the map anyway and muttered, "I'll try."

11

According to the map, up the road from where the plane had flown over them there was a trail to an old mining camp, and all that would lie between them and the facility was the long, broken line of the ridge. It was unnerving to be so close to that place—and yet, surely the whole point was to be within reach of it.

The trail, when they found it, was potted with holes, and thick with shrubs pushing their way through the hard ground. The RV bumped along as the trail switched and curved slowly uphill toward where a half dozen buildings sat bunched together. From a distance they looked solid enough and yet, as Jimmy drove closer, those buildings disintegrated: roofs rusted through, walls with missing boards, a shed caved in as though a giant fist had come down on it.

The sun had reappeared from behind the clouds. It glinted off puddles and drew stark shadows behind abandoned equipment. A faded metal sign said simply DANGER. Where the trail had branched off the highway, there had been other signs saying PRIVATE PROPERTY and KEEP OUT, and a log left across the entrance that had seemed more symbolic than anything—on his own Nash had managed to haul one end off to the side for Jimmy to drive through, then he'd hefted it back so it looked undisturbed. Just in case.

Jimmy parked behind a tall barn of a building whose wood had turned silvery, its roof corroded to the color of dried blood. Then he turned off the engine and sat with his head cocked, listening. The wind was stronger up here. It moaned past, bringing with it a harsh metallic beating. Nash peered through the window. High above, a piece of metal roofing was flapping like a wing.

With the sun shining hard through the glass, the air inside the RV was hot and stale, tinged with the foul smells of the bedroom. Nash wound down his window a couple of inches and a chilly gust swept in. His mouth felt sticky, as though he hadn't talked in days, and he ran his tongue around his teeth, said, "Well, Jimmy—"

Jimmy pulled the keys from the ignition. He gazed down at them as if no longer sure what they were and climbed out of his seat. Almost as an afterthought, he asked Nash, "Would you come with me?"

Where sunlight cut through the blinds, bright lines shone off the table, the carpet, dazzled off the metal of the sink. The rest of the RV was dim, and when Jimmy opened the bedroom door, the darkness swelled out to meet them. With it came that reek, as though it was emanating from the darkness itself. Nash held his breath against it and followed Jimmy through the doorway.

Even in the gloom it was clear what had become of Jimmy's wife: her silhouette against the sheets was enough. Those limbs bent at tortured angles, her neck crooked back. Like a dead insect, thought Nash, and recoiled. A click, and the beam of Jimmy's flashlight slid over her face. Her mouth was gaping, and from it poked a blunt tongue like a blind creature trying to escape. And her eyes—staring at nothing, the whites turned a cloudy gray. Nash heard himself say, "My god!"

Jimmy laid a hand on her forehead. He whispered, "But she's warm. She's still alive. How's that possible?"

She couldn't be. Nash wouldn't let himself believe it. Her hands were contorted into claws, arms angled out above her chest as though she'd been paralyzed clutching something to her. Jimmy took Nash's hand and laid it on her head, and fear shrilled through him. The old man was right: she was warm. As soon as

Jimmy let go, Nash pulled his hand away. "How long's she been like this?"

"Sometime during the night she stopped reacting when I turned on the flashlight." He shone the light into her face and those horror-movie eyes of hers didn't move.

A sick feeling writhed in Nash's gut as he bent toward her face. He forced himself to look away from that dreadful mouth and the pale tongue poking from it, and focused instead on her eyes. Close up they were veined with tiny gray tendrils, a mesh of them, or perhaps that was the light. With a shudder he straightened back up. "Jimmy—"

"Is she alive?"

"There's something growing—"

The beam from the flashlight was shaking. "I don't understand, I just don't know what this is. What sort of thing could do this to her? I can't—"

"Have you tried her pulse?" It was just something to say, to stop all those words.

The light wobbled as Jimmy touched her neck with his fingers, fumbling from one place to another—beneath her chin, along her neck in the hollows and ridges between where tendons stood out. At last he let out an exasperated huff. "I don't know how. You try."

More than anything, Nash wanted to escape from that room and yet he bit his teeth together and took hold of one forearm. It wouldn't unbend, and when he moved it she rocked toward him, that mouth wide, those dead eyes looming close, and he couldn't help himself, he let go.

The feel of her arm—stiff as a piece of wood yet warm, as though it had been left lying in the sun. He reached out again, this time with two fingers and his thumb, and he squeezed against the delicate frets of her wrist bones. He waited. His ears filled with the dull thud of his own blood pulsing through his body. The first time Maria had touched him—in the clinic, those delicate fingers laid across his wrist, that faraway look on her face as she counted, the slight lemony scent that hung about her—he'd fallen in love right then.

Jimmy asked, "Anything?"

"No, but I don't know what I'm doing either."

He handed Nash the flashlight and gestured for him to step back, then he tucked his head inside the delicate cage of his wife's contorted arms and pressed his ear over her heart. In Nash's hands, the flashlight tipped and sent the woman's shadow stretching nightmarishly onto the wall. He willed Jimmy to stand up and back away from her as horror movie scenarios played out in his head: the ruin of that poor woman clamping her arms around her husband, that hollow mouth latching on, that blind tongue thrusting itself into him.

At last Jimmy straightened up and shook his head. Nash didn't say a word as he led the way back to the kitchen. There they stood side by side, the beam of the flashlight shining tepidly onto the floor by their feet, and when Nash laid a hand on his shoulder, Jimmy pulled himself away.

As soon as Nash laid the map on the table, it was clear what their plan should be: to leave the RV behind and climb the ridge above the mining camp, angling along it so that they came at the facility from over the top. The slope on this side rose gently enough—the difficulty would be on the other side where it was much steeper, but surely no one would expect to be approached from over the ridge. Maybe that would be enough so they weren't spotted, out here where there was no cover, not even the darkness of night.

Jimmy set down his tea. "I can do it, easy. I'm in good shape."

"It's climbing back over the ridge with the boys that I'm worried about." Nash looked away to the dull sky outside with a frown, but it was Maria he was thinking about. If that place was a detention center, perhaps she was there. After being locked up for over a year, she'd be weak, maybe sick.

"And Ju-Yeong, we can't leave her behind." Jimmy laid a finger on the map. "We can cross here where it's lower," and he trailed his finger along a contour line, "even though we'd have to hike back a bit. It's that or climbing over the higher ground, and I don't think either of us wants to do that. Plus, it'd take longer."

"If both of us go, our only option is to come back over the ridge—that doesn't make sense. Besides, we might both get caught, and then what?"

"If one of us goes, that'd be you? On your own?"

Nash sighed. "Look—chances are we're wrong about all this, and I'll just get arrested for trespassing at some mine. But if we're right, and if by some miracle I can get them out, you need to be ready with the RV."

"That's how we're going to escape? Me driving around to collect everyone?"

"Do we have a choice? Anyway, there's your wife. Are you just going to leave her?"

Jimmy looked stung. His voice lifted. "I have to find Ju-Yeong. I have to put things right."

"You don't know she's there. You can't even be sure she's been picked up."

The old man got to his feet. "Someone took her, just like your kids. What else do we have to go on except that place?" He grabbed his cup and carried it to the sink.

"Two people are easier to spot."

"Only if they don't know what they're doing." Jimmy was silhouetted against the brightness of the window, his thin chest bulky in a fleece, his neck bent as he rinsed out the cup then set it to dry. Over by the door he crouched to rummage in a closet. From it he pulled a plastic box and levered himself back up, awkwardly, slowly, and dumped it out on the table. A compass, a GPS, a handgun, an emergency kit, and several MREs. "I'm ready to go. How about you?"

"Okay, okay." Nash lifted his hands. "I was just trying to think things through."

"You think I wasn't?" There was an edge to Jimmy's voice, and Nash looked down into his tea. He'd only drunk a little. He wrapped a hand around the cup and it was warm, though when he took a sip the tea was unpleasantly cool, and its sourness lingered in his mouth. It must have been hours since the boys were taken, and here they were, arguing.

Nash got to his feet. "Let's go, then."

"Hold on, I need a few minutes."

"Fine." Nash zipped up his jacket. "I'll be outside. I'll scout out a route."

The wind had picked up. It tore the door from his hand and banged it against the side of the RV. Sagging clouds, bruised and deflated, were being tugged toward the south, and despite the sun Nash shivered. The building they'd pulled up beside was the largest, built on the one patch of land that was close to flat. Above, others clung to the slope—sheds, a long structure that could have been a bunkhouse, buildings with rotten roofs and crooked doorways that were falling in on themselves, tired of fighting gravity.

The trail was little more than two muddy ruts overgrown with grass that led Nash zigzagging up the incline. Here and there lay the debris of other lives: corroded cans with lids crimped from being opened with a knife, the pinched mouthpiece of a pipe stem, the drum of a wheel lacy with rust and, farther up, the remains of the pickup it had evidently come from. Its tires had rotted to nothing, and the blue of its paint turned chalky and flaking. Nash shielded his eyes. The trail ended at the boarded-up mine entrance, and he was just looking away when he caught a flicker of movement. He stood so still he felt the pulse of his blood in his throat. Grass was rippling in the wind.

Beneath some old bricks, the corner of a faded tarp was fluttering. He scanned the sky for a raven or a hawk whose shadow could be skimming over this place, but there was nothing.

Soon the trail turned steeper, and on the wind came a faint keening. Close by, a falling-apart shed, and the wind was whistling through the fangs of its broken windows. Inside, a blue sleeping bag had been left crumpled in a corner, filthy but not so old. Beside it lay a small enamel plate dribbled with candle wax and stuck with cigarette butts. The next building was longer and narrow. From its ceiling, the remains of a stovepipe swung loose over a brick pad where the stove must have sat. Nash picked his way over the trash on the floor: yellowed newspaper, a broken wooden box, the head of an old shovel. A board snapped under his foot like a gunshot, and he jumped, his heart pounding.

He didn't go inside the others. There was no point risking a broken leg or a bad cut and besides, what he needed was an unobstructed view all the way to the top of the ridge. He slogged around the building closest to the mouth of the mine. From there it was clear—a route of sorts led through scattered rocks and over a fan of scree, up to where the ridge dipped. Floating in his head for a moment, an image of himself clambering over the top, getting past whatever guards the facility had and grabbing back his boys and his wife. Then again, chances were that place was just a mine. All he had to go on were the rumors Jimmy had heard, and what Jimmy thought he'd seen: the back of a white van. He hadn't even seen it himself because Jimmy had spotted that drone and they'd taken off. It seemed over the top for a mine to use drones for security, unless they were mining something valuable enough to make it worthwhile, like gold, or gems—or lithium, now that it was so in demand for batteries.

Still, when it came down to it, he had nothing to lose. If it was a mine, he'd explain he was a hiker who didn't realize he was trespassing. Most likely they wouldn't want to go to the trouble of arresting him. If the place was more than that—well, that was what he wanted: to find his family and get them out of that place because without them there was no point in heading for the border.

They'd have to be fast getting back up the steep side of the ridge, and old Jimmy Cho would just slow them down. The wind sighed past Nash's ears. Of course, without Jimmy's map and GPS, he couldn't be exactly sure where he'd come out on the other side, and without a gun he'd be helpless. He imagined himself taking that risk, weighed it against bringing Jimmy along.

No, he thought, there was another way, and he stared down the slope to where the RV shone a brilliant white in the sunshine.

He didn't have much more of a plan than letting Jimmy think they were going together so that everything would be packed up and ready to go, and then he'd make his move: grabbing the stuff— when Jimmy was in the bathroom, or when he turned his back, because after all how fast could an old guy move?—and taking off up the slope. If Jimmy came after him he'd yell it was for the best because he had a better chance this way.

The thought of it made him a little sick, but he'd do it. And if this young woman, Ju-Yeong, was there, he'd help her too, of course he would.

Coming down the slope, he leaned back where it was steep. His feet scuffed through the grass, and when the wind gusted, he kept his head bowed and followed the ruts of the trail down past the sheds and the abandoned truck, then out onto the flatter ground where the RV was parked. He swung open the door. Inside, the RV was quiet and the light muted. "Jimmy?" he called. The plastic box was tipped on its side, empty. He pulled up the blinds behind the table and glanced around, then he knocked on the bathroom door. "Hey, Jimmy?" he said gently.

From outside came the sad humming of the wind. In here, though, there was nothing except the clicking of the wall clock doling out each second. Nash gently tapped on the bedroom door and whispered, "You in there, Jimmy?" He waited, and then he eased the door open.

That vile stench bloomed out as he stared into the darkness. "Jimmy?"

The bed was empty. Nash's heart squeezed and he wheeled around, furious now, because it all made a crazy sort of sense: the map gone, the GPS and the MREs, the gun. He cried, "Jimmy! What the hell?" As he stumbled through the RV and out into the sunlight, he was close to sobbing. "Come on now," he cried, "we're in this together, aren't we?"

Behind him a bang and he jerked around—the door of the RV swinging wildly in the wind. Jimmy couldn't have got past him up the trail, not carrying his wife. Nash shielded his eyes and gazed out across the slopes stretching away from the mining camp. No sign of an old man hurrying off, nothing moving at all. Behind him, the main building, and he made his way around it, squinting against the push of the wind and the brilliance of the day. On its far side he stared out along the dirt road they'd taken from the highway. Something was coming. A white van, moving fast.

He dropped into a crouch and scuttled back around the building, and then pelted down its length. He had just passed the RV when his foot snagged and he fell flat on his chest. When he tried to heave himself up, his wrist was shoved toward his shoulder blades and one finger bent agonizingly back. How it seared, that pain in one finger, and he didn't move, didn't dare to.

"Stay still." Jimmy's voice, hoarse in his ear. On his spine, pressure pinning him down—the old man had a knee digging into his back. Nash tried to buck him off but Jimmy jerked that finger and the pain made him cry out.

A few feet away the broken neck of a bottle glinted in the sun, and a plastic supermarket bag came drifting past on the wind like a jellyfish caught in a current. Free, moving along, not like him. Then without warning, that searing pain dissipated and Jimmy pushed himself up and dragged Nash by the arm through the wide doorway of the building. Inside, a mess of broken crates, old tires stacked against a wall, a wheelbarrow without a wheel. Jimmy let go and Nash twisted away and tried to dodge past him toward the door, but the old man was waving him back, saying, "No! No!" He pointed up then laid a finger across his lips.

Nash stared toward the roof. Where it was rusted through, a blurring of sunlight, something overhead, and he understood: a drone.

He whispered to Jimmy, "It's too late. There's a van coming up the trail. How could they be on us so fast?"

"They must have sent men after us as soon as we stopped at the gate." He snatched up his binoculars from the floor and slung them around his neck. So, he'd been keeping watch. "You can still make it. Take the bag, I've packed everything you'll need." He pointed to a small backpack by the wall. "I'll run out to distract them while you head up the slope. The drone can't follow both of us."

"What about your wife?"

Jimmy looked away. "I've hidden her. They're not getting their hands on Susan."

"It's me they want. You know that, right?"

Jimmy shook his head. He got to his feet and stood in the expanse of the doorway, said, "Good luck." He took off in a stilted run, out across the bare earth. A whirr, and the shadow of the drone zipped over the ground after him. Nash snatched up the backpack. He waited a few moments before sprinting out into the sunlight and up the slope toward the mine entrance. Even as he ran it looked impossibly far.

Up ahead was the broken wall of a shed, and he threw himself behind it. On the wind, voices, then a yell. Nash pressed a fist over his mouth and stared down at the ground between his feet. Ants were picking their way over the mud, as though nothing at all was wrong. One of them climbed onto a bottle cap sparkling with rainwater and seemed to consider its own reflection.

A hum from high above, and Nash flattened himself against the wall. He was gulping down air but it wasn't enough because there, swimming through the sky, was the drone. It turned and tilted to cast its dark eye around as it searched for him, and he couldn't help himself. The moment that eye spun away, he took off across the thin grass.

He ran off the trail, sprinting over broken rocks. A glance over his shoulder—that drone was gliding toward him. It was pointless and yet he blundered on, hands groping for a hold, and even when a loud pop rang out and an instant later his thigh stung, he kept going, grabbing his way over the rocks as they rearranged themselves and floated away from him, and when he fell he didn't feel it, and when he was yanked up by the arms and dragged down to the van, all he knew was that the world had turned huge and dark, and he was lost.

12

At first, Nash understood nothing except that he couldn't move. His arms immobile, his back flat against a bed and, when he tried to shift his legs, they were weighed down. A scorching light. A blur of colors that ballooned and shifted, and he closed his eyes against it. Voices. A pressure against his forehead, fingers prying at his eyelids, and that light burning into his eyes again. Someone said, "Fuck, how much didya give him?"

Close by a woman muttered, "He's fine."

A sniff, then a man said, "Okay, get him out of here."

"Where d'you want him?"

The light blinked out. In its place, the fuzzy shape of a man's face. An upturned nose, eyes narrowed in annoyance. "Put him in the pen, for now."

The face retreated. Nash tried to follow it but he couldn't move his head, and when he shifted his eyes as far as he could, pain tore through his eye sockets. The stale scent of coffee on someone's breath, a lurch—he was on a gurney, and it was moving. Instinctively he tried to steady himself except his wrists were pinned, and he understood: he was strapped down. Overhead, long lights were sliding past. A dull thud shook him, and with a slap of swinging doors, the air turned slick with the smell of damp rock. A corridor of some kind, and the air was cooler here, the lights sparser, hanging from a low rock ceiling fraught with pipes and wires. The floor must have been uneven because the gurney juddered along, shaking Nash so hard that a knot of nausea tightened in his stomach, and he tried to call out. All that left his mouth was a groan.

His legs tipped slightly, and whoever was pushing him grunted. The soft warmth of a belly touching his head, a shove, and they were going more slowly now. Where they stopped, the air smelled of oil and iron. Without the rattle of the wheels, all was quiet except for a thin chattering noise, almost musical, so low it was hard to catch. A guy stepped past Nash to push an elevator call button. A broad back in a dark jacket, a matching ball cap above a neck ridged with fat. Nash ran his tongue over his lips. They rasped drily, and he let out a "Hey—" that was barely a croak. He swallowed to wet his throat, managed, "Hey, what is this place?" The guy didn't turn around, just took hold of the gurney again as though he hadn't heard a thing.

From far away came a heavy whirring, a clunking and rattling that grew louder until an elevator shook to a halt. The guy yanked the gate open and shoved the gurney inside. The elevator was little more than a cage: bars for the sides, bars for the ceiling, and above it the dark loops of cables moving and tightening as the elevator dropped. Just above Nash, the slight whistle of the guy's breath, the tinny sound of a distant beat, and Nash barked out, "Where the hell am I? What's going on?" The guy didn't answer, and soon the elevator stopped and swung slightly on its cables.

Down here the electric lights seemed feebler, and they flickered, flickered again as though they were being crushed out. Nash struggled against the restraints. He yelled, "Get me out of here! You can't do this." Even to him, his voice sounded desperate and pathetic.

They stopped by a metal gate bolted into the rock. From beyond it came a slight hum, and the push of forced air chilling his face, his hands, his feet—they were bare, he realized, and he shivered. As evenly as he could, he asked, "Have I been detained? Is that what this is about?"

No answer. Instead came a bright beep and a buzz followed by the squeal of hinges as the gate opened. A few feet above Nash, one solitary bulb dangled, its light weary from the effort of pushing back the darkness. Soon even that was gone, and he was being wheeled away to where the light barely reached. There was a busyness to the air thanks to the gurney rattling along, its echoes bouncing off the walls, and when the gurney stopped and those echoes died away, all was silent except for the soft tap of water falling from the ceiling, and a gentle whisper, like leaves being lifted in a breeze.

As soon as the straps were unbuckled—from Nash's head, his chest and ankles and wrists—he lashed out with his fists. Useless. His arms heavy, his head spinning. He fell to the ground, and the man hauled him up and thrust him into a chicken-wire cage. He'd only just pushed himself up onto his knees when the door closed and a padlock snapped shut. From behind the wire, the guy glanced in at him. A sullen face, thin-lipped and slack-eyed, and in his ears white earbuds that caught the meager light. The guy took hold of the gurney and pushed it away, bouncing his head to his music.

Around Nash, faint in the light of that single bulb, stood other cages, perhaps a dozen crammed into this small space, and as the guy reached the door, Nash shouted, "Where am I? What the hell's going on?"

The light blinked out. A few moments later, the gate clanged shut and once the jangling of the gurney had faded, the slight glow from the corridor snapped out too. Darkness swept in, dense as water. Nash's head filled with the sound of his own panicked breathing, and he crawled around, hands feeling their way across a wooden floor, a thin mattress, a blanket, a bucket that smelled gaggingly of shit. Slowly he stood up, and a soreness raged in the back of his leg. He leaned against the wire wall and kneaded his thigh. They must have shot him with a tranquilizer, out on that slope as he tried to escape.

Above his head, more chicken wire. He hooked his fingers through it and wrenched it about until his fingers felt bruised, and though it clinked and jingled, it wouldn't come loose. And if it had, the way out was blocked by a steel gate, and by the expanse of this facility beyond. His head filled with ideas: breaking out of this cell and attacking whoever came in—someone would have to bring food and water—and dressing himself in their jacket and cap so he could bluster his way out. Useless ideas, straight out of the movies, when he couldn't even get out of this chicken-wire cage.

He sat down on the mattress. It was so thin that the hardness of the floor pressed up against his bones. Maria might have ended up in this very facility, confined in a cage. She'd have waited for him to get her out, and as the days went by, she'd have believed that he wasn't trying hard enough, that he was going about it all wrong and that's why she hadn't been released when she was legal and shouldn't have been detained in the first place. But he had tried. Spending their savings on a lawyer, posting flyers, joining chat groups online and listening for rumors—in the end it had all been for nothing, because it was as though the air had swallowed her whole.

For him and the boys, there'd be no one trying to get them out. His closest friends back in their home countries, his dad in an old folk's home in Calgary, his brother in Vancouver with no idea they'd been detained. Even if word reached his brother, the Canadian Embassy in DC was overwhelmed by requests for help. Illegal detentions weren't even news anymore. It didn't matter that the prime minister had spoken to the president, or that the minister of foreign affairs had lodged a formal complaint. After all, so many countries had, and it'd made no difference.

Clinging to the chicken wire, Nash called into the darkness, "Chris? Robbie? Are you in here?" Groans, shouted words he couldn't make sense of. He pressed his face up to the fencing. "Who's in here? What is this place?" Laughter rang out, hard as something breaking, and a voice a few feet away licked into his ear: "*Cállate, pendejo.*" But he didn't shut up. He shouted for his boys, and he shook the chicken wire, and eventually the lightbulb flared to life and a guard came traipsing through the gate. The guard was a huge guy with a visor over his face. Behind it, his small eyes glared out. The goon from the gas station, the goon who'd taken his boys, and hope surged through Nash as he cried, "Where are they? They're here, I know they are."

The goon paused in front of Nash and didn't say a word, didn't have to, just raised a can and spray hissed into Nash's face. It burned his eyes, and the delicate membranes inside his nose, and soon furious cries were echoing around him, other people coughing and moaning. Nash snatched at his face. He held his fingers to his streaming eyes and coughed and retched. He couldn't see, couldn't think, and when the gate banged shut and the light went out, he didn't notice because he was curled on his mattress with his hands over his face.

He lay there long enough for the clawing pain to give way to stinging. Then a terrible weariness crept through him, and he slept.

Nash woke. He slept. He woke again and opened his eyes onto a darkness in which time drifted. At last, the light came back on—so dim that the people in the other cages were little more than silhouettes—and Nash heaved himself to his feet. A dull rattle—a guard wheeling a cart and stooping to slide a plate under the door of the first cage. At most there were a dozen men in here, probably fewer because he didn't stop at some of the cages. When he pushed a plate under Nash's door, Nash pushed his face up against the wire, said, "I need to see my boys. I know they're here."

The guy didn't answer. Earbuds in his ears, his face long and pointed as a rat's. He didn't look at Nash, was gone before Nash could shake the chicken wire to get his attention. Maybe that was just as well—on his belt hung a holster holding a can of pepper spray. No gun, and that made sense. If you fired off a round in here, you'd risk it ricocheting off the walls. It felt like useful information, for a few moments at least. Then the room was plunged back into darkness. Soft sounds: men eating, sighing, the crinkle of paper. Nash felt around for his food. A paper plate, and on it a sandwich, a juice box, something rectangular in a wrapper that turned out to be a cheap granola bar, barely the width of his thumb.

He ate. The sandwich was peanut butter and had an acrid aftertaste. He didn't understand why until a tide of drowsiness rose through him, and he had no way to fight it.

Nash was asleep when they came for him. Two guards yanked him off his mattress and zip-tied his hands, gripping his upper arms and propelling him out of his cage. His head was light and swimmy, his legs so heavy that he stumbled along between them past the other cages and out through the gate.

In the tunnel he blinked and ducked his head against the burn of the lights. From one of the guards rose a whiff of body spray, a clean, bright scent. The guards' hands gripping his arm were purple and sleek in examination gloves. Nash stared down at his bare feet. How grimy they looked, and the yellow coveralls they'd put him in were stained and rank. No wonder the guards wore gloves. He was already untouchable, and the realization made him shrink into himself.

They took the elevator up to a wider tunnel where they shoved him along toward a heavy door. There was a beep from the security system as it clicked open, and beyond, a floor laid with linoleum that was smooth against his bare feet. He was led through a short corridor lined with doors and into a room where the air was heavy and warm and smelled of onions. One of the guards left, and the other—the rat-faced guy—forced him down onto a hard, plastic chair in front of a desk. There was so much light that Nash couldn't look up. Beneath his feet, gray linoleum streaked darker where other men must have rested their filthy feet. Computer keys tapped delicately, and a chair squealed. A man said, "So, this is the father?" He must have leaned forward because Nash caught the smell of onion on his breath.

"Yes, Doctor."

Nash lifted his head. A dazzling light from a desk lamp. His eyes watered and a grinding pain stirred inside his head. He tried again, squinting through the tearing up of his eyes. On the other side of the desk sat a man in his thirties who looked like a wooden puppet. His face was long with an upturned nose and high cheeks flushed pink, and his mouth was strangely narrow. His dark hair had been combed back so neatly it looked painted on. This was the man who'd pried open Nash's eyelids when he'd been brought here, and anger flared up his throat. He blurted, "What the hell is this place? Where are my boys?"

From the desk, the doctor lifted a pair of glasses and slid them on. Their round lenses gave him a surprised look. He looked past Nash to the guard standing behind him, and his lips bunched in annoyance. "The lease paperwork should have been submitted as soon as he was brought in so we wouldn't have had to wait."

Behind him, the guard said sourly, "No one told us."

"Then we have a communication problem, don't we?"

In the silence there was a whisper of shoes on the floor as the guard shifted his feet. Nash felt him weighing whether he should say something back, and the huff of breath as he decided not to.

The doctor turned to his computer and nestled his hand over the mouse. From behind him, a printer whirred and sheets of paper came quivering out. He swiveled in his chair to grab them then laid them in front of Nash, and only now did he look at him again. "Mr. Preston, you've been taken into custody. You must be aware that you are in this country illegally. You need to sign at the bottom of each page." He slid a pen across the desk toward him.

"What's going on? Where are my boys?" It was dizzying to look down at so many lines of type stark against the white of the paper.

"This is the bureaucratic fallout of being detained. There's always paperwork," the doctor said lightly, as though there was a joke to it.

With his hands zip-tied together, Nash had to reach for the documents with both. The paper was still warm from the printer. "Is my wife here?"

"Your wife?" The doctor raised his eyebrows. "There are no women being held here."

Nash stared down at the documents in his hands, held them so tight that his hands trembled. She wasn't here. Something in his chest slipped—it had been a ridiculous hope. "You want me to sign? Why would I do that?"

The doctor leaned his forearms onto the desk. "Mr. Preston, your choices have consequences not only for you but for your sons. Right now, one of your sons isn't doing so well."

Nash laid the papers back down and gripped the edge of the desk with his fingers. The doctor glanced at them as though they had encroached too far. "I need to see my boys or I'm not signing anything."

"The younger is in obvious need of medical treatment, and yet you left the clinic in Glennallen despite instructions not to." He lifted a sheaf of papers clipped together. On the front, blurred though distinct, was a photo of Robbie. "His medical records only tell us so much. What happened to him, Mr. Preston?"

The room felt too warm. Light glinted off the top of the desk, off the glass of a framed diploma, caught the bright colors of a postcard pinned to a corkboard behind the doctor's head. "Long story," muttered Nash.

The doctor leaned back in his chair and wrapped his hands around one bony knee. "You do understand that you've put his life in danger, don't you? That's a criminal offense—child endangerment." Between his lips, his teeth showed small and white and even.

"How is he?"

"The news isn't good—he has deteriorated. You can't really have expected otherwise, given that you elected not to let him be treated."

A prickling over Nash's face, a painful squeezing in his gut. "This place isn't a hospital, it's a detention center."

"This is exactly where he needs to be. I can treat him. But we've lost hours because you thought you knew better."

A vastness was opening up inside Nash, expanding so fast it crushed all those ridiculous theories he'd had, all the thinking that had made him flee the clinic. He said quietly, "Is he going to make it?"

"Without knowing exactly what happened, it's much harder to treat him effectively." The doctor's small mouth flattened, and his voice dropped. "Listen, I get it—you were worried about your son, and you wanted to protect him. We want him to pull through too, but without your help, it's so much harder. Please— tell me what happened." The doctor hunched a little, as though he needed to make himself smaller to stare into Nash's face, and the light gleamed off his glasses. "What have you got to lose by telling me, Mr. Preston?"

Nash shifted his arms and the plastic ties dug into them. He shifted again so the plastic bit harder. Where to start? With the truck getting a flat and sending the boys to look for fossils. He stared past the doctor as the story came out: that thing Robbie had found, how Robbie'd held onto it all night and it had attached itself to his hand, how he'd tried to cut it off except Robbie had screamed, and later Robbie had thrown up and run a fever. He described how the thing had dried up and fallen off like an old scab, but by then a strange rash had grown over Robbie's skin. The whole time he talked, he fixed his gaze on the cork- board behind the doctor's head—a photograph of the doctor in shorts on the deck of a boat, beside it a postcard of a magnificent mountain peak against a blue sky—because that way it was easier to skirt around any mention of Jimmy Cho, in case by some miracle he'd escaped, and when at last he finished and looked across the desk, the doctor was scribbling notes onto a small pad.

"Did you keep the organism? After it released from your son?"

"No, I threw it away."

"Where exactly?"

"At the campground where we stayed outside of Glennallen."

"The state campground?"

"Yes."

"I see, I see." He tapped his lips with the end of his pen. "Tell me, where exactly did your son find this organism?"

"I can't say for sure. Somewhere close to where we got the flat. From there it took a couple of hours to get to Glennallen, but then, we were going pretty slow."

"Near Nelchina, then?"

"I don't remember." He shrugged.

"Was there anything distinctive about the location? A mile marker, a feature that stood out?"

"There was a rockfall beside the road. I pulled over because the shoulder was wider there."

The doctor frowned. "You can't be any more specific?"

"I was focused on changing out the tire."

"Did your son find the organism lying on the surface? In the debris?" The end of the doctor's pen was dancing impatiently against the pad. Just below his hairline, beads of sweat glinted.

Nash said, "Yes, lying in the debris. Does it matter?"

"We don't want other people falling victim, do we?" He pressed his lips together and glanced down at his notes again with a sigh. "It's a shame you threw away the remains, but—" and he spread his hands, the pen in one, the pad in the other "—how were you to know, right? Let's take care of the paperwork, or more time will have been lost."

"What's this for?"

"So we can treat your son."

"I need to see him. I need to see both my boys." He tried to keep his voice calm, as though that would help.

"As soon as he's out of danger, Mr. Preston, and out of isolation." He gestured to Nash to pick up the pen lying in front of him, and Nash did. He brought its tip down to the signature line at the bottom of the first sheet, but hesitated and let his gaze slip back up. At the top, like a half-open eye, was the circle logo, half green, half white. "What's this Turnback Ridge Facility?"

"We're a small operation owned by GES Holdings."

"So, this is a privately run detention center?"

The doctor shrugged apologetically. "We care for detainees under a contract with the Department of Homeland Security, among other agencies. That is how the world works these days."

Nash lifted the top sheet. Beneath was another dense with print, and beneath that another. He tried to pry free sentences. He found his name, and Robbie's, and Chris's, and the words *in violation of federal immigration law* and *detention* and *leasee*. He said, "What happens if I don't sign?"

The doctor stared across the desk at him with his eyebrows raised. "You don't want your son treated?"

Nash looked away. The pen was cheap and flimsy. He had to scribble in the margin to get the ink to flow then, as the doctor watched, he put his name to the first sheet, pressing down so hard that the tangle of his signature dug into the paper, and then he turned to the next.

13

It was dim inside the bus because the windows had been painted over and the ceiling lights were grimy and weak. As he fumbled his way along the aisle, Nash scanned the faces for his boys, for Jimmy Cho, but the men who stared back were just the same ones who'd been marched up from the cages with him. Eight of them, all silent, and when the doors had shut and the bus started off, Nash called out, "Where're they taking us?" then a few heartbeats later, "*Donde vamonos?*" Only one man turned, a hefty man with a wide face and sad eyes who muttered, "*Cállate.* No talk."

Nash was sitting close to the back on his own. He leaned his cheek against the window and it felt good. A guard had hit him twice when he'd refused to get on the bus—the guard with the narrow face like a rat's who'd stood behind him in the doctor's office. Up until then he hadn't resisted: not when they'd zip-tied his wrists again, not when they'd herded him and some of the other men into an elevator, not when he'd been lined up in a hangar where a short gray bus was idling. But when the guard had shoved him to climb on board, he'd refused. He'd shouted, "Tell me where you're taking me. Tell me!" The guard's fist had landed square on his cheek. He'd staggered, yelled, "You can't—" and the guard had hit him again, harder this time, and he'd fallen against the side of the bus.

They were heading south back toward Anchorage—that right turn just before they'd sped up onto the highway—and now the bus jolted along, carrying him farther and farther from his boys. His fury tightened. A metal grating behind the driver only let through tiny points of daylight. From the ceiling, a small red light blinked from behind a mesh cage. A camera. No wonder there were no guards back there.

Nash couldn't help himself. He got to his feet, hands cuffed and awkward as he steadied himself against the seat in front of him and started forward. A few hisses—"*Siéntate!*" "*Lárgate!*"—and then a squeal of brakes and the seats were flying past him, and he was scrabbling in the air as his hands tried to separate themselves. He landed hard, banging one elbow and his ribs. A few inches from his face, a pair of filthy sneakers with the big toe poking through. "*Loco,*" he heard and glanced up. An old man with a fuzz of gray stubble and sagging cheeks was watching, and when Nash groaned and tried to pull himself up into the empty seat beside him, the old man gave a brusque shake of the head and snapped, "*Vete pa'l carajo.*"

Nash fumbled his way back to his own seat with his arm pressed against the burning in his ribs. There, he leaned against the window to brace himself as best he could against the bouncing of the bus. They might be on the road for hours because there was nothing close by, nothing at all. He wanted to sleep but could not. The sandwich he'd eaten for breakfast hadn't had the bitter aftertaste of the others, and now when he closed his eyes, all he felt was the clenching ache of leaving his boys behind.

He had no idea how long they'd been traveling when the bus slowed. Long enough for the pain in his ribs to dull, and long enough for the utter boredom of his despair to settle in. The bus had slowed before, except now it turned and bumped over uneven ground.

Nash was the last man to file out. The light was fierce, the air so rich with smells he almost couldn't bear it. Vehicle exhaust, pine sap, wet earth. It had been days since he'd smelled anything except the reek of his own body and the flat odor of damp rock.

The bus had pulled over on the edge of the highway. Two

guards were waiting, a stocky guy he'd seen a few times wheeling the food cart, and the slighter, rat-faced man. Both of them kept their hands on their guns as the men lined up. Not pepper spray, not out here.

In the full brunt of daylight, the men standing with Nash looked brutish and dirty. The older guy with the gray stubble and sagging cheeks was the smallest, his legs short and bowed, and his face sullen. He stood between two teenagers who didn't lift their heads. Other than Nash, there was only one other white guy, a pale, nervous-looking man who kept sniffing loudly until one of the guards, the one with a large sloppy body and wrinkled jacket, wearily told him to cut it out.

The skinny guard strutted in front of them and settled his ball cap more firmly on his head. His name tag said *D. Lewis*, and he already looked pissed. "Step out of line, Preston, you motherfucker," he bawled.

Nash stepped forward. None of the other men turned their heads to look at him and Lewis sauntered close. "This it?"

"Is this what?"

"The lo-ca-tion." His voice was harsh and singsongy. "Where you found the fucking organism, you moron."

Nash glanced around. Broken rock heaped at the bottom of a slope, a hillside scarred where the rock had given way, and all around, taller hills. It looked like it, though he couldn't be sure when it felt like he'd changed that tire so goddamn long ago.

Lewis shifted closer. "Well, you fucker?"

"My son found it."

Beneath his ball cap, Lewis's face hardened. "You want to piss around with me?" A little froth of spittle showed in the corner of his mouth, and he yelled, "Because that would be a big . . . fucking . . . mistake."

That voice slapped into his face, and though Nash tried not to blink, he couldn't help it. Now Lewis pitched himself forward so his nose was just inches from Nash's, blinking furiously, and he roared at him, "You need help, Blinky? You need something to jog your memory?"

"Over there—" Nash's voice caught. "Over at the bottom of that rockfall. That's where we found it."

Lewis stepped back. He said, "Show 'em, Colt."

The other guard tugged a sheet of paper from his pocket and unfolded it. He rubbed his chin then came slow-walking down the line of men with the paper held up for them to see. It was a line drawing of the thing Robbie had found. "We're looking for more of these. Got it? *Buscamos esto.* Like the last time, okay? *Como la última vez.*" He swung his legs out so that he walked with a slight swagger, as if his pants weren't too long and pud-dled around his boots.

Meanwhile, Lewis patrolled the line. "You all fucking under-stand? Do you?" When there was only the crunch of gravel from beneath his feet in reply, he reached forward and flicked the nearest man hard on the cheek. "Do you fucking understand?"

The man was tall and broad with a mass of dark beard. He stared through the guard without a word, and Lewis ran his tongue over his lips. "Your ass belongs to us, Bemba. I can write you up. You can go on half rations, or quarter rations. You want that? You want your miserable life to get more miserable?" Bemba gazed off into the distance. Lewis tugged at his beard and then pulled him forward by it, but Bemba still wouldn't look at him. "You're a fucking worthless cunt," Lewis hissed and whacked him across the face, but Bemba gathered himself up and stood straighter.

Colt had come to a standstill with that drawing held high. He shuffled from foot to foot, eyes narrowed against the wind as he watched Lewis with a carefully blank look. He nodded a couple of times and pointed with his whole arm to the rock-slide. "Over there. *Ahi. Ver ahi.* You all go over there and look for these," he said and lifted the drawing. "But if I can't see you, you're already written up. Got it? *Intiendo?*"

Lewis drew his gun from his holster. "So go on, for fuck's sake, get going. And don't even think about running unless you want lead in your back." He gestured with the gun, and the men shambled off.

Nash followed the rest of them. No one spoke. No one lifted their head. Close by, the old man was walking with short, quick steps, stopping to bend at the waist and stare down like a bird about to peck up a fish though he hadn't reached the rockfall yet. As for the others, soon they were clambering around on the edges of the debris, kicking at rocks, crouching awkwardly with their hands tied and examining the ground in front of them. Only Bemba ventured up the tongue of broken rock. Nash followed, his feet slipping in the cheap sneakers he'd been given, the backs rubbing his heels raw. Bemba scowled down. "No room up here," he shouted. His voice stretched the vowels and trilled the *R*'s.

Nash glanced over his shoulder toward the bus. Colt was sipping from a travel mug and strolling around, and a few yards from him Lewis had his gun in one hand and was staring at his phone. Nash climbed up a little farther. Loose rock clattered and slid beneath him, and he fell onto his knees. "Wait," he called.

Bemba didn't turn around. Off he went, stamping his way over the shattered rock as though it was no effort at all.

"Listen—" and Nash scrambled after him, panting. "I just want to talk."

Bemba glanced around. He was at the crest of the debris now, and he towered above Nash. "No talking."

"They've got my kids locked up in that place. I have to get them out."

"You think I know how?" The wind fluttered his beard and he reached up to stroke it, a strange gesture because he had to move both his cuffed hands. "You think I know anything?"

"Well, do you?"

He raised one eyebrow. "You need to pay attention. GES

owns that place, and they own you. You've been rented out by the US government to earn your keep in detention."

"So it's not a medical facility for detainees?"

"Where've you been, Mr. White Guy?" He laughed softly. "It's a research facility. And sooner or later, we get to be the guinea pigs."

A shout, and Bemba gazed down the slope. Nash turned too. Lewis was striding their way, holding his gun at his waist like an old-style movie gangster. "Hey, you fuckers, you're written up. One more infraction, Bemba, and you're back in the box for a week. Blinky, get the fuck away from him and get searching"

Bemba crouched and turned over a rock by his feet. Under his breath he said, "You pretend to work, and you let them pretend they're doing their job. You play the game, and maybe in the end you don't lose. *Bonne chance.*"

"How long've you been here? How long are they going to keep us?"

Bemba didn't look up. A few yards away Lewis was shouting, "Blinky! Hey Blinky! Get down here!" His face had turned a furious red and Nash made his way back down the slope, rocks rolling away beneath his feet.

For hours the men trailed over the debris, toeing pieces aside, getting down on their knees and pretending to examine rocks when they were too tired to keep climbing over the loose rubble. In the end, it was the old man who found the first object. He'd barely left the flat area close to where the bus was parked, and when he let out a yell and raised his hands together in triumph, they all turned to look. Lewis pulled on a pair of purple gloves before he took it from him, then he turned it over and over. With his phone he took a picture and slipped the object into a small plastic bag. A few minutes later Nash heard Lewis's phone ring, and the tattered ends of Lewis's words as he talked. He gave Colt a thumb's up, his thumb purple in the glove, and Colt slouched over to the bus. He dug out a bottle of water and a chocolate bar for the old guy and stood over him while he ate. Five minutes later, he sent him back to searching.

The second object was found by one of the teens. He stood up straight from where he was squatting on the slope above Nash, then went skittering and sliding over the loose rock with his hands high. He barely had time to drink his water and eat his chocolate before Lewis shouted at him to get the hell back to searching.

Bemba had staked out the top of the rockslide, and he ventured far enough along it that Lewis shouted at him to come back. Instead, he pretended to dig at something by his feet, forcing Lewis to wait, and when Lewis screamed up at him, "You're in the box for a fucking week, you motherfucker," Bemba seemed not to hear and plodded farther away.

Nash climbed up and down over the debris, moving slowly, holding himself in because the cheap sneakers had rubbed away the skin on his heels. It was impossible to tell how late it was with the sun slanting across the sky and the light not changing. He stumbled from weariness. All those rocks. All gray, all broken. His mouth had turned gritty and dry, and his head was buzzing. He tried to suck a little saliva over his tongue and forced himself on because he'd seen what happened if you stopped: Lewis or Colt came storming over. If it was Colt, he swatted you over the head. If you were unlucky, it was Lewis and you were shoved to the ground, landing on your hip or your elbow or your face because there was no way to break your fall with your hands cuffed. It didn't matter how much you were hurt—a gash on your forehead, spitting out blood—you had to heave yourself back to your feet before he decided to kick you, too. Only Bemba didn't care, moving around with that slow walk of his, ignoring Lewis as though he were nothing more than a mosquito.

A gust of cool air and Nash paused. Clouds had been

clumping together along the edge of the sky, and now they were rolling out overhead as though they'd breached a barrier, blanking out the sun and filling the day with a dour light. Already the hills had a fuzzy look, and he wondered if they'd have to keep going in the rain.

It wasn't long until the downpour started, not gently but all at once. In an instant the rocks around Nash's feet turned dark, and a mineral smell flooded up. At the bottom of the slope Lewis and Colt were shouting, waving the men back down. Nash turned away and craned his head back to let the rain smack against his tongue, and though it was barely enough to moisten his mouth, it felt good.

Soon Nash's yellow coveralls were clinging to his skin. He shivered. Fat drops were drumming against his head, and how hard it was to see—the world smeared, the steep incline that had loomed over him for hours reduced to a shadow. Then he started up the slope, forcing his legs to move fast, his breath hissing against the rawness in his feet, but the rocks were wet and slippery, and his soaked coveralls stuck to his legs, hobbling him. He'd reached the top of the rockfall when he heard Lewis shouting over the clamor of the rain to get himself the fuck onto the fucking bus, and when he glanced back, there was Lewis charging toward him, grabbing his way up the slope with both hands.

The whole bus journey back to the facility, crawling along through the storm, Nash shivered in his wet coveralls and cradled the side of his head where Lewis had landed a vicious punch.

14

Nash wasn't returned to the pen. Instead, he had to stand to one side as the others were taken away. Only Bemba glanced back at him, and his look was full of pity.

Colt took Nash down in the elevator. The air cooled noticeably as they sank into the earth, and Nash couldn't stop shivering. His coveralls were still sodden, and torn at the knee. When Colt shoved him along the tunnel, his sneakers rubbed against the raw skin of his heels and he winced. A small stupid pain, considering how his ribs hurt, and his jaw, but the worst of those hurts was over and done with while this stinging flared with every step he took. Still, he noticed—this was the tunnel to the doctor's office where he'd signed the paperwork.

This time, the doctor was sitting on the edge of his desk looking over some documents with his glasses perched low on his nose. He seemed younger and more uncertain than Nash remembered. Perhaps it was the white coat that looked a little too big on him. Beneath it showed cheap brown pants, and the sort of lace-up shoes that are never in fashion. "There you are," he said. "Sit down."

A slight smell of sweat lingered on the air. Nash wasn't sure if it came from him or the doctor, or maybe from Colt who stood not quite silently behind him. Nash didn't sit. He leaned his bound hands on the back of the chair, said "I want to see my boys."

For a moment, the doctor simply stared at him. Then with a

sigh he removed his glasses and pinched the skin above his nose. "Roberto is in isolation, I explained that already."

"And Chris?"

"Mr. Preston, this isn't a social visit. I have questions for you." He glanced behind Nash to the guard. "Colt, you can wait outside."

The door thudded closed as the doctor went around the desk and let himself down onto his chair. It squealed as he sat forward with his arms splayed in front of him. "We're trying to analyze the organism and understand exactly how it functions."

Nash tightened his grip on the back of the chair. "How does that help my son?"

One edge of the doctor's mouth pulled downward. "The more we know, the better we can treat him." He spread his hands. "So, if you wouldn't mind, I have more questions about the circumstances under which that organism became attached to your son."

Beneath Nash's hands the plastic of the chair back felt slippery and too warm. "Haven't you asked my boys?"

Now the doctor smiled thinly. "Roberto's in no state to talk to anyone. Don't you understand that, Mr. Preston? Now sit down, or you'll be taken back to the holding pen and we'll have gotten nowhere. Time is of the essence here. Can't you see that?"

Nash dragged the chair out and sat, awkwardly. The wet fabric of the overalls pulled at his skin, and the rips over his knees widened.

"All right, then." The doctor slipped his glasses back on and took a pen from a drawer. "How long would you say the organism was immersed in the fish tank at the restaurant?"

Nash's chest felt cold, the air suffocating. "The fish tank?"

"Yes. The fish tank at the Chinese restaurant." He raised his eyebrows. "You do remember, don't you? That you took your boys for a meal, and during some sort of scuffle the organism fell into the tank. No doubt you didn't mention it because the restaurant owner and his wife are illegals too, though I must say I'm surprised that you'd put their well-being ahead of your own son's. You do understand that he's in danger, don't you? And that we're working hard to save him?"

Chris, Nash thought. He must have sat in this same chair and told the doctor everything because he wouldn't have known not to. He couldn't have guessed that Jimmy was illegal, that he had followed them out of Glennallen, that his wife was sick too. Chris wasn't ten like Robbie, and yet he'd tried to keep it all from him as if he was a kid. From across the desk the doctor was watching him. Nash shifted his hands in his lap and the zip tie dug into his wrists. He said, "If you'd wanted to save my son, you'd have had him transferred to a hospital in the lower forty-eight."

"Why do you think this facility is underground in the middle of nowhere? We have no clear understanding of that organism. We need to take precautions so there isn't a public health emergency."

"He has a right to proper medical care."

"You think anyone else out there understands these organisms like I do? I've dedicated my career to studying them!" His lips were wet, surly, and they parted to let out a sigh. "I'm trying to help—I'm one of the good guys—but you need to cooperate. We're a small facility. I have to make an argument for who we hold and why. If you aren't useful to us, then I guess you'll have to be moved somewhere else. So let's start again, Mr. Preston. Tell me exactly what happened."

"All I left out was the restaurant and the fish tank. That's all. The thing—the organism—it can't have been in the water more than fifteen minutes."

The doctor bent his head to stare at Nash over his glasses. "That's it?"

"The waiter dried it off and handed it to Robbie. He kept hold of it all night, just like I told you."

He sat back in his chair. With a weary nod, he lifted a sheaf of papers bound by a clip. "Is there anything about Robbie's medical history that might not be in here? Anything at all? New allergies? Illnesses?"

"He's allergic to strawberries and cats. Just like me."

"And his brother?"

"No."

The doctor sucked at his lip. "They look so different. Christofer is much darker than Roberto."

"Chris was three when I met my wife. I adopted him when we got married."

He looked at Nash over the papers. "So Christofer isn't your son."

A tightness in Nash's throat. His voice came out a little choked. "I adopted him. I raised him. What other father do you think he has?"

"Biologically speaking, though, he's not your son." He took off his glasses, folding them carefully and setting them on the desk. "Well, very interesting." His chair squeaked as he got to his feet. "Colt? In here." When the guard appeared he said casually, "Take Mr. Preston to the lab."

Walking ahead of Colt, keeping his feet pushed forward in his sneakers so the heels didn't rub, Nash tried to breathe evenly, to stay calm. Even so, when he asked Colt what the lab was, and why he was being taken there, he caught the strained pitch of his voice.

Colt must have heard it too but all he said was, "Way above my pay grade," and stuffed a piece of gum in his mouth.

"You must have some idea," Nash said. "I mean, you do work here."

He gave Nash a poke in the back to hurry him along and to tell him the discussion was over.

"They're doing something dangerous in there, aren't they? I sure hope they're paying you well."

"Just shut the fuck up." Colt's hand swatted him over the head, a warning more than anything, though it made Nash trip and the heel of one sneaker tore at his skin.

Colt herded him along to a room where the lights were dimmer. The walls, the desk, the flooring, everything was a dull gray so that the only spot of color drew Nash's eye—a calendar turned to a photograph of a brilliant green frog clinging to a leaf, its toes as round as spoons. It stared out at the world with a bored look, and Nash turned away.

A large vent hung from the ceiling. It drew in air with a hiss, creating a current that brushed Nash's cheek, making him shiver in his damp coveralls, sending the papers on the desk fluttering as though they were itching to be sucked up into the vent's maw, and from there to ride the ducts suspended from the ceiling out of this tiny room, up and far away into the fresh air outside.

From a doorway appeared a bony-faced man in white coveralls and paper booties with a clipboard held to his chest. He ran a finger down a sheet, taking his time, making a show of being careful, and then looked up at Colt. Over the hum of the vent he said, "What's this? I've got nothing scheduled for today."

Colt pushed Nash ahead of him. "Nash Preston. Doctor Dawes's orders."

"Where's the paperwork?" His face had a pared-down look, the skin stretched across the bones as though he didn't get enough to eat.

Colt's gum snapped in his mouth. "On its way."

"That's not how it works."

"C'mon, what d'you want me to do about it?"

"We need a written order first, you know that."

"Tell that to Doctor Dawes. All I do is deliver them, and this one's been delivered. It's the end of my shift, so I'm outta here." He turned on his heel and headed for the door.

"Just what the hell is the point of our procedures then?" the other man called after him. "If this is a screwup, it's on you."

Colt called back, "Not anymore. He's all yours."

"Prick," the guy muttered. He took hold of Nash's upper arm and steered him through a doorway to where the air smelled sweet. A familiar smell. The smell that had hung about Robbie. Maybe Robbie was close by, and excitement leaped inside him, tamping down his fear.

On the other side of the doorway was an office area where the walls were an antiseptic white, and gleaming floor tiles reflected the ducts and pipes suspended overhead. The furniture made the room look emptier: a couple of cheap desks on which sat computers and a plastic plant and, up against the wall, two folding chairs, as though this place was nothing but a waiting room.

The guy gestured for Nash to sit. He perched over one of the computers, not bothering to sit as he tapped away on the keyboard, and cursed softly as he stared at the screen. "Gotcha," he said at last, and looked over at Nash. "You speak English? *Hablas ingles?*"

"As good as you."

"Okay, then. You go in there and take a shower." He pointed to a wide door. "Wash all over with the soap in the dispenser, including your hair, then repeat."

"No one's explained what's going on. Am I going to—"

"If you don't cooperate, I call security, that's how it works here. Understand?" He sighed. "It's the end of a long day, alright? Help me out."

"Are my boys here? The younger one's only ten, dark hair, dark—"

The man jerked a thumb toward the door. "Get in there and get washing. You really don't want to piss me off."

Nash lifted his bound hands. "With these? How can I undress?"

With one motion, the guy stepped forward and took hold

of Nash's collar with both hands. The damp coveralls gave with barely a sound. What was left dangled around Nash's shoulders. "For pity's sake, they're just paper. Tear them off."

In nothing but his sneakers, Nash went through to a shower in a small cubicle. A short, dark-haired woman in scrubs walked in while he was drying off and waited for him with a hospital gown. She fastened the snaps on the sleeves around his bound arms, as though she'd done it a dozen times before, and without a word led him through to an examination room.

She had him lie on the bed while she brought over a plastic caddy. From it she took a syringe. "This won't hurt, I promise. I'm good at sticking people, everyone says so."

Nash tightened his arms against his chest. "What the hell is this? I thought I was going to see my son."

"You are, sure. But he's in isolation, right? You can't just go walking in there."

"I don't understand—" He watched as she bit her lip and filled the syringe. "Why the hell do you need to give me a shot?"

"Well," she said leaning close, her fingers cold on his bare arm, "do you want me to explain all our procedures, or do you want me to get you ready to go through?" She looked down at him with a bright smile.

He let her shift his arms, awkward with the zip tie, so one lay on the table, the other across his belly. A jab, and then cold flooded his bicep, swelling up to his shoulder and across his chest. The ceiling light flickered and he watched it, heard the woman pop open a garbage and drop in the syringe. He felt oddly loose, and when he opened his mouth to say, "What was that?" his words expanded and wobbled like overblown bubbles that floated away from him.

"You feel nice and relaxed now?" Her face loomed over him. Beneath one eye, a smudge of mascara, strangely endearing.

"Yes, yes I do," he said, or thought he said, because sleepiness was filling him, soft and heavy and blissful.

•

Afterward, what did Nash recall? A room perpetually gloomy. The heady smell of antiseptic. A sugary stink he thought he should recognize. Plastic curtains hanging from the ceiling like giant cobwebs, and silent figures in biohazard suits appearing from between them. Hands in purple gloves. Eyes staring down at him from behind visors. Curtains snagging on shoulders, on trolleys of shiny equipment. A thin wail cutting through the air, and beneath it a rattling like something shaking itself apart. Glimpses. Of a gurney being wheeled away. Of a bed where a gray creature lay thrashing against its restraints. The sight of it stirred his heart into an uneasy canter.

That rattling. On and on. Nash wanted to block his ears but he couldn't, couldn't even lift his hands. He was sure he knew what that creature was, and why they were both in this place, yet each time he tried to grasp that thought it sank away, and in its wake, dread settled over him. He wanted to run, to shake it off, but he couldn't. At last from out of the murk broke a dazzling maelstrom of fireworking colors that gathered him up and whirled him along, and the fear pinning him down fell away as he was borne off by a great fizzing happiness, and it propelled him, dancing along, bursting with joy, rising and rising ecstatically.

After hours, maybe days, the bliss drained away and all that was left was a dreary exhaustion. Each time he woke everything was the same: the smeary plastic curtains, the sharp eyes of light from machines that beeped and clicked, a relentless itch on his palm that he couldn't scratch, the ghastly sweet smell in his nose and, everywhere, that awful rattling. Behind the curtains shadows moved, and when he tried to call out, his voice shrank down his throat.

He felt his mind coming back, like binoculars being focused.

He remembered cheap sneakers and the raw mess of his heels: a hillside, rocks skittering around him as he searched for those damn objects. A sharp-edged realization—that prickling in his hand—they'd attached one of those things to him, and he tried to raise his hand only to find it was strapped down, tried to flex his fingers except they were wrapped in gauze. He pressed his palm against the mattress. No large lump, and that could mean they'd tried and failed, or that days had passed and it had withered and fallen off, and now a mesh had grown over his skin, like Robbie's.

Robbie. That gray creature fighting its restraints, so small on its bed.

A sudden agony of grief caught in Nash's throat. He thrashed against the straps pinning him down and cried, "For god's sake, untie me! Untie me!" His words came out stretched and cottony.

No wonder they hadn't explained anything before wheeling him in here. What had Bemba said? That sooner or later, they'd all be guinea pigs.

15

*Nash was dressed in coveralls then hauled out of the laboratory in a wheel-*chair—hauled, like a bag of garbage—and taken up to a different floor where puddles glimmered in the tunnel's miserly light. At least now he could see his skin. There, his left hand strapped to the wheelchair: no grayness, no strange rash. So the thing hadn't attached itself to him, no matter that Dr. Dawes had wanted it to, and a sick relief ran through him. Back in the lab Robbie was still tied to a bed, battling the thing that had infected him. Maybe Chris had been infected too, and Nash's heart seized at the thought of losing both of them.

Partway down the corridor, the guard opened a door and he was pushed into a small cell with bunks lined up against the walls. At first he crouched on the floor, too weak to move, then he raised his head. Six beds in all, and maybe the one he crawled into belonged to somebody—the blanket heaped up at the foot, the pillow dented where a head had lain—but he didn't have the strength to drag himself farther.

Against his head the pillow was oddly cold. When he reached up, his fingers found stubble. His other hand was still wrapped in gauze, and the skin beneath it itched so bad he wanted to rip off the bandages and rake his nails over it. The thought of seeing his hand pocked by tiny wounds stopped him, and he pinned his hand under his chest and lay on it, eyes closed because he was so damn tired.

He woke, perhaps hours later, when the door opened. Men trooped in, four of them, all in the same cheap yellow coveralls he was wearing. Their heads were shaved, and it gave them an unworldly look, wide-eyed as newborns. Maybe that was why it took him a moment to recognize the man staring at him: the old eyes, the skin creased around the mouth, the hands patting the air as he came toward him. Jimmy Cho. He sat on the edge of Nash's bunk, smiling hard, and called out, "Chris, it's your dad. He's here." Just beyond Jimmy, someone twisted away then heaved himself onto an upper bunk where he lay with his back turned. Jimmy's voice crept up as he said, "Chris—come on." Jimmy looked down at Nash with a frown and squeezed his arm. "We'll leave all that until later. We've been so worried, but here you are. You just lie there for now, you hear? You're going to be okay."

One of the other two men scowled at Nash. He was huge, with shoulders bulky as hams and a chest that strained at his coveralls. His eyebrows were so faint that his broad face looked unfinished. "Fuck," he spat, "so they took Octavio. That really screws things up."

The fourth man was lanky with mournful eyes and a way of tilting his head like a bird. He said, "He could just have been pulled out for a few hours. Maybe he'll be back," and his voice rose and swerved musically.

"Well, aren't you the optimistic fucking snowflake." The big guy shook his head. "He was pissing them off. I told him to cool it."

Over the edge of the top bunk showed the curve of Chris's shoulder, the pale egg of his shaved head. It was a miracle—Chris not thrashing against a bed in the lab but in here with him, so close that they were breathing the same air. "Hey," Nash croaked, "it's me. It's Dad." He started to raise himself.

Jimmy gripped him by the shoulder. "It's too soon for that. It's best to lie down."

"No," and Nash propped himself up. The room veered off to the right as though it was falling down a hill, then snapped back and slid again. "Oh crap," he muttered. A wave of nausea pushed up his throat. He bit against it and swallowed hard, and a foul taste filled his mouth.

Jimmy said, "Just lie there," and let go of his shoulder. It was like being left unmoored.

He came back with a bucket, a foul thing, and the room wheeled again as Nash stared at it. This time he couldn't help himself: he retched a vile, frothing liquid into the bucket then spat and spat to rid himself of its taste. Without thinking, he wiped the spittle from his lips with his bandaged hand and it left a glistening green smear. He coughed and fell back on the bed. A hand slid under his neck, lifting his head to bring a plastic bottle of water to his lips. Jimmy.

"Rinse," he said, "and try to drink a little." The water was warm and tasted metallic. Nash swilled it around his mouth then spat into the bucket. "Just a little, not too much or it'll come back up." He let Nash take a couple of sips then laid his head back on the pillow.

"Hey," the big man called, "new guy—"

"He's called Nash," said Jimmy.

"What did you do for work?"

Nash rolled over. A great weariness had taken hold of him and, despite the water, his mouth was still dry. Before he could say anything, Chris called out, "Sales for a cleaning products company."

"Cleaning products?"

"Yeah. Degreasers and antibacterials and stuff."

Coming from Chris's mouth, how mundane it sounded—the life of a man with small aspirations.

"Well, shit. That's not useful."

Nash looked over to where the big guy was hunched on a lower bunk. He'd propped one of his massive hands under his chin and was staring off beyond the rock walls of the cell. Not useful. Nash's life crushed down to nothing, and Chris hearing it. Nash swallowed to wet his throat, said, "It is if you don't want to get sick. Bugs are everywhere, though people just don't think about it until there's a problem. Without—"

The big guy scowled across at Nash. "I meant, not useful for us getting out of here." He shifted his elbows on his knees and let his hands drop. Across one palm lay a wide pink scar, and the sight of it made Nash wince. He'd been in the lab, too.

Jimmy let himself down on the lower bunk against the far wall. He moved slowly, as though it hurt to bend those old joints of his. He said softly, "Randall's got a plan. He's got it all worked out. Any day now, we're breaking out of this place."

The big guy's head swung toward him. "Hey, what have I told you?"

Jimmy held up his hands. "Okay, okay." Across his palm and the belly of his fingers spread red welts scabbing over.

So Jimmy had been in the lab, and most likely Chris, as well. All of them drugged up and one of those things bound to their palms, yet not one of those things had attached itself to them, only to Robbie. He shrank away from what he'd seen, his boy juddering on the bed.

The slim guy sighed. "You're paranoid."

"No, Sudeep, just careful." Something clattered from out in the corridor, and Randall held still with his head turned to the door.

Sudeep said, "Relax, it's just dinner."

"That shit they give us isn't dinner."

Sudeep shrugged and got to his feet. A slot opened at the base of the door and paper plates were pushed through. Juice boxes, granola bars, peanut butter sandwiches with deep dents where fingers had held down the bread. Nash looked up at where Chris lay turned to the wall. He wanted to tell Chris that he should have talked to him, that it would have saved them the grief of ending up here. But Chris had tried—he'd said over and over that Robbie needed to go to the hospital, and it wasn't that Nash hadn't listened, it had just felt too dangerous. Now, a couple of yards away beneath the rock ceiling, Chris was curled on his bunk, so very still he could have been sleeping, and Nash wanted to cry out across the space between them. He wanted to tell him he understood why he'd made that call, he knew he'd been doing what he thought was best for Robbie, they'd both been doing that—and for fuck's sake, they'd only had terrible options. There was no way to say any of it in front of these other men, when he'd just have been adding to Chris's shame.

Nash brought one hand up to his face and rubbed it. He dug his tongue around his mouth tasting pockets of sourness from throwing up. The thought of eating made him breathe out hard despite the gnawing in his belly.

Jimmy was shaking Chris's shoulder. "Come down and have your dinner." Chris shrugged him off and Jimmy grimaced. "What's wrong? You've got to eat." He sighed and reached for one of the plates, was lifting it to Chris when Randall touched his arm. "Don't baby him, Jimmy. He can come down if he's hungry."

"He must be hungry. This is crazy."

Nash swallowed against the smell of peanut butter that suddenly was everywhere. "It's okay, Jimmy, it's okay. Maybe he doesn't have much of an appetite right now."

Sudeep took a bite of sandwich and nodded at Nash. "You need to eat, though. You'll feel better if you do, not that there's much nutrition to this stuff. You eat it and you're hungry again half an hour later." He rested his sandwich on his knee and poked a straw into his juice box. Across his palm lay a broad scar, and as he sucked at his juice, he idly scratched it. He saw Nash watching and said, "Nearly healed. It doesn't take long. We had no idea what this was all about until Jimmy and Chris showed up."

"Yeah. Getting those fossil things to attach themselves to us."

Nash went to turn over then stopped as his stomach squeezed tight. He let out his breath, slowly, to calm the nausea. "They had me show them where Robbie found his. The work crew found two more, and straightaway I was taken to the lab."

Jimmy sucked on his juice. His cheeks caved in as he drank, then he held the juice box in both hands and crushed it. "Experimenting on us, like the Nazis did during the war. Same thing."

Randall stuffed his sandwich into his mouth and chewed. He said thickly, "Sticking those fossils on us to see what they do, it's fucking unbelievable. This is the twenty-first century."

Sudeep sighed. "I keep telling you, if it's a fossil, it's dead. Those things must be dormant."

"Whatever they are, it's still fucked up."

"No, going dormant is for when *things* are fucked up. They're a way for an organism to survive harsh conditions, a desperate way that calls for luck and patience, but a—"

A distant pop sounded, and darkness fell as sudden and complete as death, all except for one small red light high up on the wall. A camera. Of course, thought Nash, they were being watched. The sight of it unnerved him.

"Shit," Randall said. "Bastards could let us see while we eat."

That impenetrable black—it pressed right up against Nash's eyes, seemed to reach inside his head, tugging at him so that if it wasn't for the rippling squawk of a juice box being emptied to its dregs, he'd have slipped away into sleep.

At last Randall said, "Anyway, knowing what they're up to isn't going to help us. They've finished experimenting on us. Now we're just fucking slave labor until we're not useful anymore."

"You can't know that." A soft voice. Chris's.

"We're a work crew, dumbass. That means we're no longer part of their fucking experiment." Randall sighed. "If what they're up to is secret enough to do in a disused mine, none of us are ever getting out of here."

Sudeep broke in, said, "You're paranoid, Randall. There are more underground labs around than you might think. If you're studying something biological, it's a great way to isolate—"

"Yeah, yeah. Which would mean it's not just secret, it's dangerous."

"No!" Sudeep's voice rose in exasperation. "If you want to control for light in plant experimentation, for example, a mine could be perfect."

"Can't you stop being interested? For one minute, stopping being a fucking biologist, and think about our situation. If we don't get out of here, we're dead meat."

"You can't be sure." Jimmy's voice.

"You think they sent Octavio back to his wife and kids? Do you?"

Nash pulled the blanket a little higher and leaned his cheek on his bandaged hand. It smelled of vomit, and he pushed it back under the blanket. A papery rustle, a scrape of a shoe across the floor. Close by his head, someone was lifting away the bucket. The wretched stink of it floated past Nash's face, and then the bucket rang hollowly with the sound of piss.

"What have we got to lose? Any of us? Your twins must have been born by now, Sudeep. When are you going to see them?"

A foot pressed into the mattress by Nash's shoulder, and someone heaved themselves up to the bunk above his. Sudeep's voice came from overhead now, and it was taut. "You imagine I think about anything else? I want to get out of here, and for that we need to watch our step."

"Too late for that. You shouldn't have got yourself fucking detained."

Jimmy's voice cut in. "We're not getting anywhere by arguing."

"We're safer not taking any risks, that's all I'm saying."

Randall sighed. "Sudeep, do you really think they're ever going to let you out? That if you work hard and follow the rules, they'll release you? This isn't prison with a sentence you have to serve out, and time off for good behavior—it's indefinite detention."

"Come on, not even the US government can keep people locked up forever."

Out of the darkness came Chris's voice again. "Guantanamo. Some guys have been there for decades. No trial, no nothing. They're never getting out."

Randall must have shifted himself in his bed because there was a squeak, then a clatter as the bunk shook. "We're not in a high-security facility in Cuba. This is a shoestring operation, for fuck's sake."

"Come on, this is a waste of time." Sudeep's voice was tired. "We're locked in here, or haven't you noticed? We can't even get out of this cell."

"No point if we don't have a plan. It'd just be showing our hand."

Chris sniffed. "And now we don't have Octavio."

"We have your dad, so we're making do."

Nash said into the darkness, "Making do? Thanks."

Chris said, "Octavio's a black belt in *krav maga*. You aren't exactly warrior material."

Nash raised his head. "Hey, and you are?"

"Don't pretend like this isn't your fault, Dad. You landed us in this mess. You didn't tell us we were illegal." His voice cracked. "Me and Robs, we had no fucking idea."

Nash took a breath. He said as evenly as he could, "I couldn't tell you, could I? How about if Robbie told his friends? Or his teachers? How about if one of your friends knew and told their parents? Would they have turned us in? That's what's happened to thousands of people. Someone makes a phone call, and next thing they know they've been detained. And you know what?"

A moan of metal, a sigh. One of the other men must have turned over in his bunk.

Sudeep said, "You need to keep your voices down."

"For fuck's sake, Dad, I was trying to help Robbie—"

He said softly, "You were worried about him. I don't blame you."

"Sure you do." Chris's breath came hard, then he roared, "It was fucking stupid. Tell me I'm a fucking moron! Because that's what I am, and all I meant to do was save Robbie!"

Sudeep hissed, "Please, you must be quiet."

From far off, an electric hum and footsteps coming along the corridor, slow and sloppy, heels grating against the rock floor. Just outside the door they stopped. Metal slid against metal, and the beam of a flashlight winked in, gliding across the floor then up over the bunks. A man's bored voice called out, "Noise infraction. Short rations tomorrow for you guys. Keep it up and I'll write you up for three days, so just shut the fuck up, alright?" A slam and the light vanished, then the footsteps retreated, scraping away along the corridor.

Randall's voice, soft, almost buttery, whispered, "So they took you out of this place on work detail, Nash? Man, do I have questions for you."

16

Randall wanted to know everything—where they'd taken Nash on the bus, which other detainees had been with him, how many guards, their names, which one had escorted him to the lab, if he'd noticed cameras upstairs where the bus had been parked, if he'd seen any sort of surveillance control room, but Nash told him, no, no control room, nothing like that, and as for cameras—well, he hadn't thought to look. "Anyway," Nash added, "my other boy's still in the lab. I'm not going anywhere without him."

"Oh, that's just great," said Sudeep. "Now we're going to rescue someone from the lab, too? What sort of shape is your son in? Is he infected?"

"He's fine," Nash said quickly. "Weak, from the look of it, but fine."

"Then why's he still down there?"

Nash breathed hard against the tiredness in his head. "I don't know. Because he's a kid, maybe. Where else are they going to put him?"

"The way I see it," said Randall, "they're understaffed because they're running this place on the cheap."

"You're telling me they built a secret facility at who knows what cost, but they don't have the money to run it properly?" said Jimmy. "That doesn't make sense."

"You don't get it—there's no *who knows what cost*. Sure, they had to fix up the mine to use it, but it hadn't been closed for long. All the basic infrastructure was already in place." Randall grunted as he rolled over.

"They've got cameras and drones. It's all high-tech."

"No technology is going to save you if you don't have enough guards. You can set up cameras and motion detectors and all that crap, and so what? If you see a riot happening, you just watch it play out? Unless you've got the guys to go in, it's not going to help you."

Sudeep said, "Are we going to knock on pipes using Morse code to get everyone in this place to riot? Is that the plan now?"

"Don't take the piss." Randall let out an exasperated sigh. "Having more men involved would only help at the start—then there'd just be more of us competing for a vehicle to get the fuck out of here. Right? And we don't know those guys. Who knows what we'd be dealing with."

"This plan of yours is for the five of us to break out of here on our own?" Sudeep laughed.

"With Robbie," Nash added.

"No, no," said Sudeep, "that's impossible. We can't break into the lab."

"I can't leave without him."

Jimmy said, "This isn't planning. This is just more pointless arguing."

"Yeah, exactly." Chris's voice, drifting down from his bunk. "What I want to hear is this plan you've been talking about, Randall."

Sudeep murmured something, and then Randall lifted his voice. "So this is how I see it—this place is cutting corners left and right. One guard to take us to work duty. Two guards to take nine men out to search for fossils, so one of those guys was doing double duty and serving as the driver. Most of them clearly aren't trained and don't give a shit about this place, so their morale's going to be low." He let out a soft laugh. "This morning that dumbfuck Manning forgot about Chris until we were out the door. How hard's it going to be to get away from guys like that?"

"Yeah, right. Like you've done this before?"

"Listen—" Jimmy sounded irritated, his voice high. "We have to listen to Randall. It's his area of expertise."

"I'm not even sure I believe him about the camera," said Sudeep. "They could be listening in to every word."

"No, it makes sense." There was an edge to Randall's voice now. "You have cameras, then you have live feed monitored by someone at a bank of screens, right? Just like security guards in the movies. Easy. Audio's different—no one can listen to a whole bunch of audio at the same time. They'd have to go back and listen to it all separately, hours and hours of it. So no, they can't be listening in to us, they don't have the staff."

"And how about if they have software to listen in, and it's triggered by key words. Like, you know, e-s-c-a-p-e?"

"In this shithole? Where they don't even have properly trained guards? Get real."

Nash said, "We were followed by a drone when we were driving past this place. Right, Jimmy?"

"That was a fancy piece of equipment. It flew in close and stayed with us for a couple of miles."

Randall laughed. "You guys, you're so clueless. A fancy drone? Give me a break. You can program a twenty-five-thousand-dollar piece of shit to do that. You think that's a lot of money? It's cheaper than paying a bunch of rent-a-cops."

Nash rolled over onto his back. He pressed his fingers against his bandaged palm to quell the itching. "Randall, what did you do before you ended up here?"

"Security consultant."

"Who for?"

Randall took a noisy breath. "A company that'd work for anyone who paid. Lots of corporations need a whole lot of security now that they're leasing detainees. Naturally they want it on the cheap because fuck, if you're getting the detainees for almost nothing, you don't want to invest a whole bunch in personnel and equipment, right? It's all about the bottom line."

"Corporations like the one running this place?" Nash said.

"You helped them keep people like us locked up?" Jimmy's voice was sharp.

"Hey now." The metal of the bunk squeaked as he moved. "That's not what it was like. I just did my job. They don't exactly tell you they're using detainees, know what I mean? Anyway, what I did was mostly designing systems."

"Same thing," said Jimmy sourly.

Chris asked, "So, how'd they catch you?"

"I lost my status because I lost my job, and I lost my job because one of the clients I'd been working with complained when we had a video chat. My name could be Anglo—Randall Lee—but my face, not so much. This guy said he didn't want an Asian involved with the project because of *security concerns.*"

Chris laughed. "In case you ended up in one of the systems you designed?" Then he paused. "Did you work on this one?"

"Thanks, shithead. It'd be a lot more secure if I had." Randall sighed. "My wife, she's Anglo. Our daughter could pass for Italian, so she'll probably be okay. You know, when my daughter was born and everyone said how much she looked like my wife, I was pissed, but now, that's probably the best thing for her. I don't want her ending up in a place like this. My wife's a clever lady, she'll take care of her."

"Anyway . . . " Nash said gently.

"Right. The plan. The way I see it, there are twenty, maybe twenty-five of us locked up in this place, max."

Sudeep let out a laugh. "Twenty-five? You're just guessing, aren't you?"

"Estimating. The number of us on work duty. The poor motherfuckers in the pen, and there's only space for twelve men, right? Then three work crews, one for the nursery, one that goes out on the bus, and—"

"And the one that only exists in your mind."

"There's a third crew, Sudeep."

"Really? What do they do while we're off in the nursery?"

"Don't you listen, shithead? We're C crew. So there's an A and a B, right?"

"You're so sure of yourself, based on that? That's not proof, that's—that's nothing."

Nash said into the darkness, "Nursery? There are small kids in this place?"

"Not that kind of nursery. They've got trees growing down here in barrels of water with grow lights. We have to—"

Sudeep broke in. "It's a subsurface hydroponic nursery. They're growing spruce and birch saplings."

"Down here? What's that got to do with those—those things?"

"Shared space, probably. They're cutting corners." He sounded bored.

Now Jimmy spoke up. "That doesn't make sense."

Randall said, "One set of guards for all the detainees. One set of facilities. It makes economic sense. So maybe ten guards, tops, plus the workers in the lab, and there are what—two of them at any one time?"

"Not exactly very scientific." Sudeep yawned. "If all we're doing is guessing, we'll screw up and end up worse off."

Quiet descended, as though the darkness had finally sapped what was left of their energy. Nash shivered. The air down here was dank, and the blanket not thick enough to keep him warm. His hand was itching worse now, and he pressed his palms together. A breath, as though someone was about to speak, then Sudeep said, "Nash, your younger son—that thing actually attached itself to him, didn't it?"

"Yeah."

"And he's okay?"

"Yeah." He squeezed his eyes tight to push away the image of

Robbie shaking the bed, his skin the color of stone, but it made no difference: eyes open or shut, in the darkness there was nothing to distract him.

"Maybe he's not down there because he's a kid." Sudeep must have propped himself up on his elbow as his voice was clearer now. "Maybe he's the only person one of those things has successfully attached itself to." He waited. "This changes everything. You understand? He's valuable because he's a success. They had Nash lead them to the place where his son found that organism because they need more. That means they're having a hard time finding a supply, and when they do, they won't take to their hosts. If we want to get out of here, we need the boy. If we have him, we can make demands."

Nash said, "Hey—he's my son. We're not using him as a bargaining chip."

"If he's that important, they'll do anything not to lose him," said Jimmy. "That's going to be a problem."

"Not if we play our cards right." Sudeep's voice rose in excitement. "If we can break into the lab, maybe we can get out of here after all."

17

*The tunnel had the slick mineral smell of damp rock, plus a whiff of some-*thing foul. In the watery light of his headlamp, Nash could only see Sudeep's back and, farther down the tunnel, the fluttering lights of the others' headlamps glancing off the walls. Somewhere up ahead Chris was leading the way, dragging behind him a wagon of equipment that clattered and echoed in the narrow space.

Chris was the one who'd pissed off the guard. The elevator had carried them far down into the old mine, and when the door opened and the guard herded them out, Nash had noticed the way the others' eyes slid around as they took in this place: the wall of uneven rock lit only by the muted glow from the elevator, the black that stretched off beyond. It was not where they'd expected to be taken for work duty, that much was clear, but only Chris blurted, "Hey, this is the wrong floor." The guard had wheeled around and punched him in the gut. He told Chris to shut the fuck up, it was the right floor today because guess what, they were on a new work detail, and he'd laughed like there was a joke to it that they wouldn't understand.

In Nash's left hand, a shovel. It was awkward carrying it one-handed, but better that than having the handle rub against the scabs on his palm. When he'd unwound the dressing he'd winced at the sight of his flesh, stippled and sore as though he'd punc-tured it over and over with needles. At least the itching had eased a little.

He adjusted his grip on the handle. He couldn't help thinking: five men with shovels against one guard armed with pepper spray and a taser—they could overpower him, easy. The problem was how to signal each other when the wagon was making so much noise. From behind him came the slight unevenness of the guard's footsteps, the scrape of his heel over the rock: Gaetz, one of the dumb guards, or so Randall said, a runty man with hunched shoulders whose bony hands were quick to hit out. Every now and then he shouted an order, telling the men to stay together or to hurry it up, but his voice sagged with apathy.

Gaetz had a hard hat with a glaring light. The men had cheap lamps strapped to their shaved heads, despite the ceiling being so low that in places they had to stoop, ducking under rock sweating fat drops that fell shockingly cold onto their scalps.

The smell was getting stronger. Nash took to breathing through his mouth, and the reek clung to the back of his throat. When he swallowed he could taste it. His stomach clenched, and he stopped and pressed his hand against his lips. Gaetz shoved him in the back and grunted, "Fuck's sake, keep going."

Before long they were wading through puddles that came up over the tops of their shoes, and their wet sneakers rubbed and squeaked against their bare feet. The skin on Nash's heels that had scabbed over turned raw again. The slipperiness in his shoes—he couldn't tell if it was water or blood. From up ahead, the noise of the wagon had changed, louder and duller and faster, like a half dozen wagons. The feel of the air had changed too, less dense now, and just as the smell grew so strong that he held his sleeve over his nose, the ceiling overhead disappeared and the glow from his headlamp bled away into blackness.

Close to where Nash stopped, Chris was looking around him with the wagon drawn up by his feet. That dull rattling—it wasn't coming from the wagon. Nash looked around, they all did, and the beams of their headlamps flashed onto rock walls that arched up far over their heads, onto walls oozing with mold, onto the sturdy metal bars of cages. All at once the air was pierced by a high keening like a motor being run too hard, a knife of sound that made it difficult to think.

Gaetz was fiddling with something. A moment later, fierce shafts of light shot from a heavy lantern. Now it was clear where they were: a cave with a ceiling as rounded as the inside of a mouth. Along one side the ground tipped away into darkness. On the other, six large cages were raised on railroad ties, just high enough for a man to crawl beneath them. Gaetz hung the lantern on a hook driven into the rock, then he trod over to the wagon and lifted out a folding chair.

Nash muttered, "What the hell?" Randall was beside him. When he turned, his headlamp glared into Nash's eyes, wobbling as he shook his head. What that shake meant, Nash had no idea.

Gaetz had set up his chair by the tunnel. Now he took off his hardhat and was pulling straps around his head. A filtration mask. It turned his face strangely pale and muffled his voice as he yelled above the noise, "Okay, you fuckers, take a bucket and clean up around the containment units. You got it?"

The men just shrugged or nodded, and Gaetz belted out, "I said, you got it, motherfuckers? And no pissing around. I don't want to be here longer than I have to."

A murmur of "Yessirs" rippled out. Like high-school gym class, Nash thought. The shouting. The surliness. The sense of being subjected to unearned petty authority.

Gaetz settled into his chair. "Then take a goddamn bucket and get shoveling, for fuck's sake!"

The din seemed to grow louder and Nash dipped his head, as though he could escape it. With the others he clustered around the wagon. Even in the tepid light of their headlamps, it was clear the buckets were filthy. Old five-gallon buckets crusted with brown, and in the bottom, a yellowish liquid that gave off a nauseating stench. A few yards away stood six rectangular enclosures with thick steel bars. Like old-fashioned cages for lions or tigers, except they were too small, barely large enough for a person to stand straight.

Nash took a bucket and followed the pale light of his headlamp toward the enclosures. As he came closer the ground became soft and slick, and though he walked carefully, feeling his way forward in his wet shoes, one foot slid and his arms flailed. By a miracle he didn't fall, but he lost his grip on his shovel and it cartwheeled into the muck. He stood bent over, breathing hard despite the stench. A couple of yards away his shovel gleamed in the light of his headlamp, caught in the brown sludge that covered the cave floor like a wash of melted ice cream, and he inched his way toward it. With the toe of his shoe he nudged the handle up then took hold of it. Against his fingers the wood was greasy, gritty, and suddenly the reek was thick and foul and everywhere. Saliva pooled in his mouth and he spat to rid himself of it.

Chris was standing eerily still. Nash called out, "For god's sake be careful, it's slippery as hell."

Chris didn't look at him, didn't say a word.

"Chris? You okay?"

Nash eased his way toward him. The keening was filling the air, the banging so frantic that he wanted to look up and see what was in those cages. He told himself no, he shouldn't, he mustn't, was opening his mouth to tell Chris the same—but there was Chris, shovel in one hand and bucket in the other, gaping in horror. Nash cried, "Chris, no! Just keep your head down and do the work!"

Already Gaetz was on his feet. "Hey, you fuckers, get to it!"

The light on Chris's head dipped as he folded up, thudding hard to the ground and his bucket rolling away. The guard bolted toward him. "You fucker," he was yelling, "you stupid little fucker." Nash lurched toward Chris too late—he was scrambling away through the mess of muck and slime, and that was enough to stop Gaetz. The guard hesitated just short of the filth, black boots braced against the bare rock. Above the noise he laughed from behind his mask. Chris had vanished beneath the cage. In the mess of filth around it, one sneaker glowed a sad discolored white in the dazzle of Nash's lamp before it drew away out of sight. Gaetz shook his head and stalked back to his chair and pulled out a pair of headphones.

The banging and screeching had grown higher, faster, and it followed Nash as he trod through the muck to where Chris had disappeared. The noise was so close, so loud, that the inside of his head vibrated. It was impossible to think, to do anything except start shoveling. He scooped up great dripping loads of filth that slopped off into his bucket, and every now and again he glanced down to where Chris's foot had disappeared. There was no sign of him except for the furrows gouged through the mess where he'd crawled away, and Nash kept working, trying to keep at bay everything except his shovel biting into the sludge, and its weight as he hefted it up.

The others—Randall on his left, Sudeep and Jimmy beyond—were doing the same. They had their heads down, working mechanically as though the screeching, the pounding against the bars, the stench, all of it could be shoveled away if only they worked hard enough.

It felt like forever until Chris reappeared. At last, though, a dim light spread across the ground, then a hand and a shoulder, then Chris, so covered that he looked like a creature made of muck, all except for his eyes that gleamed in the lamplight. Then he set to work, shoveling furiously, carelessly, the sludge slewing off before it reached his bucket, or his shovel scraping bare rock.

Nash called out, "Chris, calm down, it's okay," but his words were lost in the din. With one hand he covered his headlamp then glanced behind him. Over by the tunnel entrance, Gaetz was lit up by the lantern, sitting with his legs splayed, his head bobbing as he listened to music. Dragging his bucket with him, Nash moved closer to Chris, working his shovel over ground he'd already cleared, telling him through the noise, "Sweetie, we'll get through this. When we're done here, they'll let us wash and this'll all be over." Gentle words, and a gentle voice, like you'd use on a spooked dog. He was within an arm's reach when Chris looked up. Nash was blinded by the glare of his headlamp and had to shield his eyes. "Chris, I know it's bad, I know, believe me."

He stepped closer, pretending to jab at something. Chris wasn't looking at him but past him, and just like that, without thinking, he swung around too. In the cage, a face. At least, part of a face pushed up against the bars: one eye staring out, gray as stone, the other dangling deflated on the cheek. And everywhere, pale tendrils—sprouting from the empty socket, from the pulpy holes where the nose had been, from the mangled mass of the mouth. For one heartbeat, it all retreated into the shadows and there was only the shrieking. Then the hands tightened on the bars—skin torn and oozing, nails broken off—and brought that face smashing against the metal, and again, and again.

Later, when the lights went out, as they lay in their bunks filthy and hungry—they'd lost shower privileges and dinner, what with Chris hiding beneath the cage, and all the talking, and taking so long to carry out their work assignment—no one said a word.

Nash wrapped his pillow around his head and pressed it over his ears, and it didn't help one bit because the racket was trapped inside his skull: the grating of shovels across rock, the banging and screaming, all of it the soundtrack to that creature bashing its ruined face against the bars. Somewhere in this mine, locked in the lab, Robbie was shuddering and jerking on a bed because that was what he was turning into. Nash cupped his hands over his head, felt part of himself retreat at the thought of it.

"What the fuck?" said Randall at last. "What the fuck? What the *fuck*?"

"You know," said Sudeep, "it kind of makes sense."

"No!" Jimmy's voice was high. "It makes no sense. Those people—what have they done to them? They've turned them into—into zombies."

Nash got to his feet and fumbled his way through the darkness to Chris's bunk. "You okay?" he whispered. He reached out, feeling where the air was warm just above where Chris lay, and brought his hand down on his cheek. His fingers touched wetness, and Chris didn't push his hand away. "We're going to get out of here, I promise you."

"That's what's going to happen to Robbie, isn't it?" Chris said it quickly, under his breath, as though otherwise he wouldn't be able to say it at all.

"No." He rubbed Chris's cheek with his thumb. "That's not going to happen to him, no way."

"Well," said Sudeep, "by the look of them, I'd say that's exactly what—"

Nash cried out, "Sudeep, for god's sake!"

Chris took hold of Nash's fingers and gave them a squeeze. "Dad, he's a biologist. We need to listen to him."

Sudeep breathed in, slowly, noisily. "Honestly? I'd say those people are infected with a fungal parasite. Whatever they tested on us and wouldn't take, it's clearly some sort of fungus. It's feeding off those poor bastards locked up in those cages."

"A fungus? Are you fucking kidding me?" Randall let out a rough laugh. "A fungus can be a parasite? I thought parasites were tapeworms and chiggers, and that weird disease you get from cat shit."

"Those stalks coming out of the mouths and eyes, they looked like hyphae, just like a fungus produces, so yes, I'd say a fungus." He paused, sniffed. "Plus, fungi can be parasites, lots of living things are. If you look—"

"Yeah, well fuck that," said Randall. "The question is why

on earth they're trying to infect us with a fungus. Other than torturing people like us, what's the point? Doesn't there have to be a point?"

Without thinking, Nash went to smooth Chris's hair. His fingers touched stubble, and the gritty filth that had dried to his scalp. He said, "They've invested so much in this place. They must be hoping to make money off their research."

"Maybe it's a cure," said Chris. "They're working on a cure for the fungus."

"No, no," said Jimmy, "that doesn't make sense. How many of those things can there be lying around?"

Chris shifted his head. "More and more, right? Maybe global warming means a whole bunch of them are showing up. They could have been buried for hundreds of years and now that the permafrost's melting, all the rain's washing them out."

"You mean buried for thousands of years," added Sudeep, "even tens of thousands of years."

Jimmy sighed. "It doesn't make any sense. Why go to all of this effort to find a cure? Your dad had to help them find more of those things, so how many people could have been infected? Not many, right?"

Nash made his way back to his bunk, taking short steps and feeling with his hands so he didn't jar his shins. "Too many," he said, "because even one is too many."

"Yeah, yeah," said Randall, "but here's the thing—now we know why they're keeping us locked up. Imagine the shit storm if word got out that they're deliberately infecting people and they turn into some kinda fucking zombie."

Nash lay down on his bunk. Everywhere hung the stink of the filth, warmed by his own body.

"So how are we breaking out of this place?" Chris spoke lightly, almost jokingly. "Because if we don't want to die here, we have to, right?"

18

It was easy enough getting the guard to open the door—Jimmy lay on the floor moaning so Manning, flustered by Nash's frantic yelling, unlocked it. Maybe Manning was counting on the camera monitoring what was going on, not noticing that Randall had covered it, or maybe he was so inexperienced that he didn't sense the danger he was putting himself in—he stepped through the doorway and gazed down at the old man writhing at his feet, was bending over when he was shoved to the ground and his ball cap went spinning away beneath a bunk.

It was a strangely quiet struggle. Randall lay on him while Sudeep jammed wadding from a pillow into Manning's mouth then forced a torn-off strip of fabric from the pillow between his teeth and bound it around his head. Manning was a hefty guy and tried to buck Randall off, and he would have managed except that Jimmy twisted his arm up behind his shoulder blades and bent back one finger.

"Holy crap, old man," Randall murmured.

Jimmy gestured with his head. "Come on, strip him, quick." Manning tried to say something through the gag, but Jimmy bent that finger harder and the guard let out a muffled cry.

It was Chris's job to take off Manning's boots, and he bent low to pluck at the laces. Nash yanked him back just as Manning kicked out. The boot only grazed Chris's chin, and for a moment he watched as Manning's legs flailed, wild, then threw himself over them, pinning them with his weight.

Together they undressed him. What an odd shuffle it was, unzipping Manning's jacket and peeling the sleeves off while Jimmy held him down by one arm then the other and Chris lay over his legs. Nash fumbled with Manning's belt. It felt obscene to touch the soft warmth of this man's body. He had to wrench the loose end to unfasten the buckle, and when it came undone it flopped to the floor, weighed down by zip ties and pepper spray and a flashlight.

When they went to yank off his pants, Manning wrenched one foot free and lashed out, sending Sudeep staggering against Jimmy. Then Manning reared up, thrashing and bellowing, pale eyes furious, and Nash was raising a hand to hit him when Randall's fist flashed out. Manning staggered and his head knocked against the edge of the bunk with a wet smack. His eyes went dull, and he slumped to the floor and lay still.

Randall shook out his hand. "Fuck," he muttered. "Well, come on, zip-tie him."

They turned him over. Nash had a zip tie in his hand, and now he hesitated. In his T-shirt and boxers, Manning looked bloated and harmless, his feet in their wrinkled socks like sightless creatures, a tattoo saying *Shawna* curled across a heart on one bicep. And he was young. On his chin, a fluff of unshaven hair so blond it was almost invisible.

"Nash, what the fuck are you waiting for?"

Nash grabbed one wrist and pulled it back, then the other. There was an odd heaviness to Manning now, and a slackness that meant he had to struggle to bring his wrists together.

"Do you think he's dead?" Chris shot a look at Randall, his lips pressed together so hard they'd gone pale.

Nash got to his feet and flexed his hands. They were trembling. "We have to get out of here, Chris. Focus on that." He tugged at the fasteners of his coveralls, pulling out his arms and shivering.

"We should check," said Sudeep, "to see if he's hurt."

Randall snatched up Manning's pants from the floor. "If he is, what you going to do? Call for help?" He held the pants up by the waist. "Fuck it, Nash, it was supposed to be Gaetz's shift. These are never going to fit you. You're built like a fucking stick."

"Does it matter? We only have to make it to the lab."

"No one's going to believe you're a guard if you're tripping over your pants."

"So you put on the uniform," said Jimmy. "It'll fit you."

"All the guards are white."

Jimmy shrugged. "Are we worried about running into other guards? Or what someone might see on the camera feed?"

"Jimmy's right," said Sudeep. He snatched up Manning's cap from under the bunk and passed it to Randall. "No one's going to notice unless we come face to face with them. If that happens we're screwed anyway, right?"

While Randall dressed, the rest of them hauled Manning onto a bunk. His T-shirt had rucked up to show a long pink scar across his lower belly. Chris pulled a blanket over him, tugging it so it covered his shoulders. "Now he looks like a detainee," he said. "You know—in case anyone looks in."

Randall zipped up the jacket and swiveled his neck against the tightness of the collar. With the cap on he looked suddenly brutish. "Jeez," he said, "you going to tell him a bedtime story too? Let's get out of here."

The door was hanging open. Across the tunnel, weak fluorescent light gleamed off the wall. Randall rolled his shoulders before he strode out. "Let's go. Line up in front of me, and don't look around like something's up. We don't need any dumb mistakes."

As they passed through the doorway ahead of Nash, the others each made a ducking motion, as though they expected to be grabbed by someone waiting outside the door. Nash felt himself doing the same—that lift of the shoulders, that slight jerk of the head. He pulled the door closed behind him. How exposed he felt out here, and when he looked up, there, just before the bend in the tunnel, was the steady red light of a camera. He winced—it should have been the guard who shut the door, not him. They were fucking up already, and they were going to get caught.

He lined up behind Chris and they marched down the tunnel ahead of Randall. All around them, the slight hum of ventilation, the soft plinks of drips falling that made Nash jump. His nerves felt raw. It had been hypothetical—grabbing a guard, stripping him of his uniform, trying to bust out of this place. Now here they were making their way down the corridor and there, so close, was the elevator.

Perhaps they'd make it to Robbie after all, and perhaps there'd be enough of him left to save. The thought of it made him feel sick with hope.

It was only two floors down to the lab and yet it felt like the elevator was plummeting into the earth's core. The massive weight of rock overhead condensed the air, muting the elevator as it clanged to a halt, compressing the light to a crystalline glare that, just a few yards beyond the crisscross elevator gate, glinted off a metal door.

They waited. There was no sound now except for the hum of ventilation, and the rasp of their scared breathing. At last Randall muttered, "Okay then, let's go," and was reaching to pull back the gate when the metal door opened and a woman in scrubs stepped through, her blonde ponytail bouncing jauntily. She peered toward the elevator. "That you, Scott?" she called. "Dawes has been waiting, he's pretty pissed."

Nash flattened himself against the elevator wall. The light inside the elevator was weak, but she was staring right at them. Surely she could see them. "Scott?" Her shoes made a soft patter as she trod closer.

Sudeep hissed under his breath, "Randall, get us out of here."

But Randall pushed the gate open and stepped out, turning deftly so that his back was toward her. "Hey, I had a problem with the elevator."

She tucked a loose strand of hair behind her ear. "With the elevator? It was fine when I came down."

"Yeah, and my radio's not working."

"Your radio?" She scratched at the side of her face, frowned. "Wait, you aren't—"

Randall was fast. He snatched the pepper spray from his belt, but she knocked it away and he lunged at her. She went reeling back against the wall and he punched her with a loose blow to the side of the head, and when she came at him again with one arm up to shield her face and the other down to guard her side, Randall feinted then kneed her in the gut. She collapsed to the ground and lay curled up and gasping. He stood over her, shifting uneasily and glancing back at the rest of them. "Well, shit," he said.

Jimmy pushed his way out of the elevator. Beside Randall he was tiny, nothing but a little old man, and maybe that was why she tried to kick him. He must have been expecting something because he stepped back just in time, then crouched beside her and covered her neck with his hand. His fingers tightened and she let out a cry.

Beside Nash, Chris muttered, "For chrissake."

"What is that, a Vulcan neck pinch?" Sudeep let out a nervous laugh and crossed his arms, as though he was merely there to watch.

"Don't struggle," Jimmy told the woman. "If you do, I'll hurt you again."

Whatever she said was muffled. Jimmy must have understood because he leaned in and she let out a quavering yell.

Chris shifted from one foot to the other, staring down at the ground. Nash lay a hand on his arm. "This could get ugly. You don't have to be part of it."

When Chris glanced at him his eyes were wet, the pupils large. He gave an odd shake of the head and ran a hand over his scalp as though to comfort himself. "Dad, we're in this together."

"Whatever we do, we'll have to live with for the rest of our lives. You're only sixteen."

"I'm old enough for them to lock up and experiment on."

"Yeah, well—" Nash gave him a sad smile. Chris gazed back, his eyes with their delicate lashes, a small scar beneath one eyebrow from when he'd fallen off a swing many years ago. Across his chin and cheeks, dark stubble was growing in. He was a man now, as tall as Nash and broader across the shoulders. "I worry," Nash said.

"As if that helps." His mouth twitched with the ghost of a laugh.

"Come on, then."

Jimmy had forced the woman to her feet. Nash and Chris followed as he propelled her toward the door, the woman dancing on her toes because Jimmy had her arm bent up behind her back. Jimmy told her, "We need you to open it."

He must have relaxed his hold because she slumped a little. Blood was trickling from her nose, two bright trails of it, and when she wiped her face and saw the red on her hand, she burst out with, "What the hell? I mean, what the *hell*?"

"Open it." His voice was gentle, insistent, and he pushed her closer to the door.

"This is a research facility." Her voice shook. "You can't go in there."

"I'm asking nicely this time, but I can hurt you again."

"There's nothing you can possibly want in there. All you'll do is set us back in ways you can't even imagine."

"I've warned you."

She shook her head and her ponytail, askew and untidy now, flopped sadly. "I can't do it. There's too much at stake."

Jimmy's face hardened as he crooked her arm higher behind her back. She cried out, her mouth gaping and showing teeth outlined in red.

"Jimmy," said Randall, "all we need is her eye." He took hold of the woman's scrubs and hauled her toward a scanner on the wall. He shoved her face up to it, and although she thrashed and grunted, she must have known she'd lost. Randall had hold of her neck, and when he squeezed she opened her eyes. A pause, as though the security system was thinking, then the scanner gave a sullen beep and the door clicked open.

19

There was so little drama to it—that's what surprised Nash. They walked down a corridor, Jimmy pushing the young woman along, until they reached the lab's small lobby. A tightness pulled at Nash's chest at the sight of this place: on the desk, papers still flapped in the breeze from the vent; from the calendar on the wall, the same bright green frog stared out. Over it all hung the odd sugary smell of earth and rot.

Randall glanced over at Nash. "Go get him. Quick now."

Blood had run down the woman's chin and dripped onto her scrubs. Her eyes had a scattered look. "You're crazy. You can't take anyone out of there."

"You going to stop us?" Nash said.

One end of her mouth twitched, and she let out a breath that could have been the start of a laugh. "The kid?" she called as Nash pushed past her. "You came down here for him? Is that what this is all about? You can't help him, you know, no one can."

Nash looked back at her. "Then what the hell have you been doing with him?" His fingers curled toward his palms. He knew what she was going to say, and dread rose up his throat.

"There's no cure once someone's infected. They just—" She tried to shrug.

Off to the left, a door opened and a bony-faced man in scrubs stared at Nash, the same man who'd processed him into the lab. Before the man could say a word, before he could register what was happening, Randall shoved Nash out of the way. "Get going, for fuck's sake, go get your kid."

The man tried to close the door too late—Randall shouldered it open, and there was a yell and a loud slam. Nash took off down the short corridor toward the door at the end. Behind him the woman was yelling, "You can't go in there!"

The door opened onto a small chamber hung with white coveralls. No, realized Nash, not coveralls. Biohazard suits. On shelves sat boxes of visors and gloves and booties, plus dozens of small plastic bottles, syringes, and tubing. A few yards away, a heavy door was marked AUTHORIZED PERSONNEL ONLY and BIO-HAZARD AREA. There'd be people on the other side—he couldn't rush in empty-handed and expect to make it out with Robbie. From the wall he snatched a fire extinguisher. Not much of a weapon, but it would have to do.

Beyond the door, it was all so familiar—the muted light, the sickly odor that was stronger than ever, the relentless rattle. Plastic curtains were suspended from tracks in the ceiling, some tied back, others hanging like sheets of cloudy water through which blurred shapes swam. A figure in white came out from behind one, face indistinct behind a visor. "Hey, what the crap? You can't be in here."

Nash lifted the extinguisher. He'd meant to fire it, except there was no time to work out how so he upended it and swung it hard into the visor. As the person staggered backward, he threw it at their head and they slumped to the floor. The extinguisher clanged down next to them and rolled away.

Nash looked around. Empty beds, two on this side, one on the other, but a couple of beds were still curtained off. He yanked back the plastic of the closest. An old man lay strapped down on his back. His skin had turned a deathly gray mottled by intricate webbing. He must have heard Nash because his eyes swiveled toward him and his tongue licked out as he tried to speak.

Not Robbie. That's all Nash could think. Behind him, voices, and he spun around, shoving equipment stands and small wheeled tables out of the way, knocking over bottles, stumbling over cords and tubes. He realized with a drowning sense of panic that he hadn't considered that maybe they'd moved Robbie to the cages, that maybe Robbie had been down there when they were sent to clear them out and he hadn't even noticed. One more set of curtains in the far corner, a clattering from behind them, and he swept them back.

A small figure was convulsing on a bed, the whole bed rocking as though it was being rolled along an uneven floor. The head was held down by a restraint that cupped the bare scalp and buckled over the forehead and under the chin. Behind it, the face seemed strange and too small, but it was Robbie. Nash felt a flash of relief just as other, murkier fears washed in. He bent toward him, said, "Sweet pea, it's me, I've come to get you." Robbie made only half-formed sounds, and when Nash lowered his head, so close that Robbie's breath brushed his ear, he caught only animal grunts pressed through dry lips. He laid a hand on his chest. Robbie was trembling, trembling, as though an electric current was coursing through him.

He leaned over him and tried to catch Robbie's gaze. "Sweetie," he whispered, "it's me, it's Dad, I've come for you." Robbie's eyes were focused somewhere far beyond the ceiling, far beyond this place. "Do you understand? We're getting you out of here."

He was pulling off the sheet and exposing the restraints strapping Robbie to the bed when someone moved behind him: Sudeep, and right behind him, Chris. Nash saw the way Chris's eyes snagged on the bed, the way his face bunched up as he understood what he was looking at. He tried to block his view, though it was too late—already Chris was wavering and Sudeep had to grab his shoulders. Sudeep called out, "That's your son?"

Nash nodded. "It's worse than I thought." A lie because he'd known, and yet he'd insisted that they come down here for Robbie anyway.

"Shit." Sudeep shook his head and scowled. "Now what are

we supposed to do? We can't take him with us like that."

"We've got to get him help, for god's sake." Nash ran his hands along Robbie's body. That awful quaking was everywhere as Robbie fought against the restraints binding his ankles, his hips, his shoulders, his head. Nash choked out, "We've got to get him out of this place, that's why we're here—come on!" When Sudeep didn't move, he took hold of the strap holding Robbie's head.

He didn't notice Jimmy come in with the woman. A cry— "No! Stop that!"—and when he looked back she was standing there with her chin dark with blood, and her hands squeezed into fists by her sides. "You've got no goddamn idea what you're doing. Don't touch him. Just leave him alone before you mess everything up."

"For chrissakes, Jimmy, get her away from me." Nash yanked on the restraints, his fingers sweaty and slipping as he tried to unbuckle them.

The woman shouted, "Don't you care about him? He's just going to hurt himself."

Jimmy pulled her back by the ponytail. "Enough of that."

One of the buckles came free, then the next. Now Robbie's head shook so hard his eyes spread in a smear, and his open mouth turned into a long oval. The broken sounds jerking from him guttered crazily. Nash held his hands to Robbie's face and that dreadful shaking traveled up his arms. Even when he clutched Robbie's head to his chest, he couldn't still him.

"This is hopeless," said Sudeep, then, more gently, "Nash, you know that, don't you? We have to leave him or no one's getting out of here." He glanced to where Chris was standing silently, half hidden by the curtain as though he couldn't bear to look at his brother. "I'm sorry, Chris."

"She can sedate him." Jimmy gripped the woman by her shoulder. "You can sedate him so he stops shaking."

"I can't give him any more. It'd kill him."

Sudeep's eyebrows lifted in surprise. "You've already sedated him? And this is how he is?"

She wrenched herself away from Jimmy and bent over Robbie, sliding the restraints back onto his head and tightening the straps. The quaking quieted to a manic tremble. She looked up at Nash. "If we don't keep him restrained, he'll give himself brain damage, and if we don't sedate him, the shaking's worse. Far worse than this."

Sudeep gazed around at the others, a nervous, twitching look. "Then the rest of us have to get out of here before it's too late."

Nash grabbed the woman by the forearm. "How do we help him? You must have some idea."

She pulled herself loose. "Once the parasite's established itself in its host, there's no stopping it. A little longer and we'll have to move him to a containment unit."

"For crying out loud, you people were trying to get those things to attach themselves to us! You must know how to stop them."

"Don't you understand? We're still researching those sclerotia—"

Nash leaned toward her. "Sclerotia? What the hell are you talking about?"

"The fungus's dormant form, those—those *things*." She wouldn't look at him. "That's what this facility is for. We don't know enough about them."

"Bull shit." Sudeep's mouth had twisted. "There's a purpose to all of this, isn't there? Otherwise, why the hell are you doing it?"

She stared down, fiddling with the restraints.

"Tell us!" Nash's voice rasped, ugly even to his own ears. "We've got nothing to lose—how about you?" He loomed over her, her neck pale and vulnerable just a few inches away.

She kept her head bowed. "Those sclerotia have been lying

around for millennia, waiting for hosts to find them. Then they come out of their dormant stage and reproduce."

"You're telling me they just use the host as part of their reproductive cycle? For protection and nutrition?" Sudeep ran a hand over his head. "Wait, it can't only be that. What the hell else does this parasite use the host for?"

Her hands were still now. She said nothing, and Nash took hold of her arm again, dug his fingers into her flesh. She said softly, "Dispersal."

"Dispersal?" Nash said. "You mean it spreads itself by turning people into—into whatever the hell those people are down in your cages, beating themselves to death?"

She wrenched her arm away and rubbed it. A little blood was still oozing from her nose, and she dabbed at it with her fingertips.

"You have to stop it before it kills my son. I mean—what the hell? It's just a fungus, isn't it?"

"I've told you, we don't know how—we've had so few successful hosts. The sclerotia wouldn't attach themselves to most of our subjects." She winced, as though only now did it occur to her who she was talking to, and her hand lifted and touched her throat. Her fingers left blood marks on her pale skin.

Sudeep's hands tried to find pockets in his coveralls, as though he'd forgotten where he was and what he was wearing. "What did you try? You did try to cure them, didn't you?"

"The thing is, at first the fungus doesn't harm its hosts. It doesn't damage the organs, it doesn't produce toxins, it doesn't provoke any serious negative behaviors. Then this happens." She nodded toward Robbie.

Sudeep came around the bed, staring down at Robbie. "You must have tried to cure them—what did you give them?"

"Voriconazole, itraconazole, nystatin." The words came tripping out of her mouth. "We even tried some meds that haven't made it through trials yet. Nothing works."

She looked away and Sudeep muttered something angry and incomprehensible under his breath, then he spat, "You've been infecting people with a fungus you can't treat? Then when the fungus takes over and they need serious medical help, you lock them out of sight in cages and leave them to die? What the hell kind of people are you?"

Her voice shook. "It's like they're possessed. Nothing we've tried makes them stop." She gazed over at Nash, blinking. "Those people downstairs—we had them restrained, you know, so they wouldn't hurt themselves. We're not monsters. But eventually they break their bones to get free, they dislocate their shoulders, they pound their heads against the bars of the containment units. After that, there's no hope. All we can do is look after them until the end comes."

"Look after them? In those filthy cages?" Sudeep's voice bounced off the walls.

Jimmy held his head in his hands. "It would be kinder to kill them."

"That would be illegal, wouldn't it." She smiled sourly.

"How long?" Nash asked. She wiped at the front of her scrubs where blood was drying. He said more loudly, "How long before he's as far gone as those people you've caged up?"

"At this stage, a few days. Hard to know for sure since he's much younger than the others." She gave an awkward shrug.

Nash stared down at Robbie, the perfection of him, those ugly straps over his head, the IV trailing from his arm, his eyes gazing up at nothing. "There must be something you can do. I mean—come on, you infected him."

Her bottom lip pulled in a little. "You can't take him," she said quietly. "It won't help, and you'll have destroyed whatever we could have learned from him."

A rustle of plastic curtain, and Randall slid through. "You still standing around? What the fuck are you up to?" He slapped his hands together. "I've disabled the cameras, I've done what I can, but someone's going to get suspicious, even with the clown cops they have in this place. Grab the kid and let's get out of here."

"Not that easy," Jimmy said. "It could kill the boy if we take him."

"You think these fuckers are looking after him? Come on, we need to hurry." Randall swung his head toward Nash. "Take him. That's why we're here."

The woman touched her hair, as if she'd only now realized what a mess it was, and then let her hand drop. "He'll just die all the sooner—you want that for him?"

Nash laid a hand over Robbie's forehead. This was his son, his little boy, strapped to a bed so he didn't shake himself to death. Sudeep was right. There was no way to take Robbie with them. And if he stayed with Robbie until he died, Chris would never get out of here, let alone to Canada. He couldn't do that to him, he just couldn't. He was lifting his hands away when Randall shoved him aside.

"For fuck's sake," he said. "This kid's coming with us. I've no idea what you people are up to down here, but you're in it to make money. That's always what it comes down to. And you're not going to make money off of this kid." He moved along Robbie's body, unbuckling the restraints over his hips, his chest, wrenching out the IV, not glancing at Robbie shaking on the bed.

The woman raised her voice. "You can't! You've no idea what you're doing!" She threw herself at him and he simply pushed her away.

Nash laid a hand on Randall's arm. "He'll just batter himself to death."

Free now, Robbie's legs scissored madly, trying to run through the air, and Randall stepped back with his arms raised to shield himself.

"You see?"

"All I understand," he said, taking the zip ties from his

guard's belt, "is that you people are fucking useless without me."
He reached for one of Robbie's ankles. "Come on, let's get going."

They zip-tied Robbie and bundled him in sheets like a giant writhing
caterpillar. His shrieks as they carried him out to the elevator
tore at Nash's heart.

Even with Chris holding Robbie's legs, Nash couldn't keep a
grip on him the way he was bucking and writhing, so he sank to
the elevator floor and cradled him. That awful noise—he pushed
his cheek over Robbie's mouth to mute it, felt the force of his
cries vibrating against his skin.

Randall was last, and Sudeep closed the elevator behind
him. "What did you do with her?" he said and gestured back to
the lab.

"Cuffed her. They'll find her soon enough." Randall punched
a button, then came the sudden heavy feeling of the elevator
hauling them up. He raised a plastic bag for them all to see.
Syringes. A yellow liquid sitting ready in front of the plungers.

Jimmy said, "What is that? Sedative for the boy?"

"Weapons."

Sudeep laughed bitterly. "Your plan is to sedate any guards
who come for us?"

"Hey, do you know what's in them? What would you do if I
tried to stick you?"

"What is in them?"

"Fuck if I know. What does it matter?"

They were close. Any moment now, they'd be hoisted up into
daylight. Randall muttered, "Shit, this is all going too well. It's
like they're not trying to stop us."

Jimmy sniffed, shifted his feet. "You said they're clown cops.
Clown cops won't even know we've escaped yet."

"Yeah." Randall's eyes drifted up. "Let's hope that's right."

Already the air smelled different. Above the rotten sugary

reek rising off Robbie, Nash noticed it: the smell of outdoors. The smell of life. Robbie must have detected it too because he thrashed more wildly now, his small knees pistoning into Nash's gut, and Nash's shoulders strained as he held on.

Randall's lips were so tight they'd vanished into a crooked line. "No alarms? No guards? It doesn't make sense." There was the snick of the plastic bag opening, then rustling. "They're one-shot deals, so use them as a threat. And don't go accidentally stabbing yourselves with them."

"You think they're waiting for us?" said Chris.

"Why wouldn't they be?"

White light flashed from above, and the elevator eased to a halt. The only sound was Robbie, that shrilling from his mouth, the soft pounding as he struggled to get free. Then through the elevator gates daylight came glaring in, blinding and brutal, flooding through the high windows of the hangar. A few yards away loomed the dark shapes of men. One of them yelled, "Don't move, you fuckers."

20

Of course. That's what Nash thought as panic shocked through him. Of course they'd been caught. Of course there were armed guards waiting, and of course those guards would include Lewis.

Lewis was shouting, "Don't move. Hands up or we'll waste you fuckers."

Colt was beside him gesturing them out of the elevator with his gun. "Come on, out of there."

Nash glanced up at Chris. "Go on," he told him, "I'll manage Robbie."

Chris arched an eyebrow, exactly as Maria would have done, then raised his hands and stepped out. As Nash got to his feet, staggering as Robbie writhed and fought in his arms, Sudeep called, "Which is it? You don't want us to move, or you want us to get out of the elevator?"

"Fucker." Lewis lashed out quick as a snake. A soft knock of flesh against metal as Sudeep fell against the bars of the elevator wall, then Lewis grabbed him by the neck and yanked him out. He turned to Nash. "What the fuck you waiting for? Put that down and get out here."

Nash gripped Robbie harder, trying to hold on as Robbie convulsed in his arms and the sheets strained around him. Lewis jabbed his gun into Nash's cheek. "Now."

Slowly, sliding down the elevator wall to keep his balance, Nash lowered himself. He set Robbie on the floor as gently as he could, was about to straighten up when he spotted a syringe lying a few inches away. His fingers snagged it, his hand bunching into a fist to hide it. Lewis was too busy yelling at him to hurry the fuck up to notice.

Nash stepped out of the elevator blinking against the harshness of the light. That syringe in his hand felt so fragile, no weapon at all against these men who'd caught them, who'd send them back underground, who didn't give a damn if Robbie died. It was all over, in this grim hangar that was nothing more than an oversized garage, where the turgid smell of engine oil fouled the air.

Lewis yanked Nash around by his arm and shoved him into line with the others. Beside him, Sudeep was breathing in quick shallow gasps.

"One of you, grab the kid." A brittle voice, familiar. Nash squinted through the sunlight dazzling off the windshield of a short gray bus, off the fenders of the vans parked beside it, but he knew who it was: that bastard, Dr. Dawes. There he was, standing in a square of sunlight coming through a high window. Against all that brilliance, he was just a ridiculous, lanky silhouette.

Beside Dawes stood a third guard, a pug-faced man with a bulging gut and thin legs, whose arms hung by his sides like a gun-slinger about to draw. The guard hollered, "Get the kid, Colt."

Colt plodded toward the elevator. He dipped his head, as though he was cursing under his breath. He grabbed the knotted sheets and dragged Robbie out. Bundled up, Robbie kicked and struggled like a newborn foal trying to break out of its amniotic sac, wrestling himself around, struggling out of Colt's grip, and Colt reared back. "What the hell?"

"Grab him," yelled Dawes. "For god's sake, keep hold of him."

By Colt's feet, Robbie was straining crazily against the sheets. A soft ripping sound and a gray leg kicked free, taut with muscle, the ankle bloodied where the zip tie had bitten in. Colt's large face turned an unnatural white. He wet his lips, shaking his head as though he couldn't believe what he was looking at. "Shit," he said, and his voice wavered. "Shit shit shit shit shit." He took a step back just as the whole sheet split like a peach being thumbed open. A riot of arms, a head thrashing through, a mouth foamy with spittle, and Robbie was bolting across the floor, the torn sheets falling away as he made for the wall, scaling it at a run when that shouldn't have been possible. A shot smacked into the concrete just below him and sent out a spray of dust, then he was gone, the high window shattering as he flung himself through it.

Dawes was sprinting to the door with a gun in his hand. "After him! Get him!" His voice was raw. "He can't escape. It'll ruin everything."

Lewis and the pug-faced guard followed at a run, yelling at each other, their voices vanishing outside. Only Colt remained, dumbfounded as he gazed over his shoulder at the window Robbie had climbed through, then back at the men lined up in front of him. At last, he remembered himself and reached for his gun.

Nash was faster. There was no thought to it, just the impulse and the action, and he was flying through the air with the syringe in his hand, bringing it down into the soft flesh of Colt's neck and pushing in the plunger. With a grunt Colt hefted him off, snatching the syringe from where it dangled in his neck and throwing it to the ground. He raised the gun and said, "You shit," but the gun was nosing the air oddly, wobbling as it looked for Nash, then Colt collapsed to his knees. One half of his face sagged, the eye expressionless and his mouth wide. He gazed up at Nash. "Look what you've done," he said thickly. On his neck, a trickle of blood was running down to his collar. His hand grabbed at the air between them. "You've got—to help me."

Colt had slumped to his side and Nash couldn't look away. He'd done this. He'd hurt this man, maybe killed him. Someone was tugging at Nash's arm—Randall. "Come on! Get in the van."

Nash pulled his arm free. "They're going to kill Robbie! We can't leave—what the hell are you thinking?"

"This isn't the way to help him." Randall wrapped an arm around Nash's neck and dragged him to one of the vans. Through the windshield, Sudeep and Jimmy were staring out.

The van's back doors were open. Chris was crouched with his arms hooked around his knees, and Randall shoved Nash inside then piled in behind him. All around hung biohazard suits that swung from the ceiling, and boxes of equipment pushed up to the sides.

As soon as Randall had slammed the doors shut, the van surged through the doorway and out into the drenching daylight. Nash peered through the small rear window. Guards were running, three of them, four, five, six, all heading to where the ridge angled up sharply behind the facility. And there, high above, was the pale spider shape of his naked son scaling the sheer slope.

Randall was right: those guards were clown cops. If they hadn't been, they wouldn't have all run toward the ridge when there was no chance of climbing up as fast as Robbie, they wouldn't have kept firing at him when he was too far off to hit, and they wouldn't have left the detainees unguarded so they could take off in a van.

Sudeep drove. He took the first switchback too fast and nearly rolled the van. He braked hard for the second, taking it so carefully, so slowly, that the others barely breathed until, at last, the trail straightened and Sudeep stamped on the gas. It was only when he cried, "Are they coming after us?" and looked back wide-eyed that Nash understood how terrified he was.

Nash was kneeling with his hands braced against the floor. Now he stared out the window at the narrow trail again. Of course there were no vehicles in pursuit, and if anyone was watching, they were too far away to see. "No," he called, "no one's after us."

"They could have called ahead," said Chris under his breath. "They could have people waiting for us. It's not like there are many ways out of here."

"Come on," muttered Randall, "let's not think we're fucked before it happens."

Chris was right, though. Maybe those guards had run for the ridge because it didn't matter if a handful of detainees took off with a van. Out here, they'd have to drive miles before they hit a fork in the road, and even then there was nowhere to hide. Nash pressed his forehead against the window and stared out at the buildings of the facility shrinking into the distance. Somewhere up there Robbie was all on his own, and he wanted to catch sight of him, to know that he was still alive. But wasn't his boy already lost? He'd been turned into something not human that fought to escape his own father. All Nash had left were the bruises and scrapes from trying to hold him, and a hand throbbing painfully where fresh scabs had been ripped from his palm.

His gaze drifted up above the ridge. Against the sky, a speck. His heart surged with horror as it moved sideways in a sweeping motion. A drone. There was no way it hadn't seen them, and yet as the van sped on, it hung on the air above the ridge until distance swallowed it. It wasn't spying on them but on Robbie, and Nash clenched his fists at the thought of him being tracked like that. He could still get to him—he just had to get to the mining camp on the other side of the ridge and climb up after him.

How long it took to escape, though: the van bumping along the straightaway, the gate to the road an impossible distance off, and beyond it a pickup driving by, and a camper van, because this day was nothing out of the ordinary. Then the gate was right ahead of them and Sudeep was stopping. Randall snapped, "What the fuck? Keep driving."

"Get the barrier."

"Drive through it. What d'you think this is? A Sunday afternoon drive with grandma?"

"It'll smash the windshield."

"Who the hell cares?"

Sudeep shook his head. "It'll make us conspicuous."

"For fuck's sake! We're in a fucking hurry!"

Sudeep sat gripping the wheel as the engine idled, and Jimmy snatched a bunch of keys from the console and got out. He fiddled with the padlock then heaved the barrier out of the way, and Sudeep eased the van forward for him to get back in, its hood pointed south.

"No," said Nash. "The other way. North."

"We need to get to Anchorage." Sudeep glanced back at Randall. "Where else can we disappear?"

"Fuck." Randall shifted beside Nash. "Things are more complicated now. There's the boy."

Sudeep grimaced. "None of us will stand a chance if we try to save him."

"North," said Nash.

Jimmy pointed, as though Sudeep hadn't understood. "That way—north." When Sudeep raised his right hand on the wheel, Jimmy snapped, "Come on! There's the old mining camp on the other side of the ridge. If the boy makes it over, that's where he'll end up."

"Listen, I understand, but even if we got hold of him, he's—" Sudeep sighed. "Sorry, Nash, we've seen what's going to happen to him."

Nash cried, "For god's sake—"

Beside him, Chris was holding onto the back of Sudeep's seat. "We can't just leave him."

"We're leaving other people too. We can't save them all."

Randall took off his cap and fanned himself with it. "How far are we going to make it if we take off down the highway? They're expecting us to head to Anchorage—all they have to do is call the cops and they'll be waiting."

Sudeep's fingers fluttered on the steering wheel as he stared out the windshield, lips pulled tight against his teeth. He gave a quick shake of the head and yanked the wheel hard to the left, and the van took off north, flying along the highway as if to make up for lost time.

21

By the time they reached the old mining camp, clouds had closed in. Sudeep parked the van alongside Jimmy's RV and sat with his hands on his knees, breathing heavily. "Hey, we've made it this far," Nash told him.

"That was the easy part." Sudeep pushed open his door and strode away across the dirt. Beside the RV he stood with his face raised to the sky, arms slack by his sides. The rest of them got out without a word.

The door to the RV had been left open, and it flapped and creaked in the wind. All around on the drying dirt, Jimmy's things lay scattered: bench cushions still sodden with rain, a pair of women's underwear, boxes of cereal, a book, all of it filthy and ruined. Jimmy stooped—his teapot, cracked apart like a coconut. He reached for part of the lid and shook his head, folding his fingers back to his palm. He said quietly, "Those men are nothing but pigs. There was no need for this, no need at all." A mosquito darted around his head, and he dashed it away as he straightened up. "We need to get out of these coveralls. I'll take a look inside and see what's left."

Sudeep was gazing around him in quick jerky movements, as if he expected to be set upon. "Really?" he said. "Aren't we in a hurry?"

Jimmy started up the steps. "They'll be looking for detainees in yellow coveralls, and one dressed as a guard."

"Okay, okay," Sudeep said and followed him into the RV,

Randall behind him. As they moved about the RV rocked slightly, and their voices sounded muffled and far away.

There was an edge to the wind, and soon rain began falling in plump, cold drops that Chris hunched his shoulders against. He stared up at the ridge. "He doesn't even know we're here. Even if he did, what chance does he have?"

"So we'll go up there and get him." Nash nodded, despite the hopelessness dragging at his heart. "This side is much less steep. Me and Jimmy, we were going to hike over the ridge to rescue you boys. At least, that was the plan." He looked away because it sounded ridiculous now.

"Really? You were going to do that?"

"I wasn't about to leave my boys." He let out his breath in a rush. "I know I screwed up. Things haven't been easy with Mom gone. Sometimes you need someone to tell you what should be obvious, but without Mom—"

"You could've talked to me."

"Yeah, I could've talked to you. The thing is, I'm used to looking after you boys, not saddling you with problems."

Chris flashed a nervous smile. "Dad, we all screw up. I screwed up too, didn't I?" In the wind the book was flapping like a wounded bird, rain speckling its pages. He launched a kick at it, and it slumped away heavily across the dirt. "I was just trying to do what was right. One of us had to do something for Robbie. I mean, he was in a bad way, anyone could see that."

His voice caught. Nash hooked an arm around his shoulders and held him hard as he shook. "Hey, it's okay. There wasn't any right way to deal with what happened. We can't blame ourselves for trying to do what we could." It sounded good, though he wasn't sure he knew how to forgive himself. He pressed his cheek against Chris's head and closed his eyes, felt the warmth of Chris's scalp against his face, the soft scrape of bristles growing longer.

All around, the smell of wet earth, the smell of things decaying. The rain was coming down harder now, cold against Nash's scalp, hitting the vehicles' roofs in a thin, lonely drumbeat. Already the world looked dreary, from the dirt trail turning back to mud, to the darkened wood of the falling-down buildings, to the slick rocks sloping up to the ridge. This might, Nash thought, be the last time he held his son. They were going to risk everything climbing the ridge because there was no safe way to end this craziness.

Behind Nash, the steps of the RV creaked. Randall was carrying a blue fleece and a flannel shirt. He'd swapped the guard's black ball cap for a brown one with a bald eagle embroidered on the front, and had knotted a green plaid blanket across his shoulders like a cape. Beneath it the uniform showed, and he shrugged. "No way anything of Jimmy's was going to fit me. Here," he said and held out the clothes. "At least from the sky we'll look like a bunch of hikers."

Chris pulled on the fleece. "Shit, can drones fly in the rain?"

Randall shrugged. "Some can. Most can't. I guess we'll find out which they have soon enough."

Sudeep came down the steps in a gray knitted hat and pink sweater, plus a pair of sweatpants that didn't reach his ankles. He glanced up into the rain and resettled the hat on his head. They'd all turned into ghosts of other people, thought Nash, all except for Jimmy who sat on the RV's steps buttoning his shirt, looking like a worn-down version of who he'd once been.

Randall clapped his hands together. "Alright then, let's get going."

"Not me." Jimmy leaned onto his knees. "I'm an old man. I'll slow you down."

"You sure?"

"Get going. Hurry now." He flapped his hands to shoo them away.

Nash caught his eye. A quick look from Jimmy, a slight shake of the head. Jimmy would slow them down, sure, but that wasn't why he was staying behind. He'd left his wife here, he'd hidden what was left of her, or tried to, and maybe Dawes's men hadn't found her. "Hey," Nash said and reached out to shake Jimmy's hand, "we'll be back for you. You know that, right?"

"Yes, yes, I know." With a thin smile, Jimmy squeezed his hand. He got to his feet and headed inside the RV, and didn't look back.

Nash led the way along the trail, hiking as fast as he could up the incline. It was eerie to take this path again: the memory of the last time was just under the surface—being chased and not running fast enough, the sting in his leg, falling and the world turning dark. He couldn't help pausing to check over his shoulder, as if a white van might be turning in from the highway, or a drone dropping through the air toward them, but there was only the trail, and the mud, and the abandoned buildings that they soon left behind.

Before long, the rain was coming down so hard that it blurred the rocks towering above them and bleached the hillside of color. Here the incline grew sharper, and he wheezed with the effort of climbing, sweating in the flannel shirt he'd pulled on over his coveralls. Every so often, he caught the smell of his own perspiration. On his right hand where the organism had tried to latch on, his skin was bleeding from grabbing onto gritty ledges and hauling himself up. It didn't help that his coveralls were so wet that they clung to his legs, hobbling him despite being ripped across the knee. Soon Randall and Sudeep climbed past, powering their way up over the rocks, and he called after them, "Shit, I didn't think I was that out of shape."

Sudeep glanced back. "We used to go rock climbing," he said. "At least, before Manisha was pregnant. Never thought it would come in useful." With that gray knitted cap and a sharp grin, maybe this was what he'd looked like before he'd been caught.

"And Randall?"

"He's just a beast." He tipped back his head to eye his route, then pulled himself up over one rock, then another.

Below him Nash heard, "Come on, Dad, we're all younger than you." It was true—Sudeep and Randall in their thirties at most.

Nash gazed down at him. "So what's your excuse?"

"Didn't want to leave you behind, old man." Chris smiled, and then that smile fell away. "Seriously, though, can't you go any faster?"

Nash heaved himself along between large blocks of rock, over others slippery from the rain, and though his lungs ached and his legs felt weak after so many days locked up, he forced himself on, taking more risks now, his feet in their cheap sneakers sliding and skidding and painful, his hands raw.

Randall and Sudeep climbed out of sight. Nash tried to follow their route, clambering along over broken rock to where the slope looked less dangerous. The rain kept falling, and it dripped into his eyes. At least it was cold enough to numb his fingers, despite his chest being sticky with sweat. When at last he spotted Randall he'd stopped, clinging to a ledge over on Nash's right, the green blanket flapping around his shoulders. He was craning his head, and Nash peered up to the ragged top of the slope where the peak jutted up like a nose. There, hazy in the rain, crouched a small shape. Robbie. Chris snatched in his breath, and Nash reached out to hold his arm. "Holy crap," Chris said, "what the hell's he doing way up there? Why's he just sitting like that?"

The rain was coming down hard enough that Nash had to shield his eyes. It was Robbie, for sure, and yet somehow not. The way his head and back and arms fitted together didn't make sense, and the sight of it chilled him. "I don't know," he said into the crackle of the downpour. "Listen, Chris—you don't have to go up there."

"Before he was all hyper and we couldn't keep him still, and now he's not moving. It's weirding me out." He shifted his feet, and a small rock went tumbling down the slope, bouncing and hopping. He looked at Nash with frightened eyes. "Dad, is he dead?"

"He just climbed all the way up there—how can he be dead?" He wiped the rain from his eyes.

"Then what the hell's he doing?"

Beneath his hands the rock felt cold and unforgiving. "I don't know."

"They're going to get him if he doesn't move. Come on, Dad." Chris clambered past him, and though Nash called for him to wait he kept going, grabbing at rocks, moving so quickly that he missed his footing and had to grab on. Nash scrambled after him. He opened his mouth to tell him to be careful, to hold on tight because he might be all the family he had left, but Chris was too far away to hear.

The rain was slapping against Nash's head, chilling his fingers while up there, at the very top of the ridge, his son sat naked and motionless, as though he knew what he'd soon become. No matter if they reached him before Dawes, there was no cure. Tendrils would burst through his mouth, his nose, his eye sockets until, driven out of his mind, he bashed his head against the rocks. Nash let his eyes close. The greasy feel of that damned find when he'd held it, that tickle against his palm, and yet when Robbie had held out his hand, he'd given it back to him. He told himself that he couldn't have guessed what that thing would do—no one could have, no one except Dawes. And instead of getting Robbie decent medical care, Dawes had kept Robbie locked up to study that thing.

Nash reached out for a handhold to haul himself up, then stopped and watched the rain slick against his fingers. Climbing to the top seemed impossible. Fear was poisoning him—not fear of falling but of reaching Robbie and seeing what he knew in his heart: that his son was as good as dead.

"Daaaad." A voice carried by the wind and torn about. "Da-ad!"

Nash let the rain hurl itself against him and laid his forehead against the wet rock. Clinging to it, a tiny patch of yellow lichen. The wind was dragging away the warmth of his body, tiring him. Soon he wouldn't be able to hold on: his toes in their cheap sneakers perched on a narrow ledge, his hands gripping a small outcropping. It was just a matter of time before he fell.

A scrape of noise, a change in the light. Chris had climbed down and was holding on just above him. "Dad, you okay?"

The ledge was biting into Nash's fingers, and along his arm burned muscles that had been straining for too long. What an effort it took to keep clinging on.

"Come on, Dad. We're so close."

"Yeah. So close." He let go with one hand and reached up for a small crevice. His fingers found nothing but air.

A hand around his wrist. Chris, guiding his fingers. It was all Nash could do to squeeze his fingers into the gap and grab on, then drag up a foot and push.

Chris was peering down at him. His eyelashes were clumped from the rain, the black of his pupils like the unlit depths of the earth. "Don't stop, Dad, or you'll freeze up again. Come on." He gave a small jerk of his head then climbed away, and Nash climbed after him, moving slowly, painfully, up to the broken top of the ridge.

So high up, the wind was fierce. The ridge sloped off dangerously a few feet away, and Nash knelt while he caught his breath. The smallness of the world was laid out before him: there, the valley they'd driven along in the van, the highway dark and shiny in the rain and a yellow truck sliding along it; over there, the scratch of trail to the research facility that had to be somewhere below him. If he fell, he'd plunge down the slope, and he leaned away from it and steadied himself on his knuckles. Only now did he let himself stare off to where the ridge climbed to its highest point: a corner of rock suspended on the edge of nothing. There, naked and pale, glistening in the rain, sat Robbie.

Chris was already on his hands and knees, making his way along the narrow ridge toward that peak, and Nash followed. A tug on his shirt. Sudeep. He pressed his mouth to Nash's ear and shouted, "I'll come with you. We'll have to carry him down," then he tapped Randall on the shoulder. Randall was squinting into the rain. He gave a nod, up to their left. The insect shape of a drone. It was tilted against the wind, skating through the air and being blown back, flying in close again to watch them, and whatever noise it was making was being whisked away. Randall tapped his wrist, though he wasn't wearing a watch: they'd have to be quick. He jerked his thumb at his chest and then at the drop-off. The guards. Dawes. Someone had to keep watch.

As Nash crept along, rain stung his face and the wind howled about his ears. To his left lay the drop-off, just a few hand widths away. Chris had just come along here, in this wind and rain. He could have lost his balance—Nash looked up, scared. There he was, hauling himself up to where Robbie was sitting on that platform of rock. No, not sitting. Perched on his knees and the balls of his feet, hands loose by his sides and his head bent back, as if to taste the air. Robbie wasn't Robbie anymore. That thing—that fungus—had taken him over and made him climb up there. What else might it make him do, if he was cornered, say? And there was Chris closing in on him. Nash cupped his hands around his mouth. He yelled, "Wait! Chris, wait!" but his words were swallowed by the wind.

There was nothing for it but to keep going, more quickly now. The rock grazed his palms, his knees, and the toes of his cheap sneakers scraped along as that wind tried to pry him loose. He was so tired, so cold that the inside of his mouth felt like ice.

He lifted his head. Chris was beside Robbie now, and Robbie hadn't moved. A flash of something to his left, and Nash swung his head: the drone, propellers whirring and the black eye of its camera panning over him. For a few seconds it bounced on the air. Then it stuttered and slipped away out of sight. Nash crept on. His hands were stuck with grit where they were bleeding, and he wiped them, one, then the other, on his shirt.

The peak was just ahead. So high up, there was nothing except for the push of the wind, the rain like splinters driven against his face, the long drop down to the ground. Nash kept moving, his wet shirt flailing and ballooning in the wind, Sudeep just behind him as he heaved himself up toward where the peak flattened. There Chris crouched, eyes half shut against the wind, and there, just beyond him, perched Robbie. His skin had turned an unearthly white, smooth as soap except for a few cuts oozing blood, no trace of the mesh now as though the rushing wind had scoured it away.

Chris was reaching out, fingers already cupped to the shape of Robbie's arm. But that wind—it swung his hand, and maybe his fingertips brushed against Robbie because Robbie reared up, balancing himself on his knees and the balls of his feet, his hands gripping his ankles, his spine arching painfully and his neck bending so far back that the ridges of his throat stood out. As though he was being pinned against his will, as though whatever had possessed him might throw him off that peak. He and Chris would need to grab him together, fast enough that he wouldn't drag them to their deaths. And to do that, Nash would have to squeeze in beside Chris up on that narrow platform of rock.

Nash was steadying himself to inch forward when Robbie moved again. He lowered himself—buttocks to heels, shins to rock—then stared out blankly toward the sky. Chris looked over at Nash, and then his gaze was yanked away and his eyes widened. Nash glanced back as well. Two guards from the facility were squatting below them on the ridge with climbing gear dropped around them, and they were helping a third man up. A tall thin man: Dawes.

A sickening pressure rose up Nash's throat: they were trapped up here with no weapons, not even loose rocks to throw or gravel to fling because the wind had long since swept the summit clean. As for Randall, there was no sign of him. If they'd shot him, most likely the sound would have been carried away. Then again, maybe they'd pushed him over the edge, and maybe that was what they were planning for the rest of them, because how much neater it would be if the escaped detainees had simply fallen to their deaths.

Dawes dropped his harness and ropes at his feet. He came staggering along the ridge with his back bent against the wind, and the guards followed. Soon he dropped to his hands and knees. Every now and again Nash glimpsed his pale face as he looked up to gauge the distance left.

A fizz and a crack. Just below Nash, shards of rock went flying away on the wind. The guard behind Dawes had a gun in his hand. Lewis. Without his cap his face was smaller, meaner. He gazed up through the rain as though deciding whether to shoot again before ducking his head and crawling on behind Dawes.

Any moment now, Dawes and the guards were going to reach them. Nash lifted his hands in surrender, for all the good it would do, and Chris and Sudeep did the same. The three of them sat there with their hands being batted around by the wind, shivering in their borrowed clothes, and to Nash it didn't seem possible that it would end like this when he'd found Robbie, and he was just an arm's length away.

Out of nowhere came another guard, a large guy, no cap, no hair, heaving himself up from the far side of the ridge. Randall, the green cape gone. He came bear-walking across the rock at a furious speed, catching up to the guard trailing Lewis and snagging his ankle, tearing him off the rock and sending him flying backward. The man's arms spun wide as he went wheeling off the edge.

Dawes must have noticed the look on their faces—he glanced back then came scuttling closer to the peak. Behind him Randall barreled down on Lewis, and Lewis lifted his gun. Maybe he fired—it was hard to tell because already Randall was flinging himself through the air, landing on Lewis and tumbling across the rock with him in a knot of arms and legs, and then—and then they vanished.

Nash craned forward. A little rain caught his neck, his cheek. In a moment Randall would climb back up, he had to. But as the wind buffeted around Nash's head and nothing moved except Dawes easing closer, the shock of it hit him. Randall was gone.

Nash stared down at his hands gripping the rock. By his fingers, a tiny puddle, its surface wrinkled by the wind. The air was full of the smells of wet rock and woken earth, and he wanted to rage, furious and heart sore, except Dawes was coming nearer, scooting along awkwardly now with something in his hand. A gun. He stopped and lifted it clumsily. It tipped in the wind as he stared up toward where Nash and the others sat cornered. The gun jerked and made a dull pop. The shot must have gone wide, and he clambered closer. This time he spread his knees to brace himself and lifted the gun in both hands. He aimed it high, up to where Robbie was perched.

Sudeep was the closest. He threw himself down toward Dawes, snatching at the gun as Dawes waved it, and then he gripped Dawes's forearm and smashed his hand down onto the rock, two times, three, until Dawes let go. Dawes lurched for the gun, but Sudeep grabbed it away and aimed it at Dawes's head.

Nash felt a shove on his shoulder. Chris. He was pointing at Robbie. He'd reared up again with his spine arched and the delicate bones of his rib cage straining, hands on ankles so that his small body teetered on his knees and the balls of his feet. His head had fallen back and his mouth was gaping toward the sky.

He was quivering, vibrations running through his whole taut body so that it trembled like a rocket about to take off.

Nash cried, "No! Robbie! Robbie!"

As they watched, Robbie's throat convulsed and his mouth stretched wider. Out of him spewed a torrent of granules, tiny and sparkling, thousands of them, millions, like steam erupting from a kettle only to be caught by the wind, and that wind bore them away, swirling over the valley in glistening ribbons. On it went, gushing, unstoppable, and Nash sank back against the rock in despair.

When finally the torrent thinned, then petered out, Robbie collapsed like a suit of empty clothes. Chris was fast. He snatched Robbie's arm and yanked him close, and Nash gathered both his boys to his chest. Robbie wasn't moving. Beneath his skin, a furious heat was fading.

Someone shouted. Nash peered down the slope to where Sudeep was holding the gun on Dawes. Over the shriek of the wind Dawes yelled, "You idiots! You've ruined everything!"

22

Though the rain had stopped, the sky stayed a sullen gray. Its gloom hung over them as they wrapped Robbie in a fleece and strapped him to Nash's back with the guards' climbing gear, then carried him down the ridge. At times Nash thought Robbie's weight was going to pull him off the rock, and he'd cling on and shut his eyes. He could see it: the way they'd go plunging through the air like Randall, tangled together, helpless. He made himself stare at the rock in front of him. Not as steep as the way they'd come up, but still his feet had to search for toeholds, his fingers grip ledges. When he glanced down to see how much farther they had to go, it always looked too far.

Sudeep stayed close to help. He kept peering down too, and Nash guessed what he was looking for: Randall. The farther they climbed down, the more Nash feared what they might see—his body sprawled against a boulder with his head caved in, or the bulk of him lying bloodied and broken on the scree. There was no sign of him, though. Not from the heights of the ridge, and not when, exhausted and scratched, they made it to the bottom. Sudeep wanted to keep looking. He even wove his way between the larger rocks, dragging his feet because he was so worn out. It was hopeless, and at last he followed Nash down the trail toward the mining camp.

Ahead of them, Dawes was trudging along in front of Chris, and though it was clear from the rigid way Chris held the gun on him that he didn't know how to handle a weapon, and had never fired one in his life, Dawes hadn't tried to escape. They'd frisked him and found a walkie-talkie that they tossed away. They'd found a cell phone that searched and searched for a signal, and that Sudeep had smashed to pieces against a rock, just in case. And yet, the whole time they'd worked their way down the ridge a worry had niggled at Nash. That acquiescent silence, that narrow mouth pinched in resignation—perhaps Dawes was simply biding his time.

Now that they were close to the old camp, it was hard not to jump at small things: a shadow skimming over the ground as a raven circled overhead, a clatter from inside a shed where the wind was blowing an empty can across the floor. By now the rest of the guards would have gathered at the research facility, and when they understood what had happened, surely they'd come after them. Then again, with Dawes missing, perhaps those clown cops would sit tight.

Wind hissed through the grass growing up between the rocks and cut through Nash's coveralls. They were torn and damp, from sweat he thought, because the rain was long since over. His shoulders were throbbing where the ropes bit into them, his spine compressed from Robbie's weight, his feet a mess of smarting skin, and yet somehow he kept going, staggering and lurching. Sudeep was a few yards farther on. He stopped now and called, "You alright? You need me to take him?"

Nash shook his head. Holding onto Robbie, straining to get him down to the camp, that was all he could do for him right now. "How's he look?"

Sudeep's gaze shifted to where Robbie's head was slumped against Nash's shoulder. "The cut on his forehead's stopped bleeding. Other than that, the same, more or less."

"More or less?"

Sudeep shrugged. "I'm not a doctor."

"I need to know if he's got any chance of making it." He steadied himself. "I mean—what the hell? What did that fungus do to him? It's like nothing I've ever heard of—it's like nothing on earth."

Sudeep was staring off to where the trail led through the mining camp. He scratched at his scalp through the hat, let out a sigh. "You know, there's a parasitic fungus that infects ants. Once it's inside, it lets the ant go about its business until, when the fungus has had time to produce spores in the ant's body, it takes over. It makes the ant climb a stalk of grass at sunset and wait at the very top. If the conditions are right, just humid enough, just cool enough, then at the optimal moment it turns the ant into a catapult to release its spores."

"What if the conditions aren't right?"

"The ant heads back down the stalk and goes about its business like nothing's happened. Then the next day, it goes through it all again."

"After it's been turned into a catapult," said Nash, "what happens to the ant?"

"It's all over. The fungus just uses the ant to disperse its spores." He looked up at Nash. "I'm sorry, that wasn't a good example. Listen, there's all sorts of stuff out there that is almost beyond belief. Wasps that turn cockroaches into zombies—"

"But what's Robbie got? That mind-control fungus?"

Sudeep pursed his lips. "As far as I know, it only infects ants. Humans would be a whole other ball game. The truth is, we don't really know what's out there. Science hasn't paid much attention to fungi—or to most parasites, come to that."

Up ahead, the trail switched back on itself before skirting around the old bunkhouse. Nash shifted Robbie's weight. "Where's Chris? I can't see him."

"He's down there somewhere."

"Can you see him?"

"No, but he can't have gone far."

"If you were Dawes, isn't this where you'd make your move?

Down off the ridge where you can make a break for it?" He turned away and started jogging down the trail, Robbie bouncing against his back.

Sudeep came racing past him, and Nash stumbled along, trailing him down around the bunkhouse. There, in the middle of the path, Dawes was waiting. Chris's face was an agony of fear, and no wonder: Dawes had the gun jammed under his chin.

Dawes herded them down past the ruined buildings with their crooked doorways and starbursts of shattered windows, down to where the RV was parked. Exhausted, Nash reeled under Robbie's weight and Dawes snapped at him to put the boy down, to just put him down for god's sake. Chris helped unstrap Robbie from the harness and ropes and carefully laid him on the ground. Without Robbie on his back, Nash felt giddy, buoyant, even as he sank down beside him.

Dawes ducked into the RV and checked the dash, the visor, cursing loud enough for Nash and the others to hear. Keys—he was looking for the keys. He slammed the door and tramped back across the mud, face bunched up in anger: here he was, stuck with escaped detainees and no phone, no radio, no way to call for help. He waved the gun at Chris and Sudeep and told them to keep their hands on their goddamn heads. As for Nash, he barely glanced his way, as though he couldn't bear the sight of him.

Around the RV, Jimmy's things were still scattered in the mud: the broken teapot, the book splayed flat, the boxes of cereal, the women's underwear. All of it had been beaten down by the rain. Just beyond, though, was a patch of drier ground where the van had been parked. Jimmy had taken off. Perhaps he'd calculated that the odds of them returning were so small he might as well save himself. Nash couldn't blame him. Still, he felt a prickle of disappointment. He'd thought more of Jimmy than that.

Dawes stalked past, over tire tracks and puddles, and the mud sucked at his hiking boots. If they were going to overpower him it would have to be now, before he could plan what to do next. But it seemed impossible to Nash, sitting there on the wet ground, his legs splayed out in front of him, that he should heave himself up and fling himself at Dawes, and manage it all without getting shot. He was just so damn tired. It was almost a relief when Dawes turned around and the moment was gone.

Gently, Nash lifted Robbie's head onto his lap then reached for his hand and laid his fingers across his wrist, the way he'd seen Maria do it dozens of times. Nothing, not even the slightest flutter of life. He told himself he was doing it wrong, and he smoothed the fleece they'd wrapped him in back over Robbie's arm. Robbie wasn't cold to the touch, but then he had no clue how long it took for a body to cool down. A dribble of blood was drying on Robbie's forehead. He dabbed at it with his cuff and cradled him closer.

Dawes had been pacing around. Now he paused and studied the drier earth where the van had been parked. "Just look at that—your friend's abandoned you. He's stolen my van and left you here." He looked strangely boyish, his hair damp and stuck to his forehead, his cheeks flushed. He called over to Nash, "There's nothing you can do for your son, you know."

The wind gusted, and Nash's arms tightened around Robbie. He leaned his cheek against Robbie's head, trying to shelter him as he stared off to where Dawes's boots were treading through the mud.

"Do you still think you rescued him? Don't you understand? You just made things worse. All the fungus wanted was for him to release its spores, and you helped it. Now that it's finished with him, it's not going to keep him alive."

A shift in the light. Dawes was standing over him, that gun aimed down at his head. "Because of you, something that was lying dormant for thousands of years has been let loose on the world. At this very moment those spores are being carried off by the wind, and who knows the havoc they'll wreak on our already fucked-up environment. But you didn't think about that, did you?"

That gun, so close—Nash willed himself not to tremble, not to blink, not to pay attention to the terrified beating in his chest. He said as evenly as he could, "You didn't try to treat him. You were just going to let him die."

"There is no cure, not yet at least." Dawes turned and stamped away, unleashing a kick that sent the broken belly of the teapot rolling off into a tire rut.

Standing by the wall beside Chris, hands still on his head, Sudeep grimaced. "You're telling us this is all about finding a cure? Come on, that makes no sense."

"You're so unbelievably clueless. That fungus has great possibilities, but you can't let something like that escape back into nature. You have to modify it first, you have to mitigate its risks so they don't outweigh its potential."

Sudeep's elbows drooped so they winged his face. "Potential?" he said. "You mean potential for profit, don't you? That isn't a government lab back there—it's a corporate enterprise, and that means it's all about money. Tell me, what are you going to sell that fungus for? Its medicinal properties?"

As Dawes pivoted, he brought the gun up. Chris flinched and stared at the ground, but Dawes ignored him and marched up to Sudeep. "You want to guess, is that it?"

"A cure for malaria, or dengue fever? It isn't, is it? See, I know that because those are poor country problems. A cure for AIDS then?" Sudeep shook his head. "Cures aren't good for business. Once people are cured, revenue dries up. What can it be, then? A new antibiotic? And this one'll get sold to agribusiness like all the others and soon become useless?"

"This is about far more than that. This is about saving the planet. Yeah, yeah, I know it sounds absurd. And you guys—you guys have got no idea the damage you've done." He touched his chin with his wrist, the gun dangling in his hand, and his face softened a little. "I'm one of the good guys, not that I expect you to appreciate that."

Sudeep shifted his feet. "Right, you're saving the planet, out here in a disused mine. That's where the real science gets done."

Dawes's voice rose. "No one in this country is funding technologies for climate change reversal. Can you get that into your dumb head? No one has the imagination to see that it's possible, let alone that there's money in it. Instead, it's all green technology and carbon offsets."

"Climate change reversal?" Sudeep's eyes crinkled, amused. He glanced at Nash then Chris, but Chris wouldn't look up.

Dawes smoothed a hand over his hair, clumsily, and stepped back with the gun aimed at Sudeep. "We're on the brink of global catastrophe. Massive storms are wiping out our crops, forest fires are devastating whole towns, rising sea levels are threatening cities where millions of people live. And I've found a solution. Not windmills and energy conservation, and that sort of pissing around, and not one of those out-there ideas like releasing particles into the upper atmosphere to block out the sun. I've found something that could truly work. Then you guys blunder in."

"A solution? Using a fungus?" said Sudeep. "That's not possible."

"Carbon sequestration." Dawes's lips were wet, his eyes shining. "The fungus sequesters carbon as it grows, and it grows fast, but it's not just that—it accelerates plant growth like you wouldn't believe." He raised both hands to demonstrate and the gun swept upward. "We can suck carbon dioxide back out of the atmosphere on a huge scale—can you imagine what that means? No need to stop using carbon fuels, no need for a radical rethink of how we live. This is what the world needs."

Dawes gazed at them in turn, as though he expected them to express astonishment, or to congratulate him, but Sudeep twisted his head away and Chris kept staring down at the mud. Nash pulled Robbie a little closer. Dawes's eager, angry look—he was getting dangerous. He was telling them too much, as if it didn't matter what they knew. With his thumb, he stroked Robbie's cheek. How pale he was, his skin a chalky white. He tucked the fleece around him and drew in his legs to cover them as best he could. Robbie's eyelids flickered, a twitch of life—Robbie coming back, or that presence that had watched from behind Robbie's eyes. Nash didn't know which, and he didn't care as long as he could lure back some part of his son, and he wanted to whisper in his ear that he loved him, whatever he'd become. Instead, he kept that thumb gently stroking his cheek, a warning to stay very still.

"What the world needs?" said Sudeep at last, so quietly that Nash barely caught it. "You were going to genetically modify the fungus to patent it, because that way the world would have to buy it from you. That's what this is about, isn't it?"

"We've invested in the research, so of course we should make money from it. Isn't that how it's supposed to work?"

"Except you can't get the fungus to reproduce without human hosts, and we've seen what happens to them." Sudeep drew a breath and nodded, his elbows bouncing as he moved his head. "Unless that's only true when you're trying to control the fungus, when you won't let those hosts release the spores. That's what's going on, isn't it?"

Dawes laughed but his eyes were furious. "You think we should let infected people loose on the world? Have them roaming around?" He let out another laugh. "Now—"

"They kill themselves trying, don't they? That fungus drives them to find a high point to release the spores, and if they can't, if they're caged up because you don't want your product out in the world for free—"

Dawes wheeled around toward Sudeep, his mouth a tight, angry curl. "Who the hell do you think you are? You're a criminal.

You broke the law. You're nothing." He raised the gun with both hands and came closer. A rut, and he stumbled, righted himself and stared down. A tire track pressed into the mud between the patch of dry earth and the building's wide door. Nash's heart beat a little faster. Jimmy hadn't left them, after all. He'd hidden the van and right now, perhaps somewhere close by, he was lying in wait.

Dawes had understood, too. "Well, well, how about that. Your old friend didn't desert you." He raised his eyebrows as he looked at Nash and the others. "Who could have anticipated such loyalty? Waiting all this time with my van and then—what? You plan to somehow make it to Anchorage to hide out? Is that it? Let's go look for your friend and find out."

That jokiness—Dawes was nervous. It must have just occurred to him that all this time he'd assumed he had the upper hand, him with a gun against three unarmed detainees, when those weren't the odds at all.

"Let's go," he cried. His face had a grim set to it now. "Open up that door."

Chris seemed to slump, but he followed Sudeep, both of them moving heavily, uneasily, and before Nash could lift Robbie off his knees, Dawes was standing over him shouting, "You too—leave the boy." The gun was in Nash's face. As he went to ease Robbie off his lap, Dawes yanked him up by the arm and Robbie tumbled to the ground. Dawes's whole body was heaving, and the gun trembled as he pointed it as Nash's chest. "Now get in there."

Fear buzzed through Nash's head as he followed Chris and Sudeep inside. If Jimmy was in here, this would be the moment for him to come raging out—from behind the broken crates, from the shadows along the wall—but there was only the patter of their footsteps on the dirt floor, and the reek of decay. This must have been where Jimmy had hidden his dying wife, in here where he'd parked the van—it sat over by the far wall, gleaming in the light that leaked down from a hole in the roof. Close by among the crates, straining up to that daylight, stood saplings taller than a man—a skinny spruce and a couple of birches whose leaves glistened from the recent rain.

Behind Nash, Dawes was breathing fast. He yelled at the three of them to keep their hands high. Nash strained his arms up over his head as Dawes backed away, dodging around the crates toward the van. He swung open the doors, checking inside, and he seemed to relax a little as he took something from the floor: a bunch of zip ties.

Nash scanned the shadows. No movement, no sign of Jimmy coming to their rescue. If they were going to escape, they would have to act now. Once Dawes had them tied up and in the van, Jimmy would have to take on Dawes on his own, one old guy against a desperate man with a gun.

Dawes was coming back around the van when he brushed against the saplings. The leaves let loose a shower of droplets that glittered over the broken crates, and he paused, then squatted and shoved aside the crates. It struck Nash: those saplings hadn't been here when he and Jimmy had hidden from the drone. And now, gleaming in the light from the hole in the roof, their pale roots were a tangled mass. Those young trees weren't growing out of the soil, they were forcing their way into it, growing too fast to push their roots into the hard ground. Such a profusion of roots for three saplings, some gray and thick and dotted with red blisters, some rearing up like stalks, their swollen tips as long as a child's hand. A familiar shape—long and slightly oblong.

Dawes swung around to the three of them. "What is this? All these sclerotia—what the hell have you done?" His lips were pulled back, his mouth menacing. Nash steeled himself—if Dawes was mad enough to use the gun, he'd throw himself in front of Chris. It might not change anything in the end, but it'd give Chris a chance.

But Dawes strode back to the saplings, kicking away the

busted wood of the crates and shoving at the massive snarl of roots and fungus, lifting it, exposing a dark stain underneath. In the doorway, the light dimmed. Nash didn't turn his head. He shifted his eyes and there was Jimmy, holding something heavy against his chest, slipping inside among the shadows.

The fungus made a sucking sound as Dawes pushed it, and it quivered, its red blisters gleaming, as if it felt Dawes's intrusion. Beneath, where the ground was stained, white sticks were laid out in a curious pattern, and he picked one up. Jimmy was edging closer. He stopped as Dawes lifted one of the sticks and shouted, "Human. You see that? Do you understand what this means?"

Jimmy's wife—Susan. Left here dead, or close to it. She'd burned that thing off her hand, and it had defended itself. Maybe it hadn't meant to kill her, and yet she had died, and the fungus had fed off her and produced those things, those sclerotia. Dormant forms were for enduring harsh conditions, that's what Sudeep had said. Not a great way to reproduce, but an act of desperation that counted on luck and patience.

Dawes tenderly touched one of the sclerotia. "Well, how about that," he said quietly. "A whole trove of them, right here." As he got to his feet a smile pulled at his mouth, and that's when Jimmy came at him. He swung a tire iron and it smacked into Dawes's skull hard enough for him to stagger and drop the gun. He clamped his hands to his head, and Jimmy struck him across the back, standing over him as he swayed, moaning. Jimmy was raising the tire iron again when Sudeep launched himself at Dawes and bowled him over, and Jimmy let the tire iron drop to the ground.

Chris grabbed it and hurled it away, and it thumped against the wall before falling into the shadows. As for the gun, he kicked it, as though he couldn't bear to touch it again. When he looked at Nash, his face was fierce.

Jimmy was dragging a red canister toward the saplings.

When he unscrewed the cap, a pungent smell wafted out. Gas. He poured it over the roots, over the fungus and, when the canister was almost empty, he hoisted it up and splashed what was left over the spindly trees. From his pocket he took a box of matches and scraped one to life. It hissed then flared, lighting up his creased face. "Time to get out of here," he said.

Afterward, Nash would remember the panic—how they'd dragged Dawes outside and left him in the dirt, how the smoke had stained the sky and it had seemed a certainty they'd be caught as they took off in Jimmy's RV. But no police cars came screaming toward them, no fire trucks. It took him miles to understand: if those old buildings burned, there was no one to give a damn.

What would come back to him more clearly, though, were other memories. The warm weight of Robbie in his lap. The fear that slid through his gut when Robbie's eyes stayed closed, though it was nothing more than the sleep of an exhausted child. The way he hugged Chris to him and whispered to his boys that they'd find Mom, he'd raise holy hell until the Canadian government helped them.

There were other memories, too. The weary sky that wouldn't darken as Jimmy drove and drove, and beside him Sudeep dozing in the passenger seat. The gravel highway climbing past the trees, the soft undersides of clouds hanging over the hills, and those hills folding away into the distance, as though this was the very top of the world. The questions that pricked at him: Had the wind carried the spores this far already? Would the fungus kill more people? Would it turn the world into a riot of green and save them all?

Later, he'd remember thinking how unremarkable the border crossing looked—a few small huts used by customs and immigration, a gate that had been locked for the night where Jimmy abandoned the RV on the roadside. He'd remember how they'd stood in their filthy clothes, quietly, patiently, until the sun hoisted itself above the hills and the Canadian border officers arrived, yawning, mugs of coffee steaming in their hands. More than anything else, though, he'd remember how, when they were finally beckoned forward, the whole world was bathed in light.

• • • • •

ABOUT THE AUTHOR

Gerri Brightwell is from southwest Britain. She has master's degrees in creative writing from the University of East Anglia and the University of Alaska, Fairbanks, and a doctorate in English from the University of Minnesota. She has worked in Greece, Israel, Spain, Thailand, and Canada, and now lives in Fairbanks, Alaska, with her husband, writer Ian C. Esslemont, and their three sons. Brightwell is the author of the novels *Dead of Winter*, *The Dark Lantern*, and *Cold Country*, as well as many short stories.

ACKNOWLEDGMENTS

Many thanks to the staff at Torrey House Press for taking on this project, and for helping me shape it. Thanks in particular to Anne Terashima, a clever and insightful editor.

Many thanks also to Dan Darrow for his help with the Spanish that appears in the novel. Any mistakes are, of course, my own.

TORREY HOUSE PRESS

Voices for the Land

The economy is a wholly owned subsidiary of the environment, not the other way around.
—Senator Gaylord Nelson, founder of Earth Day

Torrey House Press publishes books at the intersection of the literary arts and environmental advocacy. THP authors explore the diversity of human experiences with the environment and engage community in conversations about landscape, literature, and the future of our ever-changing planet, inspiring action toward a more just world. We believe that lively, contemporary literature is at the cutting edge of social change. We seek to inform, expand, and reshape the dialogue on environmental justice and stewardship for the human and more-than-human world by elevating literary excellence from diverse voices.

Visit www.torreyhouse.org for reading group discussion guides, author interviews, and more.

As a 501(c)(3) nonprofit publisher, our work is made possible by generous donations from readers like you.

Torrey House Press is supported by Back of Beyond Books, the King's English Bookshop, Maria's Bookshop, the Jeffrey S. & Helen H. Cardon Foundation, the Sam & Diane Stewart Family Foundation, the Barker Foundation, Diana Allison, Klaus Bielefeldt, Laurie Hilyer, Shelby Tisdale, Kirtly Parker Jones, Robert Aagard & Camille Bailey Aagard, Kif Augustine Adams & Stirling Adams, Rose Chilcoat & Mark Franklin, Jerome Cooney & Laura Storjohann, Linc Cornell & Lois Cornell, Susan Cushman & Charlie Quimby, Betsy Gaines Quammen & David Quammen, the Utah Division of Arts & Museums, Utah Humanities, the National Endowment for the Humanities, the National Endowment for the Arts, the Salt Lake City Arts Council, and Salt Lake County Zoo, Arts & Parks. Our thanks to individual donors, members, and the Torrey House Press board of directors for their valued support.

Join the Torrey House Press family and give today at www.torreyhouse.org/give.